HERE'S WHAT READERS' SAY ABOUT SILHOUETTE SPECIAL EDITIONS:

"The Special Editions are really special and I enjoyed them very much! I am looking forward to next month's books."
—R.M.W.*, Melbourne, FL

"I've just finished reading four of your first six Special Editions and I enjoyed them very much. I like the more sensual detail and longer stories. I will look forward each month to your new Special Editions."

—L.S.*, Visalia, CA

"Silhouette Special Editions are—1) Superb! 2) Great! 3) Delicious! 4) Fantastic! . . . Did I leave anything out? These are books that an adult woman can read . . . I love them!"

—H.C.*, Monterey Park, CA

"I used to be hooked on Harlequin, . . . but now the only books my friends and I will buy are Silhouette Special Edition."

—B.J.C.*, Mt. Airy, GA

*names available on request

0-671-53627-3

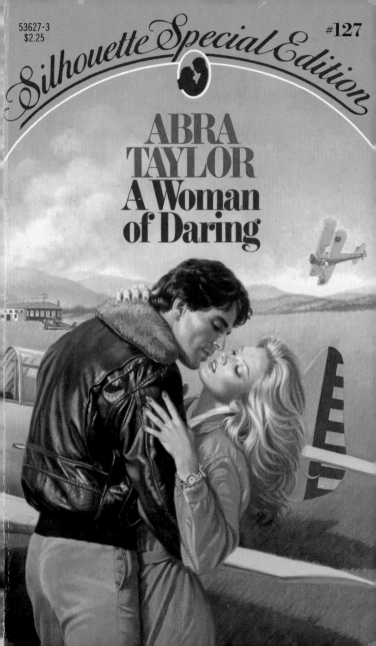

53627-3
$2.25

#127

Silhouette Special Edition

ABRA TAYLOR
A Woman of Daring

"What Shall We Drink To?"

he asked casually. "Now that the old dare is finally dealt with, we'll have to find a new one. There must be some challenge I can throw out. I should hate to bore a woman who lives as dangerously as you do."

Her gaze dropped. "I've given up living dangerously. I've decided I like the quiet life. From now on I prefer everything tame."

Gray laughed softly. "Everything? Including men? I warn you, you're going to have your work cut out for you—I'm feeling very untamed this evening. However, we'll drink the toast you propose. Here's to the taming of me!"

ABRA TAYLOR

was born in India, where her father, a doctor of tropical medicine, treated both maharajahs and British viceroys. Exposed to exotic places and unusual people from an early age, she developed an active imagination and soon turned to writing. The author of numerous romances, she is today a beloved storyteller whose books are sought after by fans worldwide.

Dear Reader,

Silhouette Special Editions are an exciting new line of contemporary romances from Silhouette Books. Special Editions are written specifically for our readers who want a story with heightened romantic tension.

Special Editions have all the elements you've enjoyed in Silhouette Romances and *more*. These stories concentrate on romance in a longer, more realistic and sophisticated way, and they feature greater sensual detail.

I hope you enjoy this book and all the wonderful romances from Silhouette. We welcome any suggestions or comments and invite you to write to us at the address below.

Karen Solem
Editor-in-Chief
Silhouette Books
P.O. Box 769
New York, N. Y. 10019

ABRA TAYLOR
A Woman of Daring

Silhouette Special Edition
Published by Silhouette Books New York
America's Publisher of Contemporary Romance

SILHOUETTE BOOKS, a Division of Simon & Schuster, Inc.
1230 Avenue of the Americas, New York, N.Y. 10020

ISBN: 0-671-53627-3

First Silhouette Books printing November, 1983

10 9 8 7 6 5 4 3 2 1

Map by Ray Lundgren

Printed in the U.S.A.

Other Books by Abra Taylor

Season of Seduction
Wild Is the Heart
A Woman of Daring

Published by SILHOUETTE BOOKS

Hold Back the Night

Published by POCKET BOOKS

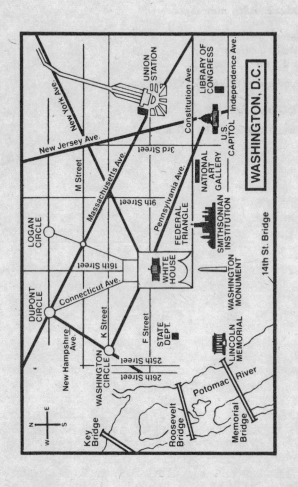

WASHINGTON, D.C.

Chapter One

The reception was overly crowded, overly extravagant, overly loud, and, to Gray Bennett's way of thinking, godawful. He hated large parties and he particularly hated *this* large party. He was there only because he had to be. The command had come directly from Dolly Winterhazy herself, who was, unhappily, the person to listen to in the Winterhazy empire. Until Gray was able to exercise his hard-earned stock options at the end of the year, Bernard Winterhazy, good-natured lush that he was, still wielded power as major shareholder in the newspaper chain Gray was attempting to control. And Dolly was the real power behind Bernard Winterhazy. Gray couldn't afford to offend her.

In the garden of the Winterhazy mansion, a massive marquee had been erected for the occasion. The reception was studded with luminaries, and tomorrow

every gossip columnist in Washington would be ec-
static with eulogies. Dolly Winterhazy's parties always
earned eulogies, even from rival newspapers.

Bored, restless, and unwilling to listen any longer to
the pontificating senator who was holding court nearby, Gray turned his attention to the vaulted roof of
the tent, which had been lined with a small fortune in
reflective silver plastic, rather like a gigantic crazy
mirror. He raked back a black forelock and narrowed
his dark blue eyes, pretending an intense interest in
the upside-down reflection of the milling, spangled
guests. He amused himself by imagining a tongue-in-
cheek version of the gushing, breathless stories that
would appear in tomorrow's society columns.

"Dolly Winterhazy does it again! Dolly, known as
the most-ogled social ogress on the Washington scene,
entertained with her usual combination of flash, pa-
nache, and lavish spending. Her theme was interga-
lactic space, possibly to compensate for lack of the
earthly variety. The packed-in guests could admire
themselves in orbit on the roof of the marquee, which
was cunningly mirrored with reflective silver plastic,
so that even in the sardine crush no one could miss
how many Truly Important People were on the invitation list. On the lunar fringes of the gathering was a
buffet table resembling a moonscape, where moun-
tains of caviar, fried grasshoppers, larks' tongues, and
other unearthly inedibles rested in monstrous moon
craters. Dolly's most precious decorator touch was
Bernard Winterhazy himself. Witty, witty Dolly! She
oozed her influential husband into a spacesuit for the
evening—such an entertainingly original idea. Who
but 'Hazy,' as his intimates have been heard to call
him, would be so affable! Dolly's name-studded guest
list included"—the guest list would follow ad nauseam
—"But wait, that's not all, my starstruck friends. As a

final diversion to titillate her glamorous guests right out of their tiaras, Dolly produced her most ingenious amusements, several of the nation's great astronauts in person, flown in from Houston for the occasion . . ."

They had been flown in by NASA, Gray knew, for a series of meetings that had nothing whatsoever to do with Dolly Winterhazy. NASA had ordered them to attend the party because *The Washington Clarion,* flagship newspaper of the Winterhazy chain, was a powerful influence in the capitol. In the silvered tent roof, Gray could see the reflections of several of the astronauts holding court near the bars, recognizable even upside down because of their uniforms, a contrast to the formal dinner jackets worn by other male guests. Clusters of women fawned over them. Bernard Winterhazy was near the bar, too, his cumbersome outfit affording an excellent excuse for not circulating—and also for a life-support system that was largely liquid, as usual. No wonder he was being affable. Gray dropped his eyes back to his drink and took a deep swallow, emptying his glass of everything but the ice.

There were two long bars in the tent, both surrounded by an enormous crush of people. Gray knew there was another bar, an uncrowded one, inside the air-conditioned mansion, in a living room so enormous it might have been a hotel ballroom. However, Gray didn't want to go inside: that was where Marina Winterhazy, heiress to all this social pretension, had last been seen. He had come to the tent, although he disliked the greater press of people out here, simply to escape her. Half an hour ago Marina had been in the midst of suggesting that they retire to her own private apartment over the coach house, so he could see where she slept, when the arrival of one of the astronauts had attracted her predatory attention. With considerable gratitude, Gray had managed to escape her clutches. He already knew where Marina slept, and that was practically anywhere. At the age of twenty-nine she had an incredibly long string of Washington scalps to prove it. She had decided to make Gray one of them.

Even worse, Dolly, who considered Gray an eminently eligible bachelor and was growing panicky to arrange a more permanent liaison for her daughter, had been encouraging it.

He couldn't afford to offend Marina, spoiled apple of her mother's eye, any more than he could afford to offend Dolly herself. For too many years he had been waiting to take control of the Winterhazy chain; he didn't want to lose it simply because of his distaste for sleeping with a female as pampered, as unchaste, as brash, and as lacking in fastidiousness as Marina. Thank God for the astronaut, who had kept her off his back for the past half hour.

Pink champagne was being circulated on silver trays by efficient white-coated waiters. Gray marveled that they hadn't been pressed into spacesuits too. He didn't like champagne, especially pink, but as a white coat passed, he relinquished his empty glass and with an air of resignation accepted the offering. It was better than fighting through to a bartender.

As he lifted the tulip champagne glass, he caught the distorted reflection of a young woman skillfully threading her way through the crowd. Was it Marina? He couldn't see the woman's face, but the bleached platinum hair could very well be hers. Did that mean she had lost interest in the astronaut? Although the press of people slowed her, she appeared to be aimed in his direction. Gray was a tall man, easy to spot in a crowd, and he had the distinct impression that Marina had run him to ground, possibly with the help of the overhead reflections. Damn!

Fortunately he was near an exit of the marquee, close to the site of the atrocious moonscape buffet. It was a service exit, through a canopied corridor that led directly to the kitchen. Servants had been coming and going all evening, replenishing champagne trays and vast craters of the best Russian beluga. Idly, as if he had been planning just such a move all along, Gray swiveled on his heel and aimed for the escape route. All he needed was a place to spend an hour or so; by then it would be midnight and safe to make his excuses for the evening.

Once he was sure he was out of Marina's line of vision, his steps quickened. During the first few months of his journalistic career, when he had been a lowly cub reporter, he had learned that people seldom stopped a man who looked as though he knew exactly where he was going. He also put a look of grim determination on his face, because he was aware that for some reason people didn't trifle with him when he wore that expression.

Seconds later he was striding purposefully through an enormous modern kitchen. A small army of caterers and helpers was holding forth, but they were too busy to spare more than swift, incurious glances at a man who so clearly knew his goal and intended to get to it.

He avoided the route that would lead to the main part of the house, instead aiming for a back hallway where there appeared to be no traffic. His expression eased once he reached it. Several doors opened off the corridor. Gray opened each of them in turn, quickly discarding each possibility as being too likely to attract some member of the household staff in search of supplies. A china pantry. A whole room full of glassware and crystal. Another containing two refrigerators and a freezer of institutional size. A room completely lined with shelves, all piled high with household linens. The mansion was like a miniature hotel, provisioned for a monumental amount of entertaining.

He opened a fourth door, and as he pushed it something crashed to the floor.

Simultaneously a shocked gasp greeted him, but he saw very little of what he wasn't supposed to see. By the time he took in the scene, with no more than one subliminal glimpse of bare breasts, the young woman in the room had already clutched something white and voluminous to her bosom. She stared at him, obviously unsettled, her eyes enormous. "This . . . this is the laundry room," she said unnecessarily.

He could see that for himself. He also saw that she had propped an ironing board against the door; it was this that had collapsed on his entrance. He stooped and lifted it, setting it against a wall, a task that drew him briefly into the room. He pulled back at once and stood with his hands braced against the doorframe, while his eyes flicked over the utilitarian space. There were several chairs, one of them occupied by the young woman. She certainly didn't look like a member of the household staff. A guest at the party, then? But if so, what was she doing here, half naked?

There were two washing machines and two dryers in the room, and one of the latter was in use. Through the glass panel in its door, Gray could see the tumble of something amber-brown, about the same color as the young woman's eyes, and several shades darker than her arresting corn-colored hair.

"My dress is in the dryer," she said jerkily, the sort of foolish explanation people offered when caught off balance. She had done an admirable job of controlling her expression, but there was still a breathless little catch to her husky voice, betraying some continued perturbation. She fingered the white cloth held to her breasts and evidently felt compelled to explain herself. "There was an accident with a drink, and I had to rinse out the dress. One of the maids gave me a tablecloth to cover myself, but I . . . I didn't want to rumple it unless I had to."

"You didn't need to rumple it for me," Gray noted sardonically, with a glint of amusement entering his dark blue eyes. "Frankly, I'd rather you hadn't."

"They told me I'd be alone in here," she said pointedly, her poise gradually returning. By now the white cloth was firmly installed. Squirming behind its cover, she had pulled it over her left shoulder like a toga. Her right hand now secured the cloth near her breast, leaving her left hand free. She gave him a stilted smile. "Would you mind closing the door behind you, please? Thank you."

Gray was amused, and he liked being amused. He walked right into the room and clicked the door closed, although he was well aware that that wasn't what she had invited him to do.

He held out his right hand, introducing himself. He knew she couldn't possibly take it without abandoning her hold on the tablecloth, but he had a perverse compulsion to keep her off balance, and an even stronger compulsion to feel her slender hand resting in his.

"My name is Gray," he said. "Our hostess sent me to see if you needed any help."

"You mean Marina Winterhazy, I suppose." She suddenly sounded cross. "As you're such a good friend of hers, will you take her a message from me?

Tell her she didn't have to spill her sticky crème de menthe all over my dress. She could have sidelined me just as easily by calling a taxi, or simply telling me it wasn't too, *too* impolite to leave this wretched party an hour after it started. I'd have gone like a shot! And now please put your hand down! I'm not about to shake it!"

Gray lifted his brows in pretended mild surprise and lowered his hand. The possibilities of the situation intrigued him. His hermit instinct extended only to predatory females like Marina Winterhazy, and he had no particular qualms about taking advantage of what might turn out to be a very interesting encounter indeed. Clearly, this woman was in no position to oust him physically, nor could she leave the room herself. For the time being, she was a captive audience, and Gray experienced a strong desire to know more about her—a great deal more about her. He unbuttoned the jacket of his lean, expensively tailored tuxedo, making himself at home. Then he pulled a chair out of position to straddle it, in order to face this fascinating person on her own eye level.

"I can't believe you're talking about my friend Marina," he scoffed. His face was absolutely straight, the dark blue eyes enigmatic, an expression he could maintain with ease as long as he was not in a difficult mood. "That brittle exterior of hers is only on the surface, you know. The shallowness doesn't go half as deep as you think."

A tiny imp of a smile started to form at the edges of the young woman's mouth, then vanished. She straightened her face and gazed at him under slanted lashes, as if unsure whether his absolutely serious mien covered a satirical intent.

It did, of course. Privately Gray was thoroughly

pleased to discover that she had a sense of humor, something he valued highly in a woman. And it sounded as though she disliked Marina too—another point in her favor. He decided to probe a little. "Surely you have no grudge against Marina for that silly accident?" he scoffed. "Why, she was even thoughtful enough to suggest that I come and keep you company for the duration."

The young woman wasn't amused by that. "God, you men are such fools," she said disgustedly. Then she shook herself a little and looked away, as if she knew her tongue had been too unguarded. She was silent for a time and he studied her while she studied the dryer, staring at it fixedly as if willing it to hurry up. The soft thump-thump-thump of the tumbling dress provided enough background noise so that the silence was not too awkward. Gray knew, as if he had read her thoughts, that she was wondering how to get rid of him.

"Thank God for wash-and-wear fabrics." She sighed. "It shouldn't be long now. You don't have to hang around, you know. Surely you can think of better things to do."

Gray stretched his lanky legs and crossed his arms indolently over the back of the chair, a posture of relaxed patience. "Of course I can think of better things," he drawled in a sardonic voice. "But I promise I'll do none of them yet. First we have to get properly acquainted."

She bit her lip and a faint flush crawled upward to her high cheekbones. He liked her looks. She had a towheaded naturalness that glowed with good health. Her corn-colored hair and amber eyes were extraordinarily attractive, while her facial planes and firm, shapely jaw held a fine blend of delicacy and stubbornness. The straight, slightly tip-tilted nose was sprinkled with the tiniest of freckles, hardly visible although she hadn't tried to hide them with a heavy layer of makeup. Her skin was clear, clean, and tanned to a deep, warm gold. From the promise of his one swift glimpse, Gray knew that a narrow bikini line interrupted that tan . . . and the curves had been fine and high and lovely, delicate mounds of pale whipped cream to invite a man's mouth. . . .

He studied her hair with particularly close fascination. It was so streaked by sun and nature that he couldn't spot two individual hairs that were precisely the same color, and that sort of endlessly intriguing variegation didn't come out of a peroxide bottle. Her shoulder-length cut was casually combed, tucked behind her unadorned ears. A few soft little tendrils had escaped, tantalizing to Gray's eye and to his imagination. He wanted to nibble them away from those ears. The unruly little wisps looked as if they might taste of lemon shampoo.

He wondered how many men had possessed her. Certainly, a lot of men would have tried; it was to be expected that a woman like this would be frequently approached. In this age of sexual liberation, some suitors would surely have succeeded. The moment of speculation left Gray with a sense of deep disturbance, the intensity of which unsettled him.

Her left hand was at rest on her lap. She wore no wedding ring and there was no indentation on her finger, no interruption of the golden tan to suggest that one had ever been worn. Not married, then. Satisfied in this at least, Gray returned to his inspection of the face whose earthy outdoor beauty attracted him so.

"You seem to think Marina assaulted you deliberately with her crème de menthe. What exactly did you do to deserve that sort of attack?" he asked with pretended gravity.

"Nothing! Believe me, nothing. I was talking to . . . to . . . to someone, and she wanted to show him a coach house or something. No doubt she thought I'd be in the way."

"Someone?"

She hesitated perceptibly. "One of the astronauts."

"Ah," Gray said softly and wisely. No doubt she wasn't volunteering the name because she didn't want to spread gossip. He didn't bother to pursue the question, because he had a good idea of the answer. He had recognized the handsome astronaut Marina had collared a short time before—Doug "Digger" Anderson, one of the men slated to take part in the next space shuttle mission, about three months from now. So possibly Marina Winterhazy had found an opportunity to show off her boudoir, after all. Gray also realized that it probably wasn't Marina whom he had sighted a short time ago; it must have been some other platinum-haired woman. The error had brought him here, and he didn't regret it.

"And did they go to the coach house?" he asked idly. If so, he would probably be safe from Marina's attentions for the evening.

"Probably. Why don't you ask her, as you're such good friends?" She sounded impatient with the subject. "Really, it's of no particular importance to me, one way or another." She was silent for a moment. "Look, Mr. White or Mr. Blue or whatever your name is, I'm quite capable of sitting here without company. In fact I'd rather."

"I have an inexhaustible supply of fascinating subjects I haven't tapped yet."

She looked at him scornfully, and he saw that her dark lashes were tipped with gold, proof that they hadn't been artificially darkened. She would be just as beautiful on first waking, he decided . . . and he wondered, not for the first time, what it would be like to make love to this woman.

"Starting with you." He paused. "By the way, the name is Gray. That's first name, not last. Short for Graydon, and the last name is Bennett. I don't believe I caught yours?"

She looked him straight in the eye. "No, I don't believe you did."

"Perhaps you forgot to tell me. You can correct the oversight now while you tell me the story of your life." He added persuasively, "People usually say I'm a very good listener. I never interrupt, I never try to top a story, my eyes never wander, and I'm fascinated by all kinds of trivia, including people's names."

She didn't respond, and Gray watched her with speculative, hooded eyes. As a rule, women were more receptive to him. Why, he wasn't sure, although he had always suspected the major factor was his status as an eligible bachelor in a city dramatically short of eligible bachelors. It could be his height that appealed to women; or his age, a mature thirty-six; or his influential position as publisher of the *Clarion*. It certainly wasn't his looks. No one, not even his mother or his three older sisters back in his birthplace of Des Moines, had ever accused him of being handsome. His features were markedly irregular, his dark hair too unruly, his nose too aquiline, his face too thin, his mouth too hard, and the womenfolk in his life had unfeelingly pointed out all those failings during his growing years, while idolizing him foolishly, uncritically, and unashamedly in other ways.

Perhaps she was being standoffish because she was at the party with a date. And yet, if she had a date, why wasn't he there, keeping her company? Gray couldn't imagine any man being foolish enough to let this fascinating find of a woman languish in solitary. "Are you here alone?" he asked.

"Obviously I *was,* until you came in."

"I mean at the party. Did you come with a man?"

"As it happens, yes."

"Boyfriend?"

"That's really none of your business, is it?" She was discouraging his questions, and Gray decided it was time for a change of tactics.

"If you won't tell me about you, lovely lady, I feel forced to tell you about me. It's not my most fascinating topic but I guarantee you I'm the world's leading authority on the subject. First and foremost, I'm a newspaperman. I'm involved with the Winterhazy chain, primarily *The Washington Clarion.*" He didn't add that its masthead listed him as publisher, nor did he enumerate the twenty-three other widely scattered dailies and weeklies he virtually controlled, barring the remaining Winterhazy interest.

She simply looked at him, but the faint compression of her lips told him she didn't fully approve of his profession.

"I'm reliable, hardworking, reasonably independent, and totally, but not determinedly, single. I have a nice quiet apartment I share with no one but my manservant. Hoshu is the soul of tact, honor, and decency, and he cooks a fantastic Japanese dinner. He keeps me fit by beating me regularly, in our daily half hour of karate. He also makes sure my shoes are well polished, my suits pressed, my socks mended, and my shirts clean. Those are my virtues." He took stock of her response, aware that to this point the list had produced nothing but antagonistic silence.

"My vices are far more interesting. If you're like most women, that's what you must be bursting to ask about. Please don't bother containing your curiosity." There was no answer. "Ah, well, I suppose it's better to keep you in suspense for now. Believe me, when you get to know my vices, you'll love them. I'll tantalize you with a hint. Here are my very worst weaknesses . . . women with dresses in dryers, females with honey-colored hair and freckles, ladies decked or undecked in tablecloths . . ."

"I'm not about to be picked up," she said with asperity, "so please spare me the catalog."

"I'm free for dinner tomorrow night." The next day was a Saturday. Gray tried to keep his weekends determinedly free of the demands of his occupation, even though the *Clarion*, a morning paper, was published seven days a week. His suggestion met with stony silence. "I could make that lunch if you'd rather, although I warn you I might have to cut it short. My mechanic has been doing an overhaul on the plane, and I—"

"Plane?" She leaned forward, suddenly intense and eager. "You own a plane?"

"—promised him I'd be out to test the results tomorrow afternoon," Gray drawled on casually without a skipped beat, letting none of his satisfaction show. He added idly, "I could take you up, if you like."

He recognized the look in her eye—the shining, the yearning, the hunger, the almost sexual fervor. Her lips had softened, and her fingers had tightened over the tablecloth. So he had finally found the chink in her armor: she enjoyed the exhilaration of flight. Or perhaps she just liked the idea of a man who owned a plane. It did tend to turn some women on.

She sounded breathy and excited as she inquired, "What kind of plane?"

"Nothing grand," he returned offhandedly. "Just an old AT-6. A trainer. It's in great condition, though."

She seemed to hold her breath for an intense moment, then let it go. "Fantastic," she murmured. She moistened her lips with a slow tonguetip, an unconscious movement that provoked Gray's strong response. He wanted to moisten that mouth too— with his.

And then her voice returned to normal. "Would you really take me up?" she asked eagerly. She added, in a second rush of words, "By the way, I have my pilot's license."

Gray almost scowled, but managed to control the expression because he knew his scowls had a way of seriously unsettling people. Maneuvering the weighty AT-6, a lumbering and unforgiving machine despite its ability to perform aerobatics, was no job for a greenhorn. She had probably trained on something modern and easy to handle and would be alarmed by the old plane's noise and discomfort. "Is it a date?" he asked, neatly sidestepping the issue.

She hesitated and then nodded. "It's ages since I've had a chance like this. But please, don't think . . ." Her voice trailed off.

"I'll pick you up at one o'clock. Where?"

Again there was a moment's pause. "I'll be out and about in the morning. I could meet you somewhere, perhaps even at the airstrip where you keep the plane."

"It's a package deal," Gray said firmly. "Food included, or the offer's off. First we lunch." After asking her preference for location, he suggested a well-known seafood restaurant in the renovated Georgetown district. Then, not wanting to press his luck, he rose to his feet. If he stayed he'd be tempted to try to find out what that mouth felt like, what the velvety-looking skin felt like. Now that he had his date, he could wait.

"By the way," he said casually, turning as he reached the door, "I must be slipping. What did you say your name was?"

The dryer chose that moment to finish its cycle, and the young woman's amber eyes escaped in that direction, causing another fractional hesitation before she answered. Gray wondered briefly if she was still reluctant to give her name, but her answer sounded candid enough when it came. "Clancy," she said.

"And your first name?"

"Sunny." She turned her head slowly back to the door and smiled at him, the first time she had done so.

Gray lifted a dark, quizzical brow. The name didn't suit someone so utterly feminine. "Sonny?"

"Spelled with a 'u.' My father started by calling me Sunshine—because of my hair, I suppose. Somehow it degenerated into Sunny. I used to be a terrible tomboy when I was growing up, and ladylike names didn't suit me. I still answer to the nickname."

She had a perfect smile, to Gray's way of thinking—beautiful, even teeth and a full, generous curve to the lower lip. It was a frank, open smile, but there was a promise of passion in that lip, an underlying hint of sensuality. Instinctively, with the sureness of a man who has had a good deal of experience with the opposite sex, he knew she was a woman with a great deal of fire and warmth to offer. It was unreasonable that he should be wishing he could have been the first to feel that fire. . . .

"Surely you have a proper name."

"I prefer not to use it." She answered with such firmness that even Gray, with his finely honed newsman's instinct, didn't press the question. He would find out the answer tomorrow.

"One o'clock," he said softly and left.

Adair Anderson's smile faded as soon as the unsettling intruder had left the laundry room. She stared at the door for a full sixty seconds, heart squeezing with excitement at the prospect ahead of her. An AT-6! A magnificent brute of a machine! A real beauty to handle! She hadn't flown one since moving to Houston, nearly five years before. In fact, two full years had passed since she'd had the opportunity to fly anything at all. Last time she'd done so, Doug had found out about it, and they'd had a tempestuous argument. The household budget didn't extend to renting airplanes at horrendous hourly rates, for one thing. For another, as Doug had pointed out hotly, the role of an astronaut's wife was to provide a secure nest for her husband, not to risk life and limb by performing loops, Immelmanns, and spins within crashing distance of the NASA Space Center.

An unfair commentary, Adair had thought, coming from a man who had earned the nickname "Digger" because of the number of holes he, or rather various experimental planes, had dug in the ground after supersonic bailouts, during his stint as a test pilot at Edwards Air Force Base.

All the same there was some justice in Doug's stand, Adair had to admit. Two years ago the space shuttle he was assigned to had been imminent—and it was still imminent after two years of delays. At NASA the powers that be probably wouldn't approve of her stunt flying, either, certainly not at such a vital juncture in Doug's life. It was impossible to guess the official reaction, of course; but there was no denying that the hierarchy *could* be remarkably sensitive at times. An astronaut was supposed to have strong motivations for returning to earth, and to the psychologists' way of thinking, that meant an all-American happy marriage to come home to, not a wife with a penchant for potentially dangerous aerobatics. Should an astronaut be worrying about the little woman's antics, the psychologists would ask, while preparing for an important mission in space? She ought to be home cooking meals and thinking about important things like what color carpet to put in the living room; or even better, planning a nice nursery, because a man with small children would have much stronger motivations for surviving a space voyage.

Doug had claimed that if his superiors knew about Adair's secret passion, they might decide to scrub him and substitute a backup man on the space mission that he was scheduled for. Reluctantly, after the argument, Adair had put her flying log into mothballs along with other matters of self-interest, until such time as Doug had had his moment of glory in space.

But what Doug and NASA didn't know wouldn't hurt his career as an astronaut. Washington was a long way from Houston. And an AT-6 . . . the opportunity was too good to resist!

As to the luncheon, Adair felt no guilt about accepting Gray Bennett's tempting invitation. Doug wouldn't be interested in her whereabouts tomorrow, any more than she would be interested in his. If events had followed a natural course, which she was sure they had, he had probably already arranged to spend the rest of the weekend with Marina Winterhazy. It was years since Adair had cared; she had been inured to such behavior long ago.

Slowly, guarding her modesty lest another intruder arrive at the door, Adair went to the dryer and pulled out the simple, inexpensive crepe evening dress Marina Winterhazy had inundated with such transparently deliberate clumsiness. The clinging Grecian folds had tumbled free of wrinkles, but the seams needed a touch-up. Adair plugged in the iron and waited for it to warm while she continued to think about the encounter just past and the prospect of the flight to come.

She hadn't exactly lied a moment ago. Clancy was not an invented surname, but the name she'd been born with, and Sunny was the nickname she had answered to all through her gangly, freckle-faced teens. She hadn't been called that for some years, except by her father. He alone insisted on clinging to the affectionate sobriquet, despite its tomboyish sound. But then, he had brought her up as the son he had wanted but had been unable to produce. He had had three tries at producing a male child, Adair the first in a line of failures. Because her father had become a widower shortly after the birth of his third daughter, he had had no more chances, and Adair, then six years old, had been brought up to fill the role of the brother she had never had. Adoring her father, she had loved every minute of her rough-and-tumble upbringing. As a youngster, she had even felt a faint, superior pity for her two younger sisters, raised by a housekeeper in a milieu of frilly little dresses, coloring books, and dollhouses.

While Adair's young sisters had been attending to more feminine pursuits, her father, Colonel Lamont Clancy—war hero, flying ace, test pilot extraordinary,

once holder of several supersonic speed records—
Colonel Lamont Clancy, then stationed at Edwards
Air Force Base in the Mojave Desert of California,
had been teaching his firstborn daughter how to ride
bareback, how to swim, how to play baseball, how to
win at poker, how to shoot a good straight game of
pool, and above all, how to fly.

Adair had disappointed him only twice, the first
time when she had eloped with Doug Anderson,
giving no warning of her intentions. "You're too damn
young!" he had roared when he found out. "And he's
too damn . . . impertinent!" But by then it had been
too late. Besides, he had liked Doug. "A helluva
pilot," he had said gruffly, his highest praise. And
when it came out, shortly after the elopement, that
Doug was being considered for astronaut training,
Adair's father had relented completely. From that
moment on, Doug might have been his very own
choice.

But if her father was having a change of heart, so
was Adair. She was learning how much her dashing
young husband caroused, for one thing—the first
discovery on the swift, painful road to realizing it was
Doug's occupation, not Doug himself, that she had
married. She had been young and starry-eyed and in
love with the pure exhilaration of flying, and because
he was a pilot, a good one, she had endowed him with
qualities he didn't possess. A whirlwind courtship had
swept her off her feet, mostly because Adair's tomboyish upbringing had left her awkward and untu-
tored in the dating game, and unusually vulnerable to
the first persistent male attention that came her way.

Doug's flattering devotion had lasted only until they
were married, when he began to spend many of his
evenings off base. The marriage had been hardly

more than two months old when, at a party in their tiny new home, she had happened to overhear a conversation between her husband and several other test pilots on the base. Doug had been boasting about his flagrant and frequent infidelities.

With horror, she discovered he had been unfaithful a dozen times over, starting in the first week of their marriage. It had hurt badly, and she had run away from her new husband when she learned of it—nineteen, confused, heartbroken, her life in a shambles, all of her illusions crashing down around her ears.

And that was the second time she had disappointed her father. It was he, not Doug, who had gone to find Adair a few weeks later and persuaded her into the sham of a marriage that she had been living ever since. Her instincts revolted against returning to a man who had betrayed her and boasted about it, but Adair idolized her father, and so she had listened to his reasons for wanting the marriage to remain intact.

"The inside dope is that Doug's right at the top of the list to make it into the space program," he had confided. "But you know what they want, don't you? Married men. Men with a stable home life! Sure, nowadays there are one or two astronauts who've gone through the divorce courts, but they're happily remarried—well settled with good, solid family ties. How does it look for Doug if his marriage goes to pieces after just two months? He looks like a high risk! If he were already established as an astronaut, with a mission or two under his belt, it might be different—they wouldn't dare kick him out then. But he's still trying to get *in*. Hell, if this news gets around, they'll strike him right off the list. Go back to him, Sunny. It doesn't have to be forever, just until he's had his first mission. My God, I know you won't disappoint me. Besides, this time maybe Doug'll toe the line. Can't you see how much this means to me?" Then he had added, his voice gruff, "You're a helluva kid, Sunny. Not like you to quit when the going gets tough. *You can't quit now!*"

Reluctantly, after several stormy sessions, Adair had been persuaded. She had steeled herself to do as her father wished, reminding herself that it was only for a finite period of time. "Until Doug's first space mission is over," her father had asked, and Adair had promised that much.

But she had returned to Doug on her own terms, which hadn't been quite to his liking, or to her father's. She had insisted on an occupation for herself, for one thing. Her father, a chauvinist of the first water, told her it wouldn't look right if she took a job. "It's up to the man to provide," he argued. That suited Adair, not because she agreed with her father, but because she didn't particularly want to work in the confinement of an office—and anyway, she had her own ideas about an occupation, one that would leave her a considerable amount of freedom for the outdoor exercise that was an integral part of her life. She had always had a strong interest in the history of aviation, nurtured by a small collection of rare photographs her father owned. She obtained the collection, started a broad correspondence to search for other rare photos, and began to compile a pictorial history of flight in hopes of selling it to a publisher of hardcover coffee-table books. Over the years the occupation and the voluminous correspondence it entailed had helped dispel Adair's sense of bleakness and desolation.

Once the shame and pain and hurt had passed and she had adjusted to the truths about Doug's character, she had found qualities in him that made it possible to share a roof. She liked and admired many things about him: his courage, his determination, his generally even temper, his intelligence. He also had the virtues of directness and honesty, and he seldom bothered dissimulating about his faults.

And after Doug had finally stopped trying to coerce her into sharing his bed, something he had promised not to do under the new arrangement, their relationship had even become reasonably comradely.

Occupying a bedroom with twin beds, as they had to do on this Washington trip because that was what the government provided, put a decided strain on the camaraderie. Doug didn't seem to think his promise to keep hands off covered windfall opportunities like that.

Doug wouldn't object to her spending the following afternoon with another man. He had no right to object. After the pact they had made five years before, Adair wouldn't even have to be dishonest, except about the fact that the afternoon would involve flying. However, Doug wouldn't want it to become common knowledge that she had been seen about town with another man. That—among other reasons —was why Adair had not revealed her true identity to Gray Bennett. The NASA psychologists again. *I'm sorry, Major Anderson, but we can't possibly send you up on the next shuttle. It's come to our attention that there are some, er, small differences between you and your wife. Oh, you didn't know she's been playing around? Well, you might have found out just before the launch. We can't risk marital upsets, can we? It seems she's become sick of this double standard we men so wholeheartedly endorse, and decided to correct the deficiency . . .*

For one angry moment, as the old bitterness rose in her throat, Adair wondered what it might be like to correct the deficiency with . . . with . . .

Yes, it had to be admitted, with the intruder. Gray Bennett. He wasn't at all handsome but he was dangerously attractive, with his thin, clever, bony face; his spare, whiplike length; his intense and penetrating gaze. His eyes were especially magnetic. They were midnight-blue and alive with curiosity, so that she'd had the feeling he was interested, really interested in her as a person, not just in making a pass. He did indeed look as though he'd be a good listener. And a good talker. And maybe even a good lover, for all that was worth.

"Oh, damn!" Dismayed with herself, Adair snatched the iron away from her dress, realizing she had rested it too long on the fabric. Appalled, she saw that the sensitive synthetic had scorched. The iron's shape was now imprinted on the dress, it seemed indelibly. She thought of Marina Winterhazy with a surge of venom and then caught herself up swiftly, realizing that this new misadventure could be blamed on nobody but herself.

And just because she had been fantasizing about something she would never, never do! A hole-in-the-wall affair didn't fit into her moral scheme of things at all. Besides, what did it matter if a man was a good lover? Doug most certainly must be one of the all-time greats, she reflected, judging by his success with the opposite sex. And yet in those few weeks when her marriage had been for real, she had always felt shy and inept, unable to recapture any of the exhilaration she had experienced during his courtship kisses. In bed she had spent a good deal of time hoping that the alcohol Doug had invariably consumed would prevent him from becoming aware of her lack of expertise and her awkwardness. Fortunately, caught up in his own pleasures, he had not seemed to notice her painful self-consciousness. Lovemaking, she had decided secretly and somewhat guiltily during those early weeks, was a highly overrated pastime. It wasn't one-tenth as exciting as aviation.

Men were rather like some small modern jets, she had concluded—thrilling to think about until you'd experienced the dull, uninspiring ride. Even had her moral code permitted, Adair wouldn't have wanted an affair.

All the same, it disturbed her not a little to realize she'd been thinking in such intimate terms about a perfect stranger, a man she had known for mere minutes.

And a newspaperman too. Well, that was a piece of wretched luck, and reason enough to fear Gray Bennett. Because of his occupation, there was no way she could reveal her identity, just in case he decided the story of her flying fetish was too good to keep to himself. It didn't even have to be a big story. Washington was the site of NASA headquarters, and even a few lines in the *Clarion*'s gossip column would likely be drawn to the attention of the powers that be. Doug's mission was now so close that it wasn't wise to risk official displeasure.

Adair shuddered and half-regretted the impulse that had led her to agree to tomorrow's outing. Possible disclosure of her hazardous hobby was not the only cause for concern. She wished she hadn't married at such an early age, graduating from tomboyish teen to betrayed wife with such dizzying speed that she'd had almost no experience in dealing with men other than Doug. By now she knew how to handle his particular brand of brash sexual overtures, but she wasn't so sure about Gray Bennett. He appeared to be mature, confident, subtle, complex, clever—a definitely dangerous man.

She could handle an AT-6, but could she handle *him?*

Chapter Two

$\mathcal{T}$he ruined dress, thank God, was excuse enough for Adair to leave the reception altogether. She was perfectly capable of finding her way back to the hotel without an escort, and she knew from experience that Doug wouldn't take kindly to being dragged away from the party so early. She wasn't able to find him anyway, or Marina Winterhazy either. She assumed they were still viewing the coach house—to lend a kindly euphemism to whatever was going on between them.

Before making her adieus, Adair wended her way through the packed crowd in the silver marquee to leave a message for Doug with someone who might be counted on to pass it along. She tried to walk as if the big brown iron-shaped mark on the bosom of her dress were a cunning part of the designer's intent. In the crush no one seemed to notice.

After a few minutes Adair spotted Peggy Wishard,

wife of one of the other astronauts. Peggy was a petite, bright-eyed brunette, mother of three small youngsters, and Adair's closest confidante in Houston. Her husband, Guy, was scheduled to go up with Doug, and Adair constantly marveled at her friend's down-to-earth attitude. If she and Doug had a normal marriage and three tiny children to consider, Adair didn't think she could have been quite so matter-of-fact about the upcoming space shuttle mission.

Peggy agreed to pass the message along. "Worry not, I'll make sure Digger gets the word," she said brightly. Peggy herself never gave the appearance of worrying. She was a dedicated optimist who saw shining silver linings in the darkest of clouds.

"Too bad about the dress, Adair." Peggy pulled a long face as her eyes turned downward to the scorch mark. Suddenly she exploded with delight. "Hey, I've got an idea! I'll help you dye it black. With your hair, you'd look stunning in black! You'll wow Doug! By hook or by crook, Adair, I'll make a siren of you yet!"

Peggy, who didn't know the truth of Adair's personal life but was too sharp-eyed to miss some nuances of her relationship with Doug, was determined to cure whatever ailed the Anderson marriage. She didn't realize it was beyond curing, and had been for five years.

Adair laughed lightly. "Not a chance. Sexy black simply isn't my style."

Peggy cocked her head. "Passionate purple, then. Or slinky scarlet. If you want to hold a man like Digger, you've got to stop dressing as if you'd like to disappear into the scenery."

"At the moment, I admit, that's exactly what I would like to do. See you, Peggy." Adair turned to go.

"Your father is sure looking well," Peggy added cheerfully just before Adair managed to sidle past the close-packed bodies that hemmed them in. "He gets more dashing every year."

"My . . . father?" Adair wheeled back, a quick joy lighting her face. "He's here?"

"Colonel Lamont Clancy himself," Peggy said, making a mock military salute. "Haven't you seen him yet? He was looking all over for you."

"I didn't even know he was back in the States!"

Peggy peered up at the crazy-mirror roof. "I think he's over by the bar, talking to the spacesuit."

Adair squeezed through the crowd, no longer conscious of her ruined dress. Her father was exactly where Peggy had said he would be, and she came to a halt beside him, her face shining. He was a great golden bear of a man, hardly thickened in the waist thanks to his military bearing. He was in his late fifties now, and the streaky blond hair was well threaded with silver, but his vitality was undiminished. Adair knew he would make no demonstration of affection in public, except with his eyes, and she wouldn't embarrass him by asking for it.

"Hi, Dad," she said casually.

"Hi, Sunny," he returned easily, and they didn't have to say another word. They just looked at each other, and they were right back to the best of all possible worlds, a relationship without stress and strain.

Colonel Clancy turned to his host. "Forgive me, Hazy, but my daughter and I have some family matters to discuss. Have you met Adair?"

Bernard Winterhazy waved his drink and nodded affably. "Pleezumeechu," he mumbled happily.

"As I've been overseas for so long, I haven't seen

her for two years. And I'm not much of a correspondent, so we have a lot of catching-up to do. Excuse us, will you?"

They decided to share a taxi to Adair's hotel, knowing that no privacy could be had in the astral environment of the Winterhazy party. Besides, Adair's ruined dress precluded the possibility of staying. As they maneuvered their way out of the marquee, she explained briefly, without telling her father about the encounter in the laundry room.

"And Doug? Where's he?"

"Oh, around and about. I told him I'd be leaving," she said, stretching the truth.

Dolly Winterhazy delayed them briefly as they exited. She looked at and through Adair with a vague smile, not recognizing her, and devoted all her effusiveness to the uniform. Colonel Lamont Clancy was no social lion, but his row of medals, trooped out for the official function, was impressive. Besides, as a war hero and former flying ace, he was not unknown. Dolly understood people with names; she collected them.

"Bloodsucking female," grumbled Colonel Clancy when they finally escaped.

"You should meet her daughter," Adair remarked drily before going to collect the light stole she had worn. Although it was September, the night was balmy.

"I'm in town to do some head-banging against the top brass at the Pentagon," Colonel Clancy informed her during the cab ride to the hotel. "I was planning to fly on down to Houston as soon as I was able. Then, only a few hours ago, I happened to hear you were in town. Someone mentioned you'd be at the Winterhazy bash, so I decided to surprise you. Pulled rank and wangled myself a last-minute invitation from

Bernard Winterhazy—I met him years ago, when he was on some committee or other. He's not a bad sort, really. That wife of his is enough to drive any man to drink."

In the taxicab he didn't ask Adair about her personal state of mind. He saved the question until they had closed the door of the hotel room behind them. It was a plain, unpretentious room—twin beds, teak furniture, everything new and neat and impersonal. Wordlessly, he relieved her of her stole and threw it over a bed.

Then he seized Adair's shoulders and smiled into her eyes. "And how are things with you? Still keeping that spunky little chin up, I hope? Your friend Peggy seemed a little concerned."

"I'm fine. A hundred percent," she answered with a brave smile. But she laid her cheek against the shoulder of his uniform, a movement that allowed her to hide her face for a few necessary moments. She suddenly felt more vulnerable than she had in some time. She didn't want to display weakness in her father's presence, and yet the sight of the twin beds was enough to remind her that the previous night in this room had not been an easy one. "Oh, Poppy," she said, calling him by the affectionate childhood name she still used when they were in private. "It's so good to see you. So good."

They separated and sat on the two beds facing each other. Adair didn't want her father to know exactly how discontented she was, but he was a party to the pact she had made with Doug, and he knew that the happy marriage presented for public view was a total sham. He knew she was living a lie.

She put off the moment of discussing her own situation. "What are you up to, Poppy? Have you been transferred back to the States?"

"No such luck. That's what all my head-banging was about. But the brass won't give me another assignment, so I'll be off to Europe again in three or four days. But not for long! I've decided to take retirement. I'm damn fed up with this cushy overseas job they shuffled me into—*pushed* me into, just so I'd stop causing trouble on the home front. I had hoped it might give me some action, but instead it's a dead end. Goodwill stuff, mostly. Even with all the traveling about, it's hardly better than a desk job. So . . . you know that flea-bitten ranch I've been eyeing in California? The one near Edwards? Well, I've finally done it. It's mine now, Sunny. Or it will be in a month or so, when the deal closes. It's a wreck of a place, but at least it's pancake flat and damn near perfect for an airstrip. And I'm having a brand-new ranch house built on the property."

"That sounds great."

"I have some other news too. Big news, and you're the first to hear it. I wanted to tell you in person— that's why I was going to fly down to Houston. I just got married again."

"Oh, Poppy, that's wonderful!" Adair flew across the space to give him a hug, her face shining. Then she settled back on her own bed, a tumble of questions on her tongue. "Who is she? Tell me all about her. Everything!"

"A woman I met about two years ago, overseas. Roberta's a widow . . . Canadian. She works for the Red Cross, and that's how we first connected." Proudly he produced a snapshot, but it was so fuzzy that Adair could determine little more than dark hair and a tendency to plumpness. "We got hitched last month, but I didn't want to put that kind of news in a letter. Besides, I figured I'd beat the mail anyway. You'll like her, Sunny. She's a helluva kid."

"Kid?"

"Well, she's not quite forty yet. Young enough to . . ."

"Young enough to what?" Adair teased.

If she had not known her father better, she could have sworn that he had started to blush. "She's pregnant," he mumbled to his uniform front, patting the pocket where he had placed the photograph. Again, Adair moved to her father's side and administered a delighted hug, noting that she hadn't imagined the heightened color. Colonel Lamont Clancy was red as a beet, right to the roots of his silver-streaked hair.

Adair learned that the pregnancy had only four more months to go. "The baby's due in January," her father admitted, still covered with embarrassment at having to discuss such things with his daughter. "Roberta wasn't going to tell me about it, but I dug the news out of her. She's a quiet little thing, Sunny, but she's a prize. A real prize."

It was some time before the conversation turned to other matters. When the surge of excitement had passed, Adair and her father talked for a time about Adair's younger sisters—Amelia, who at twenty-one was starting her last year at Vassar; Arden, who at eighteen had entered the same highly respected institution only days before. Colonel Clancy thought they were both wasting their time at a university, especially a university where females were in the majority. A dedicated chauvinist, he thought his daughters should be looking for bachelors, not for a bachelor's degree. "Waste of money," he grumbled. Adair, not wanting arguments on the subject, didn't bother pointing out that Arden and Amelia had both won scholarships to help pay their way.

Finally he introduced the touchy subject of Adair's personal life. "Digger . . . has he settled down yet?"

She shook her head. "No."

"Then I suppose—"

"You're right, Poppy. There's no hope."

"Tough luck." He sighed. "I really did think it would work out in time. I guess I shouldn't have let myself count on it so much, for I know how you felt."

You couldn't have, Adair almost said, or you wouldn't have asked me to do it. But she held her tongue, because there was nothing to be gained by going over old territory.

Colonel Clancy went on: "Don't you think Doug might actually stop sowing his wild oats if you got back together, Sunny? I mean together for real? You can't expect a man like that to settle down without a proper wife to warm his bed, and . . . well, he is a helluva pilot."

"I don't care whether he settles down or not. We're never going to get back together, Poppy. I don't love him, and I realize now that I never did. But I'll keep my part of the bargain. I promised you I'd stick with him until he's had his chance in space." She could have added that she hadn't thought it would be anything like five years, but it wasn't her father's fault that there had been so many canceled launches, so many technical difficulties, so many budget cuts, so many delays. In any case, the next space shuttle mission was now firmly scheduled for mid-December —if any schedule could be completely firm. "Have you even known me to back out on a deal? I'll see it through, Poppy. And then . . ."

Her voice trailed into nothing. There was a poignant and profound silence while father and daughter looked at each other, knowing without speaking what lay in the future. As soon as Doug's shuttle mission was over, Adair would start building herself a new life.

At last Lamont Clancy sighed heavily, conceding his inability to change Adair's mind. "Perhaps I shouldn't have talked you into staying with him at all, into going through with all this pretense." He passed a hand over his brow. "Don't misunderstand me, Sunny. I don't go along with all this loose behavior of Doug's, but there could be worse things for you to live with. Hell, he's a *man*, and lots of wives get used to that sort of thing."

"But I'm not lots of wives," Adair said. She added no more about their conflicting views on the double standard, because her father's visits were few and far between and she wanted no harsh words to spoil the occasion. At least her father had raised her to have a mind of her own, and she ought to be grateful to him for that.

Colonel Clancy had an admission to make. "Perhaps it's been selfish of me to push you so much. But you see, I . . . dammit, I was too damn old when this whole thing came along. This whole *incredible* space thing. And if I couldn't be an astronaut myself, well . . ."

He wanted an astronaut for a son. And failing that, for a son-in-law. Adair had always understood that. She moved to the other bed and put her arm around her father's shoulders, aching for him because he had never had the son he so desperately wanted. It was a role that she herself, with all the will in the world, could never fill. Poor Poppy.

She wanted to assure him, "Next time it'll be a boy," but she didn't dare voice the hope. What if it wasn't?

Doug didn't return to the hotel room that night, but he let himself in with his key first thing in the morning. Adair was well aware of his capacity for drink, but as usual he had no trace of a hangover, no circles under his eyes to show he had had anything less than eight full hours of sleep. He was fit, resilient, and boyishly handsome at the age of thirty-two, and his compact, muscular body had the bounce-back capacity of an India-rubber ball.

Adair was applying lipstick when he entered. She was already dressed for the day, in beige slacks and a casual white silk shirt. Overnight the temperature had dropped several degrees, and a navy blazer was laid out in readiness for a morning of sightseeing with Peggy Wishard, planned prior to the arrangement with Gray Bennett.

"Sorry about last night," Doug said, tossing a newspaper in Adair's direction.

She put it aside without looking at it, noting only that it was the Saturday edition of *The Washington Clarion.*

Doug rumpled his brown hair and tugged his ear in a characteristic, devil-may-care gesture. "Oh, hell, why pretend? I'm not sorry. I had a helluva time."

"Good," Adair said drily. She should be grateful to Marina Winterhazy. Thanks to her, the twin beds were presenting less of a threat.

"I came back to change my shirt, then I'm off for the rest of the day. Thank God for weekends!" Not troubling to go into the adjoining bathroom, as Adair always did when she wanted privacy for changing, he stripped off a rumpled shirt that bore bright lipstick traces. Rolled in a ball, it landed on the pillow on Adair's bed. Then he went to the chest of drawers and pulled out a fresh one. "Did your dress wash up okay?"

"I burned it with an iron," Adair answered dully, holding her resentment inside. Usually Doug's good nature kept her from being bothered by his cavalier expectations, but today the shirt on her pillow annoyed her. For some reason that she couldn't determine, she was feeling unusually hemmed in by the marital lie she lived.

"Tough luck." But he sounded distracted as he hurried with the buttons down his front.

"Dad's in town. Did you know?"

"Hey, great!" Doug looked up with a burst of enthusiasm. Hurriedly Adair began to fill him in on the highlights. Doug finally cut in as he reached for his uniform jacket, almost ready to go. "Maybe the three of us can get together some time this week. Not today, though."

"I'm going to be out today, too, Doug. This morning Peggy and I are going to hop onto a Tourmobile and have a look at some of the sights. Then I'm having lunch with—"

"Look, I can't talk long, there's someone waiting for me." He grinned, the lopsided, boyish grin that had once charmed Adair into a union that had turned out to have no charm at all. "If that Winterhazy dame calls in the next few minutes, tell her I'm on my way. And don't wait up for me tonight."

"Have a good time," Adair said, fighting down a surge of irritation. Didn't he care about her whereabouts at all?

Doug breezed to the door. "Cheers, Adair. See you, huh? Keep your pretty little nose clean. And say hello to your old man for me."

"Doug!"

Suddenly it had become very urgent to hear him answer a question that had been formulating in her mind for years, so gradually and so subversively that she had been unaware of it until this very moment. When he turned back, one eyebrow cocked, she asked curiously, "Why on earth did you marry me?"

He grinned again. "One, because you're a great-looking kid. Two, because you didn't fall into bed, and that was a challenge to my male ego. And three . . ."

"This is the big one, isn't it?" Adair asked quietly.

"Well, I'd be lying if I pretended it wasn't important. I happened to need a wife, and it didn't hurt that you were your old man's daughter. But give me some credit, kid. If I hadn't liked you a helluva lot, I'd have popped the big question to someone else." And with a wink and a cheeky salute, he was gone.

Subconsciously Adair had known it for years. Doug's whirlwind courtship had followed shortly after the grapevine rumor that a new group of trainees was soon to be inducted into the space program. Free-wheeling bachelors were unlikely to be considered, and having the legendary Colonel Lamont Clancy for a father-in-law would be a decided plus for any candidate. Adair knew that. So why had she felt the compulsion to hear Doug say it? No wonder he didn't care what she did! He had never been encumbered by any feeling of love for her, not even at the start. She was glad he hadn't tried to lie about it.

But for some reason she was also angry. Old resentments, long kept on the back burner, had been percolating with renewed vigor since the previous evening. She was angry at herself for having been so impressionable at the age of nineteen; she was angry at being trapped in a loveless charade; she was angry at the lie she lived. She was angry at having to behave herself in a manner becoming to an astronaut's wife. Answer the phone, take care of the laundry, and don't do anything to upset the NASA apple cart!

With Doug gone, Adair walked across the room, picked up the rumpled shirt, and threw it viciously at the pillow of his bed. "Take care of your own lipstick stains!" she cried passionately, to no one in particular.

But she carried the shirt into the bathroom and placed it with the rest of the laundry before picking up the Saturday edition of the *Clarion*.

"I've never met a newspaper publisher before," she was saying lightly a few hours later, once she and Gray Bennett had settled at a table in the quiet, tastefully restored seafood restaurant he had chosen. With its dark paneling, dim lights, and heavy silver, the place had an air of secluded intimacy that Adair found unsettling, but she was trying to keep the chatter easy and impersonal.

"I saw your name on the masthead," she went on, "and frankly I'm impressed. Isn't the publisher the man with the final word about everything? You must have an awful lot of problems."

Gray's voice held a hint of dry self-mockery. "I certainly do today. The most fearsome social lioness of the entire Washington jungle is on the rampage this morning. Due to a compositor's error, Dolly Winterhazy's guest list got mixed up with another item of society news. We credited her with putting all the members of an old folks' home, complete with wheelchairs and hearing aids, into orbits of ecstasy at her space-age party. Don't laugh! It's a crisis of interplanetary proportion."

Adair laughed. She had seen the page—"People in the News," it was called—but flipped away from it quickly, disliking the whole tone of innuendo in some of the columns and the mealy-mouthed gushing in others. Privately she was of the opinion that Gray ought not to allow that sort of trash in an otherwise respectable paper, but she didn't know him well enough to criticize, so she kept her peace. "The trials and tribulations of a publisher! And I thought your most serious headaches would involve nothing worse than tricky union negotiations, dwindling advertising revenues, rising newsprint prices, and dropping circulation."

"Strike the last problem, but otherwise, yes, that's more or less the life of a publisher. Actually, though, I prefer giving headaches to getting them. I always try to put them right back where they belong—into the heads of union negotiators, purchasing departments, and circulation managers. Fortunately I have an excellent staff. I'm a great believer in doing absolutely nothing that someone else can do better."

"It sounds like the story of your manservant all over again! Do you always delegate everything?"

"Not everything. As I came up through the editorial side, I still devote most of my energy to improving the newspaper's contents."

Adair almost mentioned the sleazy society page, but thought better of it. "What else didn't you tell me about yourself?"

Gray's smile faded, his eyes becoming penetrating. "Not half as much," he said in a soft, incisive voice, "as you didn't tell me about *you*. Where would you like to start?"

Adair's heart skipped a beat, and her eyes fled to study the soda-and-lime she had ordered. With an afternoon's flying ahead, it was nonalcoholic, but now she felt she could have used something with a little more bite. Had Gray been asking questions about her? With a newspaper's files to call upon, he might very well have found out the truth. "There's very little to tell," she temporized.

"There's no point holding out," Gray warned. "I have you all figured out now—well, almost figured out. I'm a newspaperman by training, remember. First of all, I saw you leave the party last night. Due to the crowd, I couldn't quite see your companion's face, but I saw his hair—silver mixed with a streaky gold very like yours—and his colonel's uniform. Even from the back, he looked vaguely familiar. With the last name Clancy for a clue, I was pretty sure I knew his identity, but I decided to make sure. It wasn't hard to get hold of the complete Winterhazy guest list. I simply asked my society editor."

Adair's heart halted and then began to hammer too quickly when he added, "Fortunately she had the most updated list, complete with penciled additions at the end. There was only one Clancy on the whole thing, and that's where it was, last entry on the list. As I always work backward, naturally I spotted it right at the start. Colonel Lamont Clancy. Clearly you're not his wife, so you must be . . . his daughter?"

Adair's eyes had flown back to Gray, wide with a consternation she could not conceal. She nodded wordlessly. Gray murmured, "Why didn't you tell me before?"

"I didn't think you'd care," Adair said, managing a quick recovery. His piercing blue eyes were puzzled, mildly curious. Had he still not made the connection? She held her breath, waiting for him to identify her as Doug Anderson's wife.

"Not care? How could I own a plane and *not care?* Come now, be reasonable. Your old man is practically a flying legend. And you know I have an interest in flying. What was your reason for hiding the connection? Modesty?"

Adair shrugged and answered with a wisp of a smile that could have meant anything at all.

"No, it can't be that—you looked too shocked just

now. Were you afraid I might print something that would embarrass your father? 'Air Ace's Daughter Surprised in Secret Striptease.' That sort of thing?"

"Maybe," Adair said guardedly.

Gray's voice was sardonic, lightly edged with mockery. "I wouldn't risk my afternoon's date with you by printing an exposé like that. If you'd thwarted me in my goal of becoming better acquainted with you, however, you might have found yourself in print. Anything to achieve my purpose! Which, I have to warn you, is exactly as wicked as you think it is. I freely admit that tablecloths arouse my most primitive instincts. I often tell myself that nature never intended us to use them, which may explain why last night I found myself with a very heathen urge to dispense with the wretched things altogether. With uncivilized thoughts like that going around in my head, do you think I'd have stopped at a little yellow journalism?"

Was he simply playing her along? Adair kept her eyes turned to her soda while she tried to think. He might not yet know that she was an astronaut's wife, but if he knew she was Colonel Lamont Clancy's daughter, he was certainly on the right track. The connection was a matter of public record, so it was only a question of time until he made it. She considered backing out of the afternoon's flying, but then she thought of the AT-6 and the old longing rose in her throat.

Gray was talking again, with the relaxed, engaging manner of a man who knows how to set others at ease when he chooses. "At least this explains some things about you. You came by your flying honestly, didn't you?"

"Yes." Adair nodded, still tingling with tension, too apprehensive to extend the answer.

"I suppose your father took you up almost as soon as you could toddle."

She affirmed it, this time without words. There was an electric tension in the air between herself and Gray Bennett, and she had the idea that Gray felt it too. He had leaned forward, and his hand had crept closer to hers on the tablecloth. He didn't close the gap, but her skin quivered, reacting to the impact of the single inch between their hands. She had the feeling his fingers were about to shoot forward and clamp over her wrist, pinioning her to the table while he triumphantly disclosed his knowledge of her true identity.

"I suppose you teethed on air force jets?"

Tension still gripped her throat, preventing an answer. When she failed to respond, Gray sighed. "Well, I suppose you wouldn't tell, even if you had. That would be against regulations, wouldn't it? So I'll simply have to make my own guesses. Your father has broken every other rule in the book—why balk at giving his daughter a few joyrides in military aircraft? As I recall, it was because of various infractions— most of them far, far worse than that—that he got himself booted off into limbo overseas."

Adair finally got her voice together. She didn't want Gray Bennett making guesses about how many rules her father had broken. "Dad owned an old World War Two Mustang. His *own* plane. He bought it in a war surplus sale. There was also an AT-6 on base that was privately owned. I trained in it."

"So you do know how to handle the beast. I wondered." His fingers at last made a physical connection, but without force. With his thumb, he probed gently and started to draw soothing circles over the palm of Adair's hand. Her mind rejected the softly persuasive contact, but for some reason she could not bring herself to pull her hand away, as she knew she ought to have done.

Gray was looking thoughtful, as if he hadn't noticed what his hand was up to. His thumb continued to adventure, now stroking the exposed pulse at her wrist. It was ticking at an alarming rate, and she could only put it down to her fear of having him home in on her exact identity. There was something about Gray Bennett's physical presence that caused her brain to whirl just when she ought to be thinking most cautiously. His dry comments about yellow journalism had been satirical, and Adair didn't really take them seriously; nevertheless, she felt he was dangerous. There was a hard, compelling, possibly unscrupulous man beneath that easy manner of his. A man she couldn't trust.

Suddenly Gray smiled broadly. The expression emphasized the long, interesting grooves in his thin cheeks and deepened the little indentations feathering out from the edges of his eyes. When he wasn't smiling, the flesh in those tiny crevices was paler than the rest of his tan, now dark from a whole summer's sun. His teeth were strong and even, Adair noted, and his mouth had a wonderfully firm and interesting line. But he wasn't good-looking at all, so what was it that made him attractive?

All those thoughts passed like quicksilver through her mind, in the the second before his grin changed into conversation. "Are you afraid I'd expose your father's old infractions? You needn't worry. I've broken more than a few rules in my own time. Besides, I'm one of your father's staunchest admirers. I'm sure he would have made general long ago if he hadn't spent so many years bucking the establishment. About fifteen years ago I did some research on him for a series of articles I was writing on the history of supersonic flight. At the time I flew out to Edwards Air Force Base and met him. In fact, I was at your house."

Adair had bent her head in order to escape his visual magnetism. Now she glanced up, alarmed. He did know a lot about the Clancy family, then. Here it came, the denunciation. If so, she would have to beg off the flying.

"I suppose you were one of the three little moptops I saw peering over the bannisters? As I recall, your sisters are all just as entrancingly towheaded as you are."

"Yes," she conceded, feeling numbed except in those inches where their hands met. There, her skin seemed to be suffering from high-voltage electric impulses, further contributing to an inability to think clearly.

The waiter chose that moment to arrive with steaming bowls of clam chowder, rescuing Adair. Gray at last pulled his hand away, restoring function to her fingers. She started to toy with the creamy soup, hoping that he wouldn't notice the trembling of her wrist, the legacy of a touch that had affected her, she tried to tell herself, mostly because of her inner tension.

Over his own soup Gray eyed her speculatively. "Now all I have to do is guess which one you are. It's a long time in the past, so I've forgotten all of your names, I'm afraid. I'll have to work by process of elimination. The youngest . . . I'd hazard a guess that you're not young enough to be the youngest. Which one is she?"

Adair dabbed her mouth on a large linen napkin and mumbled the answer through it. "Arden," she said. And now he was one step nearer to the truth.

"One down and two to go."

Adair felt held and hypnotized by Gray's mocking gaze. His lashes were thick and black, like dark curtains over his heavy-lidded eyes. No man had a right to lashes like that, Adair thought . . . and then reminded herself forcibly that Gray Bennett wasn't handsome at all; there was no reason to be devastated by his male attractions. The fascination he exerted must be like that of a snake charmer, mesmerizing her into a state of trance.

He glanced at Adair's unadorned ring finger, his eyes thoughtful. "Let me see . . . didn't one of you marry an astronaut?"

Adair's heart skipped a full beat, but his close attention to her hand suggested that the missing wedding ring might have misled him. People did put an awful lot of stock in wedding rings. "Yes," she said. The word sounded mangled to her ears.

"Which one?"

It was a moment for split-second decision. "Adair," she heard herself say—as if she were talking about someone else altogether.

"Hmm. Yes, I saw your brother-in-law at the party last night. I suppose your sister Adair was there too?"

Adair nodded a wordless yes. Gray went on: "And that explains why you and your father wangled in at the last minute, I suppose? I wondered, because snobbish socializing isn't Colonel Lamont Clancy's usual style. Adair . . . she must be the oldest, I imagine?"

"Yes."

"Which puts you squarely in the middle. Now are you going to tell me your real name?" Gray Bennett requested persuasively. "By now you must know I can find out easily enough. All I have to do is set some reporter to asking a few questions. I'd prefer not to do that kind of prying—although I will, if I must. Sunny may have done for a tomboy, but it's wrong for a woman like you. Besides, my curiosity about you extends a lot further than nicknames."

Adair licked her dry lips. "Amelia," she said. A slightly defiant tone covered her sense of guilt. Well, why not? Amelia wouldn't care, and it certainly solved the identity crisis of the moment.

She embroidered the lie with some truth. "I was named after Amelia Earhart. I don't think the name suits me, though."

Gray looked her over carefully, his eyes astute. "No," he agreed after a moment. "No, it doesn't, particularly. But Sunny . . . no matter how you spell it, it sounds as though the gender's wrong. You deserve something infinitely more feminine, I think. I refuse to call you Sunny."

Adair was afraid she might fail to respond with sufficient promptitude if he called her Amelia. "You could invent a nickname for the afternoon," she suggested.

"I'll have to think about it. Whatever I decide to call you, it's got to last a lot longer than one afternoon, and it's got to work in situations a great deal more personal than we'll encounter in an AT-6."

His voice was grave. He wasn't being facetious at all, as he had been about tablecloths. Adair felt a peculiar thrill flow through her but tried to tamp the feeling down, reminding herself of the trouble she had gotten into the last time she'd succumbed to a man's declaration of serious interest in her. Gray was looking at her in that probing way of his, and although his expression was neither suggestive nor particularly seductive, Adair felt as if he had seen into her mind and discovered all its offbeat, out-of-the-way corners.

She felt the heat begin to rise in her face. Gray saved the moment by saying quietly, "Don't worry, I'll settle for Amelia, for the time being at least. Now tell me more about what you do with your time—besides flying, that is."

"Nothing else I do is particularly interesting," Adair said, hedging.

Gray gave her a deep look, presaging a return to the lightly bantering mood of before. "I have an insatiable need to know endless amounts of information about you. Stick to the really important things. For instance: do you bathe in tubfuls of pure cream . . . and do you use lemon shampoo . . . and have you ever counted the freckles on your nose . . . and . . ."

Adair laughed, delighted, in part because she had expected harder questions. "No, and yes . . . and no to the last!"

"*I* have," Gray said somberly. "There are exactly seventeen, except when you wrinkle your nose, as you do sometimes when you're concentrating. Then the tiny one at the top of your nose vanishes. I'm always breathless until it reappears. Now, can you really think I'll be bored by anything at all to do with you?"

He wasn't. Through lunch he listened and Adair talked, unfolding unconsciously, opening like a flower in the warmth of his genuine interest. Mostly she spoke about flying, for she wanted to prevaricate as little as possible. She also told of her morning's sightseeing, which had begun with the important public monuments and the famous Japanese cherry trees ringing the Tidal Basin, on the Tourmobile trip shared with Peggy. On her own, Adair had also made a quick inspection of Georgetown's interesting old Federal and Victorian houses and found herself charmed by the district's boutiques, bistros, and sidewalk flower vendors. "It's lovely the way the old buildings have been restored. Like this restaurant! You know, this is my first trip to Washington, and it isn't exactly what I expected. It seems to stretch out, not up. And the most astonishing thing for such a big city is all that greenery, everywhere you look."

There were a few lies that couldn't be avoided. Amelia attended Vassar, but Adair didn't know enough about college life or Poughkeepsie to juggle her way through that particular pretext. And it would be ghastly if Gray took a notion to contact Amelia some day!

Nor did she want to give Gray any idea of where she herself lived, and yet she had to tell him something when he asked. She did some quick thinking when he pressed her for an answer. "I travel a lot," she said. "All the time, in fact."

"Did you win a lottery, or is it just an occupational hazard?"

"I . . . occupational hazard." There were more mental gymnastics, for she didn't want him asking what company she worked for. "I . . . investigate hotels and tourist attractions for travel agencies. You know, give them ratings and so on. It's a freelance thing. I have a few clients."

"Odd you've never gotten to Washington before."

She smiled and gave a helpless little shrug. "I go where I'm asked. I have a new client who's interested in Washington accommodations."

"You must have a home base."

"New York, at the moment," she invented quickly. It was a big, impersonal city where there must be pages and pages of Clancys in the telephone directory. "But by next week or next month . . . well, frankly, I'm not sure. I recently gave up my apartment, for I was almost never there. A home base is a waste of money for someone who's always at a different hotel."

"Elusive female," he said with a groan, looking at her glumly. "I suppose you're not going to tell me how I can get in touch with you after today."

Adair considered admitting baldly that she had no intention of allowing this acquaintance to extend beyond the afternoon. Instead something impelled her to say, "You could write to me in care of my sister. She would forward a letter."

"Which sister?"

She gave him the address in Houston. "Adair will know where I am," she said, pleased with her round-about ruse. Of course, there would have to be some internal analysis later on, most of it to do with why she would want to continue communication when she had no thought of becoming involved.

But for the moment Adair was simply living from one instant to the next, by this time enjoying the game of misleading Gray Bennett. Her face was becoming animated and her eyes had begun to sparkle, and it didn't even occur to her to consider that Gray's admiration might be the cause. In impersonating her own sister, she was flirting with danger, discovering an exhilaration that increased in direct proportion to the success of her daring.

"Any other men in your life?"

Adair was still pondering an appropriate response when Gray went on, his keen eyes fixed thoughtfully on her lips. "No, on second thought I retract that question. Of course there are other men—in fact, in view of that arm's-length reception I got last night, I imagine the competition is pretty rough. However, I like a challenge. I intend to make you forget them all."

So she didn't have to prevaricate about Doug. But Adair did tell Gray another lie, or rather a part-truth. It occurred to her that when Doug went up on the space shuttle, she might attract publicity as his wife. A man in Gray's position likely had little time for watching TV, but if he happened to see a press photo at some point, he wouldn't miss it.

She thought she could muddy the issue in advance. "I'm fascinated that you remember all the little Clancy sisters. We're all look-alikes, you know."

"Yes, I remember. Quite striking, that Clancy hair."

"Sometimes people mistake me for Adair."

"I wouldn't make that mistake."

"You might . . . from a distance."

"There can't be two exactly like you. Besides, I can count freckles across a crowded room."

Under those perceptive blue eyes, Adair knew a swift, uneasy moment. She had the idea he was stating no more than the truth.

Gray kept his AT-6 in a hangar filled with painstakingly restored planes, most of them of World War Two vintage. It was a private flying club, he had explained during the drive to the small airstrip in Virginia. Its members were able to share facilities, trained mechanics, and even difficult-to-come-by parts.

Adair was giddy with delight. Because of her interest in the history of aviation, she recognized all of the antique machines in the hangar, despite the cheerful coats of fresh paint that were a far cry from camouflage khaki. There was an old P-47 Thunderbolt, a pair of flashy P-51 Mustangs painted bright blue, a PT-19 Cornell, a gull-winged Corsair. There was a Tiger Moth and a Stearman biplane.

"And a Fairey Firefly," she breathed out excitedly, tiptoeing up to peer at the strange wing structure of a sleek silver machine. "I've never seen one before."

"Then I'm surprised you recognize it. It's a distinctly rare bird."

Adair pirouetted away, filled with a reckless happiness that made her forget she was supposed to be a staid married woman, the emotional anchor that tied an astronaut to earth. She felt sixteen again, carefree as a girl. "And where's yours?"

It was, he told her, at the far end of the hangar. They walked past planes from which grease-stained men grinned at Gray, calling out good-natured male insults. It all sounded warm and familiar to Adair, who had made a mental spiral right back to the days prior to her marriage. She felt utterly free-hearted, a tomboy again, as if all her growing up were ahead of her, and none of it as painful as it had actually turned out to be.

The lumbering AT-6 had already been moved out onto the runway. She could see it through the open hangar door. It was painted a bright canary color, but even so it looked like a huge, faintly menacing bird of prey. The polished glass on its canopy glinted in the sun. A man in overalls was about to climb out of the rear cockpit, having completed a last-minute instrument check. Gray called a greeting, and while Adair waited in a state of high anticipation, he and the mechanic exchanged a few words.

Before leading her to the plane, Gray escorted her to a shadowed corner of the hangar and halted at a large metal locker. Opening it, he disposed of his suit jacket, which he had been carrying hooked over his shoulder. He relieved Adair of her blazer and handed her an armload of flying gear. "It may be a little large," he warned, "but it's the best I can offer."

Adair pulled the baggy, unflattering flight overalls directly over her street clothes, obviating the need for a changing room. Excitement was beginning to bubble inside her, the anticipation that for her always preceded the marvel of flight. The excitement was still contained, but once in the air those emotional bubbles would be released through her bloodstream, causing a "high" that was headier than champagne, more potent than kisses, more exhilarating than any embraces of love she had ever experienced. It was the ultimate experience. Or at least, that was how it had always seemed to Adair.

She zipped up the front of her overalls and turned to find a parachute, knowing herself quite capable of strapping it on without help. However, Gray had picked up both chutes to carry them closer to the plane. "After you," he said, waving her toward the apron where the AT-6 waited.

The mechanic's arrival in the hangar delayed Gray for a few moments while Adair went out to the plane. She walked around it, slowly looking it over, admiring its excellent condition. With Gray no longer in sight, she was paying little attention to his doings, so the hands that closed over her upper arms came as a surprise. She stopped stock-still, stunned by the sensuous thrill that had reached her right through the heavy layers of clothing she wore. A few of her internal bubbles leaped into premature release, and the surprise of that left her too frozen to object when he began to buckle her into her parachute.

"Hold still," he murmured into her hair, the words stirring little wavelets of air that fanned her ear. Her earlobe felt extraordinarily sensitive, like radar receiving invisible signals and amplifying them a thousandfold.

And then he began to affix the parachute. She had

never thought of this as an intimate procedure until now. But the straps had to pass over the shoulders, around the body, even between the legs.

She closed her eyes when he eased that lowest strap through the niche, his hands slow and sure, his breathing echoing the thud in her heart. She couldn't believe that she wasn't protesting, that she wasn't seizing the fastenings from him. She felt every movement of his hands as if there had been no layers of cloth at all. It all seemed to be happening in slow motion, too, his arms remaining around her for ages as he fastened the recalcitrant buckles, checked the D-ring at her breast, released the ungainly weight of the parachute to hang behind her, turned her in his arms for a quick visual check.

Her eyes were still feverishly closed when he turned her, and her face was flushed too. She was dizzy and exquisitely short of breath, and she could not remember experiencing these exact bodily sensations before in all her life. Even with her eyes shut and the sun warm on her lids, she was utterly aware of Gray, but she was unaware that her lips had unconsciously parted—moist, trembling, expectant. It was the look of sexual fervor she had worn the evening before, stronger and sweeter than ever because the expectation was more intimate and more immediate.

Gray looked and couldn't mistake what he saw. He knew when a woman wanted to be kissed, and many years had passed since he had gained the expertise and patience to do it in the exact way women wanted.

His long fingers already had firm possession of her shoulders, so there was little to do but slide his hands slowly around to her back. And then he bent his dark head, moving his open lips slowly over hers. He had spent a lot of time thinking about this moment, and although he would have preferred it to come about in some more private place, he wanted to savor it to the full.

Adair had ceased to think at all. No man's touch had ever affected her like this, possibly because no man had ever touched her so tenderly, so reverently, so seductively. Gray's slow, explorative patience made no sudden demands. His flattened palms slid over her shoulders as warmly, as gently, as if they had been moving on bare skin. And his tongue compelled with the most insidious of temptations, tutoring her in the responses he wanted, seeking the inner velvet of her mouth only as she became helpless to withhold it.

And even then he probed with a gentle mastery, plumbing the depths as if to draw all the sweetness of her into his own mouth, but giving more sensuous pleasure than he took. She forgot all but the primitive senses of touch and taste as he explored the vulnerable inner lip, the polish of her teeth, the warm cavern of the hidden recess beyond. And suddenly Adair was awash with an intoxication of bubbles—wild bubbles, bursting bubbles, beautiful bubbles, a freedom of feeling such as she had never known except in flight.

She reached for the sweet sensation as mindlessly as if this had been her first kiss. She wrapped her arms around Gray's neck and twined her fingers into the good vitality of his dark thick hair; and with her lips, she invited the passionate deepening of the kiss. Her tongue tangled with his in increasing ardor as latent and long-suppressed urges swept through her, compelling her to forget that she had any past to remember at all.

She pressed close against Gray, submitting all her senses to the masculine feel of him, the whip-lean, supple height of him. He was spare and hard and muscular, and he smelled of potent male things— soap, after-shave, the detectable aroma of the black leather jacket he had donned for the flight. The scents and the tastes and the textures of him dizzied her. His long fingers stroked her nape with slow, erotic skill, drawing from her a wildness of response she had not known herself capable of. And then he touched her ears, the slight roughness of his thumb bringing to life a thousand undiscovered nerve endings, pulling her into a whole new vortex of quivering, delirious sensations. Her body trembled beneath the exquisite, expert domination of his moving hands. Her reason fled beneath the skilled incursions of his tongue. Her mind spiraled at the strength of his lean, muscular thighs, at the virility that every feminine intuition told her she could swiftly arouse. She wanted to feel him aroused. She hadn't known she could want that so much. . . .

"Hey, Gray!" called a voice from somewhere. "Ain't you going to take that crate up?"

Chapter Three

$\mathscr{T}$he kiss had been a bit like a bad spin, Adair decided a short time after takeoff. In a good spin, a planned spin, everything worked, even in that dizzying moment before a pilot made the decision to exercise control. The world whirled, the ground raced up too quickly, the head reeled sickly; and all the time the hand hovered over the stick, and the reeling brain stayed clear and cool, because in a few more seconds it would be too late to pull out of the spin at all.

But in the spiral of that kiss, her head had been anything but clear and cool. Her hand hadn't been hovering over the stick, ready to pull back. She had lost control; in fact, she had never had it at all. She had been like a neophyte on her first flight, so overwhelmed by the sensations that thought had been blotted out altogether, causing a paralysis of the mind. She had the feeling she would have abandoned herself completely to pure feeling, had she and Gray been in some more private place. Thank God for the mechanic's timing!

Next time she would know better—except that there wouldn't be a next time. But if there *was,* if it happened that Gray took advantage in some moment when her guard was down, she wouldn't lose control again.

And what could she say to Gray if he tried again? I'm sorry, I didn't mean to respond? Keep your hands off, mister, this property is temporarily taken? I haven't told you the truth about my marital status? She decided it was best to say nothing at all. Just avoid compromising situations from now on, she told herself sternly.

Gray had assigned her to the forward cockpit, while he occupied the rear, normally the instructor's seat. Buckled into a familiar haven, with her parachute folded into the yawning cavity of the seat to form a cushion beneath her, she was at home and in control. Enclosed by the canopy and with earphones in place, she was still only partially protected from the bone-rattling noise of the AT-6. Adair was used to it. Her brain was cool and clear now, but it was so much occupied in thinking about the kiss that many of her reactions during takeoff were automatic, the result of long training since earliest youth. Her experienced feet made no mistakes on the rudder pedals; her left hand was sure on the throttle, the mixture, and the propeller pitch controls; she kept a close visual check on the instrument dash and an eye on the needle/ball/airspeed. But she was so absorbed in thinking about the exhilaration she had experienced during the kiss that she didn't notice she had very little left over to devote to the flight.

Gray was keeping in touch on the pilot-to-pilot intercom, but he was giving few instructions except those necessary to guide her away from crowded flight corridors. The earphones of the old helmet she wore were a far cry from the sophisticated space-age technology of newer equipment, but Adair was accustomed to distinguishing words through the interference of heavy static. She listened carefully because Gray was familiar with flying conditions, restrictions, and visual landmarks in this area, and she wasn't.

Even in competition with the static and the thunderous noise of the engine, his tone came through cool and controlled, as if the kiss had never happened. In fact, thought Adair with a sudden flash of anger, he was too damn cool. And too damn practiced with his embraces! Did he kiss every passing woman that way?

Suddenly she remembered Marina Winterhazy and remembered that Gray had introduced himself as her friend. He had defended her too. Had he had an affair with that shoddy little baggage? Probably. Like Doug, he couldn't see her for what she was—or perhaps he didn't care. Men were all cut from the same piece of cloth. How *could* she have allowed herself to respond to Gray with such abandon?

Irked, she did a slow half roll and dropped to a lower altitude, flying upside down. Below, as close as Adair's common sense allowed, were the ruffled waters of Chesapeake Bay. She wanted to disrupt Gray's composure as he had disrupted hers. She wished she had her father's flying skill—even flying upside down, *he* could have dropped so low that the skin would prickle at the prospect of a particularly big wave spraying the plane's canopy.

"If you can give me a few more feet," crackled an unperturbed voice into her earphones, "I'll get out my fishing tackle."

Gray's chuckle annoyed her and she eased downward by the few feet he had so ironically requested. Did he think she wouldn't dare? A few seconds later he added, "By the way, there's a fishing trawler dead ahead."

Adair was already rolling into a right-side-up position and climbing swiftly away from the path of the trawler. "I saw it," she said tautly.

"I was absolutely sure you did," came the dry retort. "I was only trying to aim you properly. With a little luck, you might have sheared off the mast with your wingtip. Correction, *my* wingtip."

"I never take foolhardy risks," Adair said crisply into her mouthpiece, only to hear the maddening rumble of Gray's chuckle sounding again in her earphones.

They were high and flying toward the mainland now, and she executed a series of lazy rolls, with the blue bay far below them, and Virginia and Maryland a patchwork of green and brown seen from on high. Rivers and estuaries trailed away from the bay like delicate and haphazard blue ribbons, the Patuxent, the Potomac, the Susquehanna, others she couldn't identify. Outside the distant cities, roads were pale threads, cars were crawling mites, huge factories were tiny toys. She banked and aimed back out over the water, climbing again.

"You say you never take risks?" Gray's taunting voice sounded again in her ears, all the more disturbing because she couldn't see his face. "In other words, you don't have the courage to accept a dare?"

Adair bristled, all the tomboy in her rising to the challenge. "Of course I do!"

"Good! I was afraid you wouldn't."

She looped and then asked curiously, "Well, what's the dare? I'm still waiting."

"Dinner," crackled the earphones. "I told Hoshu to cook for two tonight."

"Two?" she repeated blankly, stunned into momentary stupidity.

"A nice even number. My favorite, in fact."

Adair felt a sudden weakness in the pit of her stomach. It traveled through her legs and tingled her breasts as the memory of Gray's seductive kiss overwhelmed her. There was Doug to think of . . . but Doug had no right to object. Thanks to him she had a long, empty evening ahead of her. There was nothing to prevent her from accepting. . . .

She pulled herself together, reminding herself that two was a very dangerous number indeed, especially when Gray Bennett was one half of the number. "If you want two at your table, you'll have to invite your man Hoshu to eat with you. I can't accept."

"It's not an invitation, it's a dare. You told me you were ready to accept a dare."

Adair dealt with her immediate feelings by executing an Immelmann—a half loop, followed by a half roll to bring the plane right side up again. With the stunt complete, the plane had changed direction by a hundred and eighty degrees. She banked back to her former direction of flight, then bent into her microphone and cried, "I won't accept *that* dare!"

"Coward!"

The word was like a gauntlet flung in her face. They were over the water now, with nothing below but blue sea. She pulled level and did a strictly forbidden snap roll, a maneuver that could pull off a wing if improperly done. The wild vertigo of the sudden violent roll, over before a passenger could realize it had started, stirred dust from the cockpit floor, leaving the air hazy. Adair was ready for the sensation; she hoped that Gray wasn't.

Not a word from the rear cockpit. She hoped he was terrified out of his wits. "Don't you have anything to say about that?" she asked angrily.

She thought she could hear the clucking of Gray's tongue. "Shows I'm a mighty bad housekeeper. Would you care to do it again, with the canopy open? We might be able to shake out some of the dust."

She went into a tight turn. The plane shuddered, stalled, and broke out of the turn by falling into a crazy spin. "If it's a drink of the briny you want," Gray drawled as the sea rushed up at them, "I can ask Hoshu to add it to the menu."

She pulled out of the spin, angry because she hadn't succeeded in shattering Gray's cool. She was sure she heard soft laughter in her earphones. Damn him for laughing at her, with danger staring him in the face!

"Don't ask Hoshu to do anything, because the answer is still no!"

"Coward," he repeated.

She flew low and level for a minute and then climbed again, right through a puffy cumulus cloud, the only one in the near sky. In that white blanket the verbal static in her earphones started again, making her flesh prickle. "Hoshu's cooking—now there's a *real* adventure. This playing about in the air is tame compared to the wild and wonderful things he does in a kitchen. Are you afraid to say yes?"

"No!"

"I knew I'd convince you."

"I mean no, the answer is no!"

"You have other plans for tonight? You'll have to cancel. Last night I told you food was included in my invitation. I meant dinner too."

"The answer is still no!"

"Coward," he said for a third time.

"I'll make you eat that word!" She had climbed to a

height where the atmosphere was growing thin. She banked and turned, aiming in a great slow arc back toward the lonely cloud that was now far below, using it as a target in the sky. All around it, blue sea glittered in the sun, the indented coastlines safely in the distance. Adair's father had taught her to confine her aerial stunts to unpopulated areas.

"And how do you plan to make me eat it? By proving I'm more of a coward than you are?"

"Exactly!"

"And if I don't admit defeat? I have to have some incentive in order to keep my hands off the controls."

"If you touch your controls, Gray Bennett, you lose. If you don't, I lose."

Because it was a trainer, the plane had duplicate controls. There was no automatic override, but from his cockpit Gray could exercise some restraint over Adair's daredevil flying, if he chose to fight for control of the pedals and the stick. And he would choose, she thought—if he got alarmed enough about their safety. She intended to give him a good scare, enough to force him into seizing control of the plane. It would be a concession of defeat on his part, and then he would have to stop pressuring her. In Adair's frame of mind it seemed easier than sticking to a simple, unequivocal no. She felt alarmingly close to accepting the dinner invitation.

"In other words, either I eat my words or you eat Hoshu's dinner?"

"Yes."

"Done!"

She put the plane into a sudden dive, and the great, heavy AT-6 streaked back down toward the lone cloud, plummeting like a stone. As the plane burst through the fog of white, she kept an eye on her altimeter because water was deceptive, particularly when a slanted sun caught its surface and sent distorted visual messages winking back up at a plane. Even pilots flying at a slow speed over calm water had been known to crash, thinking they were a safe hundred feet off the surface. But the speed and the wild angle of the dive greatly magnified the dangers.

When she started trying to get the plane back in control, she knew a millisecond of cold fear. Perhaps her timing was off from lack of practice; perhaps it was the sun on the water; perhaps she was rattled by Gray's disruptive taunts; perhaps her insides were screaming at his insistence on a dinner she didn't dare agree to. Whatever the reason, her feet and her hands felt frozen on the controls, just as a beginner's limbs sometimes froze.

The water was still coming at her, rushing at her, blinding her. The plane was gathering speed with every fraction of a second. The sea was too close now . . . much too close . . . too late . . . *too late* . . .

She made a hair-raising recovery with no margin for safety at all, and found herself shaking as the plane swooped within skimming distance of the water and zoomed upward at tremendous speed, hurtling up to three thousand feet before full momentum was lost.

She decreased the airspeed, through with all stunts for the day. And maybe for life. She hadn't intended anything quite so foolhardy, and she had frightened herself very, very badly indeed. She was too shaky to care whether Gray called her a coward or not.

"Well?" His even voice managed to sound like a mocking murmur, even against the interference and the plane's incessant boom. "Do I win?"

It seemed a small thing now, because Adair knew that she had almost lost more than a bet. "You win," she conceded, hoping the crackle of Gray's earphones would cover the tremor in her voice.

Habit and sheer force of will held her together for the next half hour, until they were down. There were no more close calls, although the landing was a little bumpy, not the effortless exercise Adair usually achieved.

The hangar was a haven, a goal in itself. She taxied to it slowly, automatically following Gray's directions. She inched the great machine into place on the apron, came to a standstill, and cut the engine. After the deafening noise, the cockpit filled with the thin, whistling whine of gyros.

"Thank God for solid earth," a dry voice said into her earphones. "For a while I didn't think I'd see it again. You really are your father's daughter, aren't you?"

Adair hardly heard the sardonic remark. She unbuckled her helmet and pushed it off, cutting the aerial communication system. Then she seized the canopy handle and pushed it back, but in the same moment an immense weakness seized her limbs and she started to tremble, unable to move. The blood seemed to have drained out of her head, the air out of her lungs, the strength out of her cold fingers. And so she simply sat there, shaking like a leaf.

Gray emerged from his cockpit and divested himself of his helmet and parachute, handing them to the mechanic who had materialized to help. Quickly he zipped himself out of the black leather jacket he had worn, all the time keeping an eye on Adair's cockpit. A heavy frown gathered on his brow as he saw that she was making no move to climb out. The mechanic was looking in Adair's direction, too, starting to move, looking concerned.

Gray waved the man away and swung himself up to Adair's side. She took one look at his lean, dark face swimming toward her, saw the grim expression and the white line about his mouth, and realized he was very, very angry with her . . . so angry . . . and she couldn't remember why.

"You crazy little hellion," he muttered, his voice tight and fierce. "Why didn't you tell me you were feeling faint? You're white as a sheet."

She licked her lips to tell him she was all right, but she couldn't say a word. She thought she was going to pass out.

"You frightened the hell out of me," Gray admitted during the drive back to Washington. Now traveling through spreading suburbia, past one of the bedroom communities of the nation's capitol, they had not yet reached the Beltway and the inner spokes of the avenues that radiated from the city's core. "The first time during that dive, and then . . . are you sure you're all right?"

Adair had had to be pulled from the plane, her parachute unbuckled, and her clothes loosened before she had recovered from her spell of dizziness. She thanked her stars that she hadn't fainted, but she knew she had been very close. "I'm fine," she insisted, just as she had at the time.

"Do you always put life and limb on the line every time you go up? That last dive practically had a Kamikaze finish."

Adair's eyes dropped. "I know. I miscalculated. Usually I'm very careful."

"Careful!" Gray's laugh was harsh, disbelieving. "Frankly, my fiendish friend, you damn near killed both of us."

"I'm sorry," Adair muttered, still under stress but trying to hide it. Her knuckles were tightening until they turned white.

Gray glanced sideways and saw. "If you were anyone but Colonel Lamont Clancy's daughter, I'd suspect you were suffering from a case of nerves."

"I'm not," Adair insisted, but her voice was still tremulous. "All I have now is a headache, and a couple of aspirin will cure that. I told you, it was just that last long dive. It's a while since I've flown and it made me very dizzy. That's why I didn't pull out sooner."

Gray's manner was grave. "Have you ever been that dizzy before? While flying, I mean."

"No."

"Or frightened?"

"No, never," Adair said, feeling suddenly confused as an old recollection pricked at her. Her eyes escaped to the passenger window of Gray's car, a quiet dark blue Jaguar four-seater. Had there been a moment of terror at some point in her life? She pushed the memory away, not wanting to feel it, not wanting to know about it. "Never," she repeated more positively, turning back to Gray.

He glanced at her narrowly, his lean face very sober. "Much as I'd like to hold you to our arrangement, I think I'd better take a raincheck on that dinner. You're still too pale, and you've had more than enough excitement for one day. I couldn't promise you an evening as tame as I think you need. You should be in a quiet bed, preferably bundled up in blankets. And without a companion."

Adair couldn't disagree. And yet she wondered why she should feel so little relief to be freed from her promise, after the intense emotions she had experienced while Gray had been trying to press her into accepting.

"I do intend to hold you to our agreement, though. I deserve some reward for the bone-shaking you put me through! How about tomorrow night?"

"I . . . I'm leaving Washington first thing tomorrow." It was a weak lie, an escape of the sort Adair hated, but she didn't have the strength to admit she was going to be in town for some days yet. Nor did she feel she had the inner fortitude to face an intimate dinner with Gray, her promise notwithstanding.

"You *will* be back in town at some point, though?"

"I . . . yes." She had no reason to return to Washington at all, certainly not within the next few months. But she had to give Gray some answer, and if the answer was no, he might change his mind and insist on the bargain she had made for tonight. She liked the city and it wasn't hard to contemplate a return at some future date, possibly after Doug's mission. And by then she would be free, her part of the bargain fulfilled, the sham marriage at an end.

"And you won't welsh on the deal."

It was a flat statement, not a question. "No, I won't," she agreed, and the promise wasn't too hard to make. Never in her life had Adair backed out on a lost bet, and she wouldn't have to back out on this one. She would simply be putting Gray on hold.

"I'm an importunate man," he warned, "and all this sounds a little too indefinite for me. I do travel a fair amount because of the different Winterhazy newspapers. I could meet you in another city, any city. You name it."

"I'll call you next time I'm in Washington."

Gray sighed. "You're about as easy to pin down as a politician after an election promise. Well, are you going to tell me what hotel you're staying at? I have to see you safely somewhere, and I refuse to make it a street corner."

The real name of the hotel popped out before Adair's mental processes caught up. She could have chewed her tongue off, but it was too late. And what did it matter, anyway? If he phoned and asked for the name Clancy, he wouldn't reach her.

She wanted to be dropped at the canopied front entrance, but Gray was absolutely rock-firm. "I'm seeing you to your room," he insisted. He swung his lanky legs out of the driver's seat before Adair could escape, and left his Jaguar illegally parked at the hotel entrance. The doorman, discreetly pocketing a very large tip, promised to have a car jockey move it if trouble materialized. Short of making a difficult scene, Adair couldn't think how to get out of being escorted inside. She prayed they wouldn't run into anyone she knew.

He guided her through the foyer, holding her elbow in a no-nonsense grip. Adair was devastatingly conscious of Gray's touch and his lean length beside her, of his urbane attractiveness in the steel-blue business suit he wore. She wasn't sure whether to attribute the continuing weakness of her knees to past dangers or present ones. At the moment the present ones seemed overwhelming. How was she going to keep him from walking her up to her hotel room, where traces of Doug were everywhere?

And if she'd had reason for concealment before, didn't she have double the reason now? That last suicidal stunt, unintentional though it had been, was hardly fit behavior for an astronaut's wife. She could imagine Doug's justifiable anger and the possible furor at NASA if the word leaked out. And what a tidbit for the *Clarion!*

They were waiting for an elevator when Adair

heard a shriek of delighted feminine recognition behind her. "There you are! I've been looking for you everywhere! I thought you might . . ."

Adair turned, alarmed. Gray turned too. Peggy Wishard's voice trailed away as she became conscious that her friend was not alone. Her perky smile faded and her eyes widened as they lifted to Gray's face.

". . . lend me your pearls," Peggy finished in an unnatural voice, staring up at Gray as if he were an alien from some other planet.

Adair's brain marked time for about two seconds and then started to work again. She realized the game was not yet lost, for Peggy had given away nothing in her greeting. And perhaps this chance meeting could be turned to advantage. "Sure," she said quickly. "Come on up to my room, Peggy, and I'll get them for you. I was just saying good-bye to my friend anyway."

"I haven't met your friend," Peggy said, still looking strange, with her eyes fixed on Gray's face.

"Peggy, this is Gray. Gray, this is Peggy."

Fortunately at that moment the elevator doors glided open, ready to start an upward trip. Several people moved in, passing Adair. She turned to Gray. "Thanks for the ride, Gray. Will you excuse me? I'm sure you're in a hurry to be on your way."

Peggy edged onto the elevator, not taking her rounded eyes off the small exchange between the other two. Gray's long fingers were still firmly locked over Adair's elbow, allowing no quick escape. "Good-bye," she said pointedly.

Gray simply raised his free hand and propped it against the elevator door, preventing its closure. "Not so fast," he murmured laconically. The fingers restraining Adair's arm moved, instead capturing the nape of her neck. They threaded into her hair, warm and gently persuasive. His dark blue eyes smoked.

Stars began to explode in her head, for she knew full well what he intended to do even before his lean, angular face closed in. She couldn't seem to think or move as she saw his mouth descending.

His lips were expert and softly sensual, promising rather than demanding. The kiss, delivered in full view of Peggy and anyone else who cared to watch, deepened only briefly. But there was no mistaking the intent and the intimacy of it, the wooing seductiveness of Gray's open, moving lips. It was the kiss of a man who has kissed before, and who intends to kiss again.

Peggy was still agog when the door closed on an elevator containing several bemused spectators. "Well," she muttered. "Well."

Adair fought to come out of the internal spin that had dizzied her once again, causing reactions out of all proportion to the lingering but not extremely erotic caress. She struggled for self-possession, wondering how to put a good face on things. Playing for time, she licked her lips and tasted Gray's maleness on them, the tangy, salty flavor that seemed to be so distinctively his. The taste didn't help her thought processes at all.

As the elevator sped upward, soon disgorging all other passengers, Peggy continued to stare at her with a peculiar expression. "Well!" she exclaimed again when they were alone. "You could bowl me over with a feather, Adair Anderson."

Adair pulled herself together. "Thanks for saving me," she got out jerkily. Then she added, "Sorry to disappoint you, Peggy, but I didn't bring my rope of pearls to Washington. I just wanted an excuse to get away from that man. Actually, I'm feeling a little under the weather. Can I retract the invitation for you to come to my room?"

"No, you cannot," Peggy said firmly, grabbing

Adair's arm as the elevator opened on the floor where both their rooms were situated. A dynamo of energy when she chose to be, Peggy steered Adair toward her door with the determination of a mother hen.

"Now, tell me what all this is about," she ordered when they were alone together. She parked herself on a bed and impaled Adair with a stern, fixed expression. "Shoot," she directed, "and I mean straight."

"There's nothing to tell," Adair returned, collapsing on her own bed.

"Look, if you're having an affair behind Doug's back, that's bad news!"

"I'm not having an affair," Adair protested. "I only met the man last night."

"In that case, I'd say things are moving a little too fast in the direction of B-E-D. I'm not blind, honey. That man is unh-unh dynamite, and I mean *dynamite*. That thin face and those deep eyes and that long, lanky body . . . he is definitely dangerous. Just the type who blows women's minds."

"Not mine," denied Adair, but without enough conviction.

"Was that who you hurried off to have lunch with today?"

"Yes," Adair admitted.

"You idiot!" Peggy's lips thinned into a disapproving line. "I bet you'd swallow poison, too, if it tàsted good."

Adair was beginning to feel angry and defensive, trapped by her friend's persistence. Peggy's intentions might be good, but she didn't know all the facts. And how could Adair tell them? "I won't be meeting him again," she said stiffly, but she knew it wasn't the truth, and so her eyes were not entirely steady. They fell beneath the sharp, disbelieving look she earned.

Peggy made no secret of her outrage. "You'd better

not," she warned, "or I'll personally wring your neck." Then her voice became level and crisp. "This isn't idle meddling, Adair. I have a vested interest in this whole thing too. You think I want to bring up three orphans? My husband is going up there with yours, remember! I'd hate to see *either* of them blasting off in a bad frame of mind. And if Doug found out you were fooling around . . ."

Adair looked up, her face flushed. "He wouldn't care," she said tightly. "Go have a look at the shirt lying on the pile of laundry in the bathroom! Those lipstick stains aren't *mine!*"

Sympathy briefly touched Peggy's face. "Adair," she said quietly. "I know, honey."

"Do you? I don't think so! Guy is true blue; he'd never look at another woman."

Peggy's mouth twisted ruefully. "Oh, wouldn't he? Do you think I'm married to a saint or something? Guy is one hell of a man, and he sure has lots of temptation put in his way. Why would a hunk like him be faithful to a dull hausfrau like me? Frankly, I don't ask whether he gives in to his baser nature, for I don't want to know. But I do see lots of women flirting with him. And if I can learn to look in the other direction, why can't you? It's all in the rules of the game."

"Is it?" cried Adair, too agitated to hold her tongue. "*Is it?* Well, for your information, I got fed up with the double standard when I hadn't been married for ten weeks. Doug and I haven't slept together since!"

Peggy exploded, pounding the bed with her fist. "Then no wonder he fools around! No wonder you have a rotten home life! My God, Adair, you're even dumber than I gave you credit for! You deserve everything you get if you refuse to sleep with the man! I used to feel sorry for you, but now I think it's Doug who deserves sympathy! My God, he must be tied up in inner knots! How *dare* you leave him frustrated?"

"How *dare* you pass judgment!"

They glared at each other, hot-eyed, good friends who had known each other too long to mince many words. Adair was white-faced, trembling badly. It had been a long, difficult day and Peggy's censure was the last straw.

Peggy said tightly, "I have every right to pass judgment. What goes on or *doesn't* go on in your bedroom, honey chile, might just happen to affect Doug's judgment up there in space. You damn well better start giving him his conjugal rights, or I'll yell this to the rooftops! I won't have *your* marital problems putting *my* husband in jeopardy!"

Adair leaped to her feet, caution scattering to the wind in the face of severe stress. "What rights?" she cried. "He doesn't have any rights! Doug and I are divorced, Peggy! *Divorced!* He hasn't been my husband for five years!"

Chapter Four

$\mathcal{A}$t least it explains the lack of a wedding ring," Peggy observed morosely when the worst of her shock had passed. "I never did completely buy that story about your being allergic to gold. *Nobody's* allergic to gold."

Peggy's temper had simmered back to normal, but her usual bouncy optimism had not been restored. She was looking as deflated as a pricked balloon. Adair had the feeling her friend was still worrying about the effect all this might be having on Doug's state of mind, and consequently how it might affect her husband, Guy.

Adair had calmed, too, the surge of adrenaline having given way to a weak sense of relief. She knew she ought to be aghast at herself for betraying her huge secret against all promises, but somehow she wasn't. She had held the truth inside for too long, and the past five years had not been easy ones.

And now, having revealed the most important part, she felt a strong need to tell more, and not only to reassure her friend. It was as though a dam had given way at a weak spot, letting the truth spurt through. Under the severe pressure of recent events, the crack was swiftly spreading. Adair had contained a flood of difficult feelings for too long, and they badly needed release. Besides, she trusted Peggy.

"A wedding ring was one piece of pretense I didn't think I could bear," she said in a low voice. She started to recount the whole story, beginning with the discovery of Doug's infidelities, which had followed so swiftly on the heels of their marriage. "I overheard a conversation. I didn't want to hear but I couldn't help it. It was when we were first married, living on base at Edwards. We were having a housewarming party, outside on the patio. A big crowd turned up. I had gone inside to fetch more highball glasses, and because we'd just moved in, I had some trouble finding them—they were in a packing crate, in an unused room. I was in there when the doorbell rang. Before I could untangle myself from the packing paper and the cartons, Doug had come through the house and answered the front door. There were several new arrivals, other pilots, all bachelors. The men stood there and chatted, having a few minutes of man talk before they went outside to join the other guests. I heard Doug's voice, and the remark he made stopped me cold. It was about some woman he'd been with the night before. He was . . . boasting a bit, describing details that—" She stopped briefly, choked by remembrance. "And while I stood there frozen, he went on, and on. . . .

"In order to leave the scene, I would have had to pass right through the hall where the men were standing, joking as if they were at a stag party. They would all know I had heard. And so I stood where I was and listened. It wasn't just one infidelity, Peggy. Some man made a joke about the number of Doug's other recent conquests, asked him how he could manage so much action with a new bride at home."

"My God," Peggy muttered grimly.

"In answer, Doug made some remark about our wedding night. About *me*. He said I'd been a virgin, and because of that he didn't want to spoil the fun by teaching me too many things all at once. I felt sick. I felt nauseous. I wanted to die."

Peggy slid across the space to sit beside Adair, one arm around her shoulders to lend quiet support.

"It felt like . . . like I'd bailed out without a parachute. Poppy was away on an extended tour at the time, not on the base at all. I felt I had no one to turn to. I was too ashamed to tell anyone, even my sisters, of the things I'd overheard. So a few days later I bolted without confiding in a soul, although I left a note for Doug. I told him I was going to Reno, and why."

"And what did he do?" Peggy prompted gently.

Adair cast her eyes to the ceiling and uttered a small, mirthless laugh. "He told everyone I'd gone to Nevada to visit his family—that's where they lived. He didn't want the truth to come out, you see, because by then he was being seriously considered for the space program. A divorce would probably have wrecked his chances. By phone, he tried to talk me into coming back to him, but I wouldn't agree."

Adair told about her father following her to Reno a short time later, about the pressure that had been applied. "The divorce proceedings were already well under way by then; in fact, the thing came through right after Poppy found me. He wanted me to remarry Doug, to give him another chance."

"Why?" Peggy murmured wonderingly.

Adair sighed. "My father admired Doug's ability as a pilot and thought he was sure to get into the space program, provided I didn't walk out on him at that crucial point in time. I guess the bottom line was that Poppy wanted an astronaut for a son-in-law. But he said Doug would never make it without me, without a stable home life."

"It seems to me—" Peggy bit her lip and kept her comments to herself, resuming the role of uncritical friend. "Go on," she said.

"Anyway, I couldn't be convinced," Adair said, bitterness creeping into her voice. "How could I marry Doug again, after what had happened? How could I live with a man who cared so little for me that he . . . described our wedding night? Boasted of his success rate with other women? But I could see how badly I was letting my father down, so I did agree to a charade. Only three of us knew about the divorce—me, Doug, and my father. And if we didn't tell, how would anyone know?"

"How, indeed," Peggy said, with an element of steel in her voice. Her face had tightened, but her anger was no longer directed at Adair.

"I agreed to the pretense. The promise only goes until Doug's completed his first space mission, at which point a marriage breakup isn't so likely to wreck his career." A cloud crossed Adair's face as a sudden spasm of restlessness returned. "I didn't know it would take five years."

Peggy was sympathetic. "All this must have been hell for you."

"Oh, not really. The arrangement has worked out all right, most of the time. Separate bedrooms and all that. And Doug isn't a complete villain; it's just that he likes a wingding good time and isn't ready to settle down. He's still a bachelor at heart. As to his frustrations . . . when I agreed to go back to him, he agreed to deal with them elsewhere. Don't you see, I couldn't possibly sleep with him again?"

"I sure can," came the feeling answer. But Peggy still looked morose.

Adair put a gentle hand on her friend's arm, wanting to reassure her. "You don't need to worry, Peggy. Nothing in our relationship is going to endanger that space mission. My connection with Doug is strictly friendship now. Gradually we've become good pals. He doesn't love me and he never did, not even at the start. I've known it for years, and he's as much as admitted it in words."

Peggy looked up sharply. "Then why in God's name did he marry you?"

"Because he felt he needed a wife, if he was going to be considered for astronaut training," Adair said steadily. "You know, the old hearth-and-home bit. He picked on me because of Poppy. Son-in-law of Colonel Lamont Clancy! Can't you imagine how that would help move him up in the running? Doug didn't marry me, he married my father's daughter."

"Then he really wouldn't care if you did carry on," Peggy concluded slowly, "as long as you were discreet about it."

"No. But I meant what I said, Peggy. I'm not about to have an affair. Good Lord, Gray doesn't even know exactly who I am." She told about misleading him as to her identity. "He *could* find out the truth easily enough, but I don't think he'll try, because he believes he already knows it. He's nobody's fool, but the missing wedding ring did the trick—that, and seeing me leave the reception with my father. It didn't even occur to him that I might be Adair. I've left him with the impression that Amelia hops around a lot. And he won't expect me to be in Washington this week; he thinks I'm checking out in the morning. So you see, it's not going to amount to anything. He doesn't know how to get in touch with Amelia. And I certainly don't intend to get in touch with *him*. At least, not until after the space shuttle, when I'll be free again. And then . . ."

"Then?"

"I've promised I'll look Gray up next time I'm in Washington. We have a sort of . . . date. But that'll be months from now. Maybe years, if there are many more delays." She laughed ruefully, her voice shaky again. "By then he'll probably be lined up with some other woman. He's not going to spend all his time panting breathlessly for some female who's made herself deliberately scarce."

"Oh?" Peggy murmured with a faraway gleam in her eye.

Adair was worried about that gleam. She had seen it before, when Peggy had been trying to stage-manage an improvement in the relationship between herself and Doug. Was she going to play amateur matchmaker again?

Suddenly Peggy's eyes started dancing with impish little lights, and her mouth curved into a positive smile, announcing the restoration of high spirits.

"Oh, yes, you are," she announced firmly. "You're going to have the damnedest affair this side of outer space. And don't think I'm going to let you get out of it!"

If Gray phoned the hotel during her remaining days in Washington, Adair had no way of knowing it. As he didn't know her last name or her room number, a call was not to be expected. Besides, he didn't think she was in town. And yet during the rest of the week, she was conscious of an occasional stab of disappointment, a sense of hurt that he had not tried a little harder to penetrate the fog of evasiveness in which she had wrapped herself.

Worried by the gleam in Peggy's eye, Adair had told her friend almost the entire story of her acquaintance with Gray Bennett. The forbidden flying, the dinner bet, the fear of unwanted publicity from Gray's newspaper: Peggy was now aware of all these things. "Do you think he'd betray you, if you told him the whole truth?" Peggy had asked. "I don't. I thought he looked very trustworthy."

"You're the one who said he was poison!"

"Nice poison," Peggy had recanted philosophically and without shame. But at Adair's insistence, she had promised not to meddle in the course of the relationship.

The week in Washington brought its highlights. Most memorable for Adair was a visit to the National Air and Space Museum, where she thrilled to the dramatic beginning of flight exemplified by the *Spirit of St. Louis,* the Wright Brothers' famous plane, and its soaring culmination—the Apollo II command module. She felt she could have spent the whole week in that one place alone.

But there were also trips to the Museum of Natural History, Arlington House, the Botanic Gardens, Ford's Theatre, and the Smithsonian. There were tours of the House and the Senate, with a few minutes spent in the visitors' galleries of each. There were a hundred sights, many seen on the fly, or from the open seats of a Tourmobile. Even with this energetic schedule, Adair felt she had hardly touched the surface of the city.

The week also brought a pleasant dinner with her father, an occasion for which Doug managed to drag himself away from Marina Winterhazy's attractions. During this meal the talk covered flying, flying, and more flying, and in the interstices there were a few mentions of the new Canadian wife. Colonel Lamont Clancy looked like a kid at Christmas when Doug told him he was bound to produce a son this time.

"I should be finished with my overseas duties a month or so before Roberta's time," he informed them. He turned to Adair. "Roberta wants to meet you, Sunny, but she won't be in any condition to visit Houston when we first get back. Besides, we'll be aiming north to spend several months up in Ottawa, visiting with her relatives until our new ranch house is finished. However, when I leave the service, I'll have to clean up some loose ends at the Pentagon. You think you can manage another trip to the big town? We should hit Washington in early December."

"Of course," Adair promised, and then remembered her prior promise to Gray Bennett. Well, it was too bad, but she simply couldn't keep that bargain—at least, not until after Doug's space shuttle mission. It didn't matter. Gray wouldn't even know she had been in town.

"Unfortunately that's likely to be a week or so before your space shuttle, Doug, or I'd press you to come along with Adair. Roberta will be heartbroken, of course. You know what women are like! She's dying to meet a real honest-to-God astronaut."

Doug grinned and punched his ex–father-in-law on the arm. "Go on! That new kid of yours'll be into a spacesuit before he's out of diapers. Ten bucks says he'll be the first man on Mars!"

Colonel Lamont Clancy beamed and brought out a cigar to celebrate.

After Washington, Adair felt so changed inside that she almost expected Houston to have changed too. It hadn't. Home was the same: the suburban sprawl, the low ranch house Adair had decorated largely with her own spare-time efforts, the swimming pool Doug had built largely with his. The routine was the same: the outdoor exercise, the hours of concentration on historic aviation data, the inevitable household tasks. Life was the same: the easy socializing with a few valued friends like the Wishards, the occasional coffee parties with other astronauts' wives, the talk that concentrated on the meaningless issues and skirted the really important ones.

Or rather, *the* important one.

Everything that was taboo revolved around one central issue, the hazardous occupation of the husbands. No one shared the fears about having a man whose goal in life was to expose himself to the risks of space travel, because to share those fears was to admit they existed. It was rare indeed for a wife to confess anxiety, as Peggy had done during her angry scene with Adair. But the concern was always there, and it was real, and it could be sensed like a strong undertow beneath the sea of chatter concerning babies' formulas, supermarket specials, recipes, and light gossip. The wives stuck together because they all understood, without saying it in so many words, that the familiar topics were a life raft, floating safely over the surface of a reality that was too powerful to be dealt with in easy conversation.

It was a conspiracy of silence that had always seemed a little unreal to Adair, although she understood the reasons for it. She knew she was not quite like the others—"the Wives," as Peggy called them. Adair empathized with them and understood them and liked them, but barring her friendship with Peggy, she didn't feel she was really one of them—and of course she really wasn't; her marriage was only a sham. In many ways she envied the Wives enormously. There was love and real caring in their lives, a river running deep beneath the trivialities of everyday existence, and the fullness of their existence underscored the emptiness in hers.

The small separateness she felt was in part because most of her days were spent not in scrubbing small faces and talking to kindergarten teachers, but in intensive research, in sorting and cross-indexing pictures of early pilots and antique planes, and in maintaining the vast correspondence that helped her unearth new photographic finds. But the greatest difference, she realized, was her lack of true emotional involvement with Doug, and the fact that she was not married to him at all. If she had been, would she have felt the same need for that conspiracy of silence, that protection against fears that were too terrible to contemplate?

Adair had learned to be fond of Doug, even if she didn't love him. She felt some apprehension for him regarding his occupation, but kept it to herself, mostly out of respect for the other wives. Her concerns were more objective than most, she had always thought, simply because she had a more realistic attitude toward aviation of all kinds. She had no fear of flying.

Or did she? It wasn't until her first night back in Houston that she allowed herself to examine her reactions to the near accident in the AT-6. She lay in bed and thought about it until her hands grew clammy with cold perspiration. Was there an old memory tugging at her mind? Something involving terror? And someone's voice shouting at her?

She had the idea that pain had somehow been involved, and an agony of shame in case she disappointed her father. But the memory was too evanescent, too lost in the mists of the dim past to be fully recaptured.

And yet she sensed there must have been fear at one point, perhaps the first time she had been encouraged to do a difficult aerial stunt. Possibly she had done it wrong, or possibly she had not had the pluck to do it at all. She must have been quite young, as she couldn't remember the details. And she had learned to overcome the fear because she had to, in order to win her father's respect. He had expected so much of her, and she had learned to give it. Calmness, courage, and cool control in the face of danger—the attributes of the son he so desperately wanted.

She had learned to love flying to please him, and she did indeed love it. It wasn't mere pretense. There was a purity of joy to be found in the free air, a release from the earthbound cares of ordinary mortal existence. But the more dangerous daredevil stunts, such as the forbidden snap roll, and that last crazy dive she had performed during the flight with Gray Bennett . . . what were *they*? It came to her, in a moment of painful insight, that it was some years since she had done anything even remotely so hazardous in the way of aerobatics. Since reaching adulthood, she had been satisfied with relatively safe loops, rolls, and Immelmanns. Yet at a younger age she had taken enormous risks to impress her father. Were they attempts to earn respect and approval?

At the time of that near-fatal dive, she had told herself she was trying to escape Gray's persistence, but was that just a disguise for her true motives? Had she really been trying to impress him?

The thoughts were difficult and distressing and there seemed to be no answer for them, and when she fell asleep her dreams offered no escape. What started as a kiss, with softly persuasive lips moving erotically over hers, became a long spin in Gray's arms, a downward spiral, a dizzying plummet to certain destruction.

She woke unrested, a headache nagging at the back of her eyes, feeling unready to face the day. Breakfast was a ritual that had become automatic, although today it was somewhat behind time due to the late-night return from Washington. She hurriedly served up bacon and eggs for two and carried them to the table in the yellow-papered breakfast nook, a production almost exactly timed to Doug's entrance. He walked into the kitchen dressed, shaved, and ready to face the day.

"Helluva pile of mail while we were away," he grumbled, sliding into the booth. Due to their late arrival the night before, he had not gone through the correspondence properly. After extracting a few official-looking letters, he had placed the rest on the table for more careful perusal at breakfast. He riffled through the envelopes, frowning at the bills, tossing the circulars aside, making a pile of the letters addressed to Adair, some of which might contain new material for the book she was compiling.

"Hey, what's this? A letter for Amelia?"

Immediately Adair's eyes were riveted to the envelope and the bold, spare handwriting that must be Gray's. Her stomach did a roller-coaster dip. "Oh? Let's see." She held out her hand.

Doug didn't relinquish the letter. He turned it over,

examining the return address on the back flap. "Looks like a personal letter too. Some man friend, I guess. He must have forgotten her Vassar address." He patted his pocket, found a pen, and scratched out the Houston address. Then he looked up at Adair with the pen poised expectantly over the envelope. "I can mail this on the way to work. What's the name of that residence again?"

Adair couldn't pretend she didn't know her sister's address by heart. "The letter's for me, Doug," she said evenly. She held out her hand again. "Let me have it, and I'll tell you what the whole thing is about. I can tell you right now if you have time, or later, if you don't."

Doug was staring at her with a puzzled expression on his face. "Now," he said, handing the letter over. Adair tucked it into the pocket of her jeans, to be read later in privacy.

When she had told the story, with all mention of flying carefully deleted, Doug was thoughtful. He pushed his emptied breakfast plate aside. "Well, well. There are times, Adair, when you surprise me. So the frustration is finally beginning to get to you, is it?"

Consciousness of the unread letter burned at her hip, much as if Gray's fingers had been there. "There's nothing serious about this, Doug. He's just an acquaintance."

"For God's sake, don't get defensive. Hell, I don't give a damn if you play footsie with some dude, as long as it's on the Q.T. At this point I can't afford the flak if you start playing around and the word gets out."

"I know that."

"Just reminding you." He glanced at her uneaten bacon and eggs, at her tense fingers, at the stiffness of her posture. His eyelids drooped as his gaze returned to her lips. "There's only one thing I can't understand," he drawled.

"What's that?"

His hand closed over Adair's, drawing it away from her coffee cup. "If you're getting ripe for an affair," he suggested in a meaningful murmur, "why not have it with me? We could have a helluva time, kid."

Adair snatched her hand away. "I've told you, I'm not interested in affairs, with you or anyone else!"

Doug shrugged, yawned, and picked up the morning paper. "Just asking," he muttered. But Adair saw his faint, knowing smile and knew that the coming night was not going to be an easy one.

She read the letter from Gray after Doug had left for the day. Her hands were trembling as she opened the envelope. There weren't many words on the notepaper. For a moment she closed her eyes, feeling she could not bear to read them. If the message was too personal, she would be upset, and if it was too impersonal, she would be devastated.

"A dare is a dare," he wrote in a bold black scrawl. "When am I going to collect? Yours, Gray."

That was all. No words of affection, no pretense that their relationship presaged anything more than a casual encounter. Adair put her face in her hands and started to shake. Was that all she meant to him? A bet to be collected? And she knew what he thought he would collect. Getting her into his apartment was only the first step toward inveigling her into his bed. Did men never want anything else? With a sudden surge of rage she picked up the note and ripped it into a hundred tiny bits.

That night was every bit as difficult as she had anticipated. It didn't help that Gray's next letter arrived the very next morning, with Adair still disturbed by memories of Doug's unwanted persistence.

"I'm still waiting for that dinner," Gray had scrawled this time, "and getting very lean and mean about it. Yours, Gray."

Adair scrunched up the note and aimed it at a wastebasket. Why did he have to pretend it was a dinner he was hungry for? At least Doug was honest about what he wanted from her!

In the days that followed, the letters continued to arrive. Adair hadn't expected such persistence. She didn't wish Gray to start an active search for Amelia Clancy, so she provisioned herself with a number of postcards. She knew it wouldn't be too hard to arrange for them to be mailed from different places; because of her interest in old aviation photos, she had correspondents all over the United States, and some overseas. She would simply ask some of these people, on one pretext or another, to drop the postcards in a mailbox. As they were formally addressed to Gray as the publisher of the *Clarion*, she didn't think the contents would arouse particular curiosity.

On the cards she wrote vague, businesslike messages of three or four words that could be answers to things he had written. "When I get to Washington" or "Soonest possible" or "Slight delay unavoidable"— the simple words were carefully thought out to imply little, to promise little, and yet to allay any growing suspicion that the promised dinner was not going to materialize in the near future.

Peggy took to uncomfortable probing. "You look really drained," she said when Adair was visiting one day at the Wishard home. It was afternoon nap time, and for once all was peace, the loudest background sound being the contented snuffles of the dreaming Wishard family cat. "And don't bother telling me it's nothing! If you had Doug's real interests at heart, Adair, you'd take the bull by the horns and do something positive to make yourself happy. Oh, you try to hide it, but the discontent is there. How do you think Doug likes looking at *that* over the breakfast table? It would do him good to see you cheered up."

Adair tried to sidestep the well-intentioned meddling. "The only thing Doug notices at the breakfast table is whether his bacon is crisp enough. Don't you have any problems of your own to think about?"

"Sure," Peggy acknowledged. "Three of them. Susan, Tilda, and little Tommy. Do you know he can almost pull himself up to his feet now? One of these days he's going to go headfirst out of his crib, and . . . oh, my God, I think he's done it!"

An enormous howl rent the house, and Peggy raced off in response. The cat perked its ears at the sound, then unfolded, stretched into a great lazy arc as only cats can do, and settled down for a good wash, recognizing that the time for peace was over.

When Peggy came back to the living room, she had nine-month-old Tommy in her arms. He was still hiccuping away his tears. Peggy dandled him on her knee, played pat-a-cake for a few minutes to cheer him up, and then put him down on the floor to crawl about on all fours, chasing the cat. The feline sidestepped out of reach, looking bored by it all. Peggy turned her attention back to Adair.

"You claim you're not moping, Adair, but you can't fool me. I know you too well. When you smile these days, you look like your face is going to crack. You really are in love with that man, aren't you?"

"Good heavens, no," Adair said, truthfully

enough. She knew she was obsessed with thoughts of Gray, but believed it must be due to the almost daily arrival of letters for Amelia. It was hard to put a man out of mind when he persisted in pursuit.

"Well, I've had enough of this braver-than-thou exterior of yours. Why don't you fly off to Washington and have your fling? Do us all a favor! When the Wives see you looking pale and wan, how do you think they feel? They don't know the truth, so they think it's because Doug's about to go up on his . . . Tomm-eee! No! No-no-no! Little boys do not eat pussy cats' tails!"

Adair solved the problem of the other wives' feelings by staying away from coffee parties and most other gatherings. She worked out furiously in the swimming pool, punishing herself by increasing the number of laps to the point of pain. She threw herself into the organization of photographic material with such vigor that the passage of time became confused, one week sliding into the next, each marked by exhaustion during the day, restlessness at night, and a tendency to internal loop-the-loops whenever she heard the day's mail being pushed through the letter-box.

Only during those times when Doug was home did she manage to quell her own feelings and concentrate on his. He had grown unusually tense and morose in the past few weeks, as if something had started to trouble him shortly after the return from Washington. He was preoccupied and his behavior had become very erratic. Either he stayed out all night, not even returning home for dinner, or else he returned home early and didn't go out at all. Adair knew his distraction had nothing to do with herself. The overture made some weeks before had not been repeated, nor was he aware of the letters that had continued to arrive each day. Her friendship with Doug was intact; in fact, during those quiet evenings at home, he seemed to relax somewhat in the companionable atmosphere she tried to create for him. She had not been able to put her finger on the cause of his brooding mood, but since noticing it, she had been making extra efforts to smooth his home life.

Her weekly visit with Peggy was the one piece of socializing she didn't forego, simply because her friend wouldn't allow her to. If Adair tried to be evasive, Peggy would simply turn up at Adair's door, complete with the bouncing burden of her youngest child. Tommy was the only one of the Wishard children who had not yet reached at least nursery school level, so Peggy's visits always took place in the morning, right after she had driven her other children to school.

The trip to Washington was a full six weeks in the past when one of these unannounced visits occurred. "I'm cleaning out the oven," Adair complained, holding up her rubber gloves to prove it.

"Fine, I won't stop you." Peggy marched right into the living room, set up a portable playpen, and settled Tommy into it. He gurgled happily as she dumped a bagful of toys in beside him. Normally Adair was entranced by the baby, but not today. She compressed her lips and returned to the kitchen, followed a few minutes later by Peggy.

"Your mail's here," Peggy said, to Adair's immediate consternation. "And what's this? A letter to Amelia—from *Gray Bennett*? Adair! You sly fox!"

Under pressure, Adair admitted that it was only one of a long string of letters mailed to Houston, ostensibly for forwarding. "And no, I'm not going to open it now," she added with asperity. "Just put it on the kitchen table, please."

Peggy struck her head dramatically. "The man's that interested—and you're going to let him get away? You've got to do something, Adair. There are too many women looking for that kind of catch! Why, it's like seeing a big game fish in the ocean, aiming right for *your* line and ready to swallow the hook. And you won't even use bait!"

A short time later the ring of the phone broke into Peggy's stream of chatter. "Oh, damn," muttered Adair. On her hands and knees, with gloves covered in caustic solution, she could not easily answer, although the phone was right in the same room. "Can you get it, Peggy? Find out who it is. I don't want to clean up if it's only someone selling magazine subscriptions."

Peggy picked up the phone. "Yes, this is the Anderson house. Mrs. Anderson? Who shall I say is calling?" Covering the mouthpiece, she explained to Adair, "Someone's secretary, from the sound of it."

Adair came to her haunches and watched narrowly, noting the way her friend's eyes suddenly started to dance. "Actually, this is Adair Anderson speaking," Peggy said promptly.

"Who is it?" whispered Adair.

Peggy just winked, and in the same moment Adair heard the faint rumble of a male voice on the other end of the line. She could hear only Peggy's answers, given in a slightly faked accent: "Yes, this is she . . . oh, yes, of course I know who you are! Don't I always forward your letters? Well, isn't it lucky you called! It just happens Amelia's staying with me right now. Wait a minute, Mr. Bennett, I'll call her to the phone."

Adair was in shock. "Peggy, how dare you!" she hissed sotto voce, but already she had started to peel the rubber gloves from her fingers.

Peggy's hand was over the mouthpiece. "What have I done wrong?" she asked, her expression beatific. "I didn't give away a thing. In fact, I've been a great help to you. He'll never think to question your identity again!"

Adair rose and moved toward the phone. Peggy handed it over with a knowing grin. "Make hay, Sunshine," she whispered. Then she said, audibly, "I'm off now, Amelia. See you later!" And before Adair knew it, Tommy, toys, and playpen were being whisked out the front door, leaving her alone with the phone.

"Gray?" she asked shakily.

"I can't believe my good luck," murmured a low, husky voice that sent quivers down to Adair's toes. "Can it be that I've actually run you to ground?"

"Not . . . not exactly. I'm just visiting Houston. Passing through."

"In that case perhaps I'll visit Houston too. So cancel all plans for this evening, because—"

"I'm only here for the day," she broke in. "I'll be gone by dinnertime. I have to catch a flight this afternoon."

Gray groaned. "You're doing dreadful things to my constitution, Amelia Clancy. Where are you off to now?"

"Dallas," she fibbed, and then realized it would be just as easy for him to decide on a stay in that city. She cast about wildly for a suitable escape route. "That's just to make flight connections, for I'm aiming right on to South America. I'll be there for several weeks, on a tourist raft starting at the headwaters of the Amazon. One of my travel agencies wants a full report." She paused and let all that sink in. "There's no point sending any more letters to Houston, Gray. For the next month or two my sister won't be able to forward them to me."

Gray was silent for a moment. When his voice started again, it was deceptively casual. "Well, send me a postcard, will you? Glad we connected, Amelia. Now I have to go. There's an emergency I must attend to."

When she hung up, her hands were trembling badly. She had been trying to fool herself into putting Gray Bennett out of mind, but there was no use pretending she hadn't been affected by the sound of his voice. It must be a case of nerves induced by the unexpectedness of the call, she told herself, cursing Peggy for putting her into such an equivocal position. Oh, why had she ever become involved with the man? The deception had started out as a simple thing, a charade played for an afternoon's adventure, but Gray's persistence and his romantic interest had given the whole thing an importance out of all proportion. The little lie had become a very big lie indeed, and now Adair was so embroiled in her tangled web of deceit that she could think of no easy way out.

She threw herself into a day of cupboard cleaning she hadn't planned, interrupted only by a phone call from Peggy. "You deserve to be hanged, drawn, and quartered," she told her friend heatedly. "But I have an even ghastlier punishment planned. I'm not going to tell you a single thing he said!"

"Great!" Peggy laughed. "Now I know it must have been good! Censored conversations are always the best."

In the early afternoon, unable to find an unattacked closet in the house, Adair dived into the pool for a quick forty laps to wash off the accumulated dust and grime of the day. Her make-work projects had not completely calmed her, and she wanted a full restoration of equilibrium before Doug returned home later in the day. *If* he returned home later in the day.

The doorbell rang moments after she had stepped from the pool. Her hair was soaking, her body beaded with moisture. As she had just removed her bikini top, she wrapped herself in a thigh-length terry robe and went to answer. Hair dripping wetly on her shoulders, she peered through the small window in the door. Her visitor must be standing out of view, to one side, but she could see a man's long shadow falling over the flagstone walk.

A man? Concern for Doug knifed sharply through her. Although his occupation was not always dangerous on a day-to-day basis, there were times when he went spinning off in supersonic jets, just to keep his pilot's hand in practice. The foreboding increased as she remembered Doug's recent unnatural gloominess. When accidents happened, the news never came by phone. A man at the door could mean bad, bad trouble.

She turned the handle with some urgency, and froze into disbelief when she saw the tall, lean figure that loomed at once into her line of vision.

Gray! At her own front door!

Gray's impatient expression melted into an amused smile. "Did I surprise you? My intention exactly, Amelia Clancy. Well, are you going to invite me in?"

He walked through without waiting for an answer and pushed the door closed behind him. His smile faded as he folded Adair into his arms with a low groan. "I've come across half a continent for this," he breathed thickly as his demanding lips began to descend.

Adair was in a whirl of shock. Stunned by his arrival and overwhelmed by the impact of his lean, hard body against hers, she didn't try to fight free, but she maintained enough sense to turn her head away, evading the kiss. "No, Gray, no . . ."

"Why?" he murmured, tightening his hold. His face buried itself against the wet line of her throat. "Are you afraid your sister might walk in on the scene? By now she must have a very good idea of my intentions regarding you."

"She . . . she had to go out. But—"

"No buts," Gray muttered. Before Adair could utter another protest, her mouth was covered in a deep, hungry kiss that betrayed some of the need that had been building in Gray for many weeks. His tongue taunted her lips apart and plumbed the depths thirstily. Adair's swirling reaction was without reason. Overcome by his impetuosity, she didn't respond actively, but she submitted as if she had no will of her own, even when his hand probed at her neckline, discovering the state of her undress. It was some moments before she realized that his long fingers had tugged at the terry tie and parted the front of her robe. His hand slipped through the opening and closed over her breast, thumb gentling the nipple with an expertise that further affected Adair's swooning senses.

And then his other hand moved to her buttock, beneath the robe. He pulled her hard against him and insinuated his fingers intimately beneath the verges of the tiny bikini, caressing the soft depression.

Adair knew she had to stop this. She had to!

Being in her own home, surrounded by all the reminders of her life with Doug, gave her some strength she might not have possessed in different surroundings. Quivering in every nerve, but with her brain already starting to seek an escape from this impossible situation, she managed to wrench herself away. She pulled her robe closed and retreated a few feet, reverberating beneath the message contained in Gray's dark, smoldering eyes.

"Gray, you shouldn't have come to Houston! I . . . I'm in a terrible hurry to get dressed. I was visiting with Adair and we didn't notice the time, until she got a call reminding her she was supposed to be somewhere. Now I'm in a panic because I have to catch my flight."

He glanced disbelievingly at her hair, the gold of it slicked and darkened by water. And he had felt her wet bikini bottom. "You were visiting in a swimming pool?"

"I . . . we were sunning. I dived in because I was hot, and I thought I'd have time to dry my hair if I hurried. And I *must* hurry. You'll have to leave at once."

"I do intend to leave—with you. Why do you think I'm here? I've come to offer the services of the Winterhazy jet . . . oh, not all the way to South America; I couldn't manage that. But I'll give you a lift as far as Dallas."

Adair stared at him for a moment, heart plummeting, and then chose the only instant course she could think of. She had to get Gray out of Houston, and she had to do it at once. "I'll be ready in a few minutes," she said, escaping to her bedroom.

An hour later, ensconced in a lounge chair in a luxurious private Learjet, she was still catching her breath. It had all happened so quickly that she'd had no time to think. The snatched shirtwaist dress, the suitcase into which she'd thrown a miscellaneous armload of clothes to give it some heft, the quick note left for Doug, telling him she'd be out for dinner and would phone to explain . . . to this moment, she had only been able to think of one problem at a time. Her blow-dry had been so quick that her hair was still half damp.

After takeoff a steward had brought a carafe of coffee and then departed, with crisp instructions from Gray not to return unless called. And then Gray himself had vanished forward to ask the pilot the estimated time of arrival in Dallas. For the moment Adair was alone in the Learjet's lounge, a comfortable space fitted out like the living room of a private home. When Gray chose to act, she reflected, he was like a tornado; it wasn't safe to be in his path.

Luckily Gray hadn't had time to investigate various flight departures before leaving Washington, because he had dropped everything to speed down to Houston. He had told her this, while asking what time she left for South America. Adair had given him a departure time that was pure invention, cutting the hour fine enough that it would leave a minimum of waiting time at the Dallas/Fort Worth airport.

And now Gray would expect to see her onto the imaginary flight bound for imaginary destinations, with only an imaginary ticket to get her to the imaginary goal. How was she going to get out of the corner she had painted herself into? She was in an impossibly tricky situation, and she had to invent a way out. And she had very little time—by jet, Dallas was only a hop, skip, and a jump.

Gray returned to the lounge before she'd had an opportunity to think her way through the dilemma. "Some flights are too damn short," he said drily. He doffed his suit jacket and threw it aside, revealing a pinstripe cotton shirt that molded his broad shoulders and tapered to fit neatly against the flatness of a stomach where no ounce of spare flesh resided. Loosening his tie, he came to sit on a sofa immediately adjacent to Adair's chair. His closeness was disruptive to her reasoning processes, for she was by now thoroughly aware that beneath that deceptively easy manner of his, there was one very determined man who let nothing stand in his way when he saw something he wanted.

"Will you be flying back to Washington at once, after you drop me off?" she asked hopefully.

"No, I won't. Fortunately I have the best excuse in the world for this little junket. There's trouble brewing at one of the Winterhazy weeklies, in a small town just outside Fort Worth. I should have put in an appearance every yesterday for the past three weeks."

"Then you'll be in a hurry when we land?"

Gray eyes drooped with lazy mockery. "Not so much that I can't see you onto your flight. However, I do admit I won't be standing still after you take off. I'd like to flatter you by pretending the whole trip was on your account, but frankly, if it had been, I couldn't possibly have justified the use of the company jet. Even the trip to Houston wasn't without purpose, for I dropped off our science editor, who's going to do some feature stuff on the space shuttle." Amusement crinkled the edges of Gray's eyes. "Mind you, he squawked a little at the sudden assignment, especially as I snatched him from his desk and gave him no time to go home and pack a toothbrush. I told him to charge a new one to me. I decided it was a small price to pay for an hour of stern conversation with you.

Does all this convince you, Amelia Clancy, that I'm not going to let you get out of your promise to dine at my apartment?"

"Yes," she agreed faintly.

"And exactly when are you coming to Washington to keep our date?"

"Uh . . . as soon as I get back from South America."

"And when exactly will that be? I'm getting very fed up with your procrastination."

"I don't know my precise plans. I . . . I'll send you a postcard."

"I have even more antipathy to postcards than I do to tablecloths. From now on I expect person-to-person phone calls, charges reversed." Gray assumed a grim face, driving deep grooves into his angular cheeks. He fixed her with a stern eye. "Do I make myself clear?"

Adair's eyes fled for safety. "There are no phones where I'm going." Thank God she had picked the Amazon! "But I'll call you as soon as possible, I promise."

"And that means the very moment you get back to civilization." Gray leaned forward and captured her wrist, his fingers clamping it firmly. "Understood?"

"Understood," she agreed, because she felt she had no choice.

His thumb began to slide softly over her flesh. "You'll have to give me a better assurance than that," he said coolly, "or I intend to give the pilot new directions, and kidnap you to Washington without further ado."

"You wouldn't!"

She turned alarmed eyes back to him and saw that his face now wore no mocking smile. There was serious purpose in his lean, grooved cheeks, determination in his chin.

"Oh, yes, I would. Do you think I'm given to idle threats?" he asked softly. "I'm an absolutely intransigent man, Amelia Clancy, when I decide on a course of action. Now come over here and let me give you some very good reasons for keeping our date. I need tangible proof of your good intentions, or off to Washington we go."

She had the strong feeling he really did mean it. "Gray, I—"

"No more chatter for the duration of this flight," he ordered. "As it is, the trip is far too short for the things I want to do. If you force me to waste time in talk, I'll do my talking to the pilot, and then you'll simply have to forego that foolish raft trip. I told you, I'll stop at nothing to get what I want. You have a simple choice—be kissed, or be kidnapped altogether."

His fingers tightened, drawing her forcibly forward. In response to the enormous sexual attraction he exerted over her, Adair's reason was already in flight, but still, she tried to resist. She reminded herself that if she succumbed to his undoubted skills, the pleasure would probably evaporate as soon as she found herself in a position too compromising for easy extraction.

The tug on her wrist was sucking at her as a whirlpool sucks at a floating reed. "Come here, woman," he growled huskily, and his low voice thrilled her to the core.

Whether impelled by his threat, his obdurate grip, or his hold over her senses, moments later she found herself collapsing against him, heart palpitating insanely, limbs in a tremble of wanting, lips already parting to meet the importunate, seeking ardor of his kiss.

She had intended to resist. But when his tongue probed, her hands tangled into his hair to bring his face yet closer. When his warm palm slid over her spine, her backbone melted like candlewax beneath a flame. When his fingers counted a downward path over the buttons of her shirtwaist, she shifted to ease his task.

"Oh, God, you're beautiful," he muttered darkly as he undid her brassiere. He turned his mouth to her ear and whispered what he wanted to do to her, the stirring erotic suggestion sending a wave of incredible heat sweeping through her body. The damp probe of his tongue examined the little hollow below her earlobe, then stabbed its way softly past her throat, over her collarbone, downward toward her breasts. Under the bikini line they were pale as milk, softly rounded yet firm with frequent exercise, the texture silky but for the sepia tautness of the nipple. It excited her unbearably to see Gray's thin, deeply tanned face with its harsher male textures descending against the creaminess, and she arched unthinkingly to make herself available to his mouth.

The first touch ignited her, causing her nipples to bud and harden with desire. He eased her gently to a prone position and kneeled beside the couch, the better to achieve his lovemaking. Beautiful bubbles of excitement were sweeping through her bloodstream, and the skilled tonguing of a nipple only amplified the incredible flood of erotic sensations. His maddening slowness, as he moistened and manipulated the sensitive flesh of her breasts, bathing and nibbling and biting gently at each in turn, aroused her as no man had ever aroused her. She longed to be fully naked,

suffering the sweet torment of his mouth and his
hands over every bared inch. In the grip of her wild
sensual excitation, it seemed that the greatest cruelty
he inflicted was in moving too slowly to suit her.

She moaned, groaned, writhed, and twisted beneath the marvelous ministrations of his mouth.

His fingers continued to slide down the row of
buttons, so skillfully that she was hardly aware of it,
until he tugged to push her tiny briefs lower on her
hips. With one hand teasing her stimulated breasts,
and the other tangling at her thighs, his mouth now
dropped a stream of wet, sensuous kisses toward her
navel, while each inch of dampened flesh cried out for
a return of his erotic skills.

She thought she would go mad with the beauty of
what he was doing to her, and yet she twisted away
when his touch became too bold. "No, Gray, no . . ."

"Yes," he murmured thickly, "yes . . ."

She was not a virgin and he must have discovered it
at once, for his fingers grew even more importunate.
Her twisting thighs could not deny him, and soon her
desire was a captured bird trembling and fluttering
beneath his hand. . . .

When at last he eased himself into a prone position
beside her on the couch, her unfulfilled need had
become an aching emptiness within her. It was not
enough to feel the full length of his clothed body
pressing hard against her. He was supremely aroused,
the potency of his manhood felt through the textured
cloth, driving her to a forgetfulness that would have
made the conquest easy, had he chosen to claim her at
that moment.

Instead he merely clasped her hips close against his,
forcing her to feel the extent of his molded strength,
the fullness of his desire. He had grown still except for

the slow slide of his palm against the thin layers of fabric covering her buttocks. Against her mouth he muttered hoarsely, "That's how I feel about you, how I've felt from the first."

He did no more and he said no more, only lying in intimate tandem so that Adair could feel the pit of her being weak with awareness of his strong but well-leashed sexual drive. Despite his leanness, his chest was hard and warm and strongly muscled, and through the thin silky fabric the maddening texture of crisp hair could be felt. She started to pull urgently at his buttons, but he stilled her fingers with his hand.

She longed for him to continue; she begged for him to continue. "Gray, please . . ." And yet, even when she sought his mouth eagerly and let her hips stir restlessly, becoming for a time the aggressor, he made no move to undress himself and give her the satisfaction she sought.

Gradually she grew conscious of other things—the heavy thud of his heart, the ragged fan of his breath against her cheek, the tremor of his firm fingers pressed to her buttock. Slowly, as she lay enclosed in his arms, her urgency changed to drugged compliance, and compliance changed to raw disbelief. Had she been out of her mind, to come so dangerously close to capitulation?

Gradually, unstopped by Gray, she eased away from the virile body beside her. Gathering the folds of her dress against her bared breasts, she left the couch and returned to her lounge chair. Her fingers fumbled as she ineptly secured the fastenings of her brassiere and her dress. She could not look at Gray, who had swung into a sitting position to nurse the after-effects of his self-induced frustrations.

"This isn't the time or the place," he said hoarsely,

"especially with the plane about to descend. If this had been a longer flight, nothing in the world could have induced me to stop."

"Then perhaps you shouldn't have started," Adair said unsteadily, still concentrating on her buttons.

Gray's small harsh laugh belied his difficult physical state. "A matter of tactics, my danger-loving friend. If you can play at brinkmanship so can I! I told you I intended to give you a good reason to hold to your promise—and that, I hope, was it. I wanted you to start wanting me as much as I want you. After this, can you pretend you don't? And can you still fob me off with those tantalizing, stilted messages? My God, one of your postcards traveled a grand distance of forty miles. Why didn't you tell me you were going to be in Baltimore? I could have driven there in an hour, blindfold. How close can you get to Washington without actually tripping over it?"

Adair glanced up at him, troubled, the glaze of desire still moistening her well-kissed lips. She tried to think, but could remember no correspondent in Baltimore. Perhaps someone had moved, and a letter been forwarded?

"I . . . I was in a terrible rush at the time," she temporized. "I won't do that again, I promise."

Gray was once more in control. The edges of his hard mouth lifted into a faint, purposeful smile, and his eyelids drooped over speculative blue eyes. "No, I don't believe you will," he murmured with unsettling self-confidence.

They were in the approach to the landing strip, and Adair recaptured some of her aplomb by attending to the seatbelt attached to the lounge chair. She took a lipstick from her purse and began to apply it, struggling to steady her hand. And she still had to solve the problem of getting away from Gray. How on earth was she going to manage that?

By the time her face was restored, so were her wits. She waited until the plane had taxied to a halt, then swiftly unfastened her seatbelt and rose to her feet. "Gray," she said, "I absolutely detest long-drawn-out farewells, especially public ones in places like terminals. Do you mind if we say good-bye right here and now?"

Her new evasion caused Gray to wince inwardly, for he had to wonder if she'd arranged to meet some other man. A companion for her South American trip, perhaps? But for the moment he had done all that was in his power, and at this point he could only hope that he'd given Amelia Clancy some reason to compare his embraces favorably with those of other men. She was an independent woman with an independent mind; moreover, she had such a decided taste for adventure that she was unlikely to thrill to an overly possessive male who allowed her no freedom of movement. Nothing more could be accomplished by following her into the terminal.

As to that old dare, at this point she would either phone him or she wouldn't; she would either come to Washington or she wouldn't; she either would live up to her promise or she wouldn't. Gray had his pride, and he wouldn't do any more chasing. If she didn't respond to twenty or thirty letters, a hell-bent trip halfway across the States, and the most skillful lovemaking he could manage short of the actual thing, he would simply have to face the unsavory fact that he wasn't in the running. He knew he might never see Amelia Clancy again.

He remained seated, his face masked, to all outward appearances controlled and enigmatic. He shrugged as if her suggestion were a matter of little moment. "As you wish," he drawled, ringing for the steward. "Frankly, I hate terminal kisses myself. Anton will help you with your suitcase. Will you forgive me if I don't rise to my feet? I have a briefcase full of papers to look over before I get off."

Minutes later Adair was in the Dallas/Fort Worth terminal, insisting that the obliging Learjet steward leave her beside an information booth with her suitcase. "I'm meeting someone who has my ticket," she explained with a fixed smile, although she knew that Anton would most likely report the imaginary arrangement to Gray.

Her thoughts were in a turmoil as she watched Anton move reluctantly away. Doug had made her a woman in the technical sense, but he had never awakened her as Gray was now awakening her. As a bride, she had never thought herself exactly frigid, but she had felt that her awkwardness and inexperience were interfering with enjoyment. Because of her tomboy upbringing, she hadn't particularly cared. There had been other pleasures in life. But now . . .

Could it be that Doug, despite all his macho success with women, simply didn't have the technique and patience to arouse a woman who wasn't already sexually fulfilled, who wasn't fully aware and confident of her own womanhood? Doug was absolutely straightforward about sex, dauntingly direct in his approaches, and unsubtle in his methods. Whereas Gray tempted and taunted and trapped a woman into response . . . Gray, with his persuasive hands and his dark, smoking eyes and his warm, adventuring lips . . .

When Anton had vanished, she went to a pay phone and tried to reach Doug at the Space Center. "Oh, is that you, Mrs. Anderson?" asked the woman answering the phone. "I've been trying to reach you for ages. Your husband asked me to let you know he wouldn't be home for dinner."

And that meant he probably wouldn't be home for the night. All's well that ends well, Adair decided with an audible sigh of relief. She had pulled the crazy stunt off with no harm done, barring some physical reactions that hardly bore thinking about.

Now all she had to do was get back to Houston.

Chapter Five

The announcement that the space shuttle had been postponed yet again came near the end of November, shortly before Adair was supposed to fly to Washington. "Now it's scheduled for mid-January," Doug groaned gloomily, his depression even deeper than it had been on the occasion of previous delays.

"Not again!"

"Yes, again. And it's not even a technical difficulty this time. Just bad long-range weather forecasts, and some crazy trouble with a tracking station in Botswana. Wretched, isn't it?"

It was only a one-month delay, but seeing Doug's deep disappointment, Adair almost canceled her plans to visit Washington. In truth, she had been hunting for an excuse to cancel ever since the flight to Dallas, for the alarums and excursions of that hectic day had cured her of thinking she could risk being anywhere within spotting range of Gray Bennett. Although Washington was a huge, impersonal city where chance meetings were highly unlikely, she had the fatalistic feeling that he was perfectly capable of pulling the wildest of coincidences right out of his superbly tailored sleeve.

However, a few days later a special delivery airmail letter arrived from Adair's father. Colonel Clancy announced that he and his new wife would be arriving in Washington imminently and staying there for less than a week, due to the progress of the pregnancy. The letter was vague but its tone was worrisome. Doctors in Europe had forecast possible difficulties because of Roberta's age and advised no travel, except for very short car trips, during the final month. Adair's father urged her to come to Washington immediately, as he and Roberta would be leaving for Canada far sooner than expected.

The concern she read between the lines led her to decide she couldn't forego the trip to Washington. Her trip was to be short anyway, because the household budget wouldn't extend to a long visit. She would go on a weekend partly because it would be easier for Doug to mess about making his own breakfast then, and partly because in Washington—unlike many other cities—the hotels were likely to be emptier after the work week was over, when lobbyists and others with government business had departed. She thought two or three days in the capital would allow ample time for getting acquainted with Roberta, and also for a good reunion with her father.

She made her reservations, phoned Peggy Wishard to beg off a quiet weekend dinner, packed an overnight bag, wished Doug well, and caught a flight that would arrive in Washington in the midafternoon on Friday. She didn't expect to be met. She had booked a room in the same hotel where her father and his new wife would be staying, but she hadn't informed them exactly when she would be arriving, simply because she didn't want anyone to go to the trouble of coming out to the airport.

Despite some turbulence caused by a new storm front moving in slowly from the northwest, the flight was a few minutes early landing at National Airport. The airport, which handled most of Washington's domestic traffic, was beautifully situated on a willow-fringed bank of the Potomac, but the terminal was extraordinarily crowded. It was the first time Adair had seen it, for on her previous visit, traveling with Doug, she had landed at Andrews Air Force Base.

Along with a crush of other incoming passengers, Adair pressed around the baggage ramp, watching for the blue suitcase on which she had pasted a bright orange sticker for easy identification. She was feeling low in mind and morale, thinking about Gray and the promise she wasn't intending to keep—although perhaps it would have been extraordinary if she *hadn't* been thinking about Gray; for months he had filled her mind in all its unoccupied moments.

She saw her suitcase coming along the conveyor and reached out to get it, but a man's hand shot out from behind and got there before her. "Hello, Amelia," said a soft, deep voice above her ear.

She whirled and looked up at its source, and the ground dipped. The world spun crazily for a moment. And then a rush of intense feeling filled her. "Gray," she whispered. "Oh, Gray, it's you . . ."

"Don't look so surprised. Couldn't you have guessed that I might decide to meet your plane?" He was smiling with cool amusement, but his expression didn't completely conceal the raw hunger in his eyes. His voice dropped to a husky murmur heard by Adair alone. "I'd welcome you properly, Amelia Clancy, but I remember you don't like being kissed in terminals. Now let's get out of here. I can only promise to keep my hands off you for about sixty seconds, and by then I'd like to be in my car."

At first Adair's brain was in too much of a whirl to question how he had known of her arrival. The simple, staggering fact of his physical presence precluded all other considerations. And by the time he had maneuvered her to his Jaguar, he had answered any questions she might have asked.

"Nice of you to let me know you were back from South America," he remarked drily as he swept her through the terminal, "but would it have been so very difficult to phone yourself? Your sister has a pleasant voice, but it wasn't the one I'd been hoping to hear."

Adair was too dazed for instant comprehension. The long, lean legs beside her were moving at a dynamo pace, impelling her toward a fate she seemed incapable of resisting. With her suitcase in Gray's possession, and with his fingers clamped forcefully over her arm, she could not have escaped him even if she had tried. And she was too overwhelmed to try.

Then understanding came. Her sister—there was only one person Gray could mean. Adair was weak with incredulity. How could Peggy have broken her promise? After the episode that had sent Adair on a helter-skelter chase to Dallas, Peggy had solemnly sworn that she would not interfere again, *ever*. "At least, not until after the space shuttle," she had added with a twinkle.

Adair was distraught to think her friend would betray her so. And yet she tried to hide her deep disturbance from Gray, to whom she could explain nothing.

"When did . . . Adair . . . phone you?"

Gray didn't break stride. "This afternoon. She got through to my office only half an hour ago. My secretary called me out of a hot and heavy board meeting she wouldn't have dared interrupt for any other reason. Good secretary. She gets her priorities straight." Gray's swift sideways glance smoldered with meaning. "Mind you, I had told her in no uncertain terms exactly what the priorities were."

Adair was breathless at the pace he was setting. "What exactly did Adair . . . tell you?"

"Only what you told her to tell me—your flight number and your ETA. She said I'd have to ask you which hotel you'd be at, how long you'd be staying, and what your plans were. But you're having dinner with me tonight, and I'm not taking no for an answer."

"Oh . . ." It was a trembling "oh," a compound of consternation and numbness, yet she could not have said a firm no if she had tried.

"Don't bother telling me you have another date tonight, because you're not getting out of the date with me. You owe me one. Besides, my secretary phoned Hoshu to tell him to cook up a storm. He'll be working like a fiend to get the dinner ready on short notice. I could never pacify him if his efforts went wasting a second time. He'd make me pay in our next workout—and he's a black belt first class, trained in the best karate schools of Japan. He has a mean chop. I've risked a lot for you, Amelia Clancy—a reckless ride in an AT-6, a mad dash across the continent, a wild drive to the airport just now—but I see no reason to risk a mess of broken bones. I'll hog-tie you and drag you to my apartment if necessary!"

Gray's whirlwind force was such that Adair felt as if she had been hog-tied and dragged already. She saw the brown Jaguar now, parked in a blatantly illegal zone, as if he had pulled up in great haste in the first likely spot he had seen. Its red warning lights were flashing, a ruse that had fooled no one, for several nearby taxi drivers were looking angry, and there was a traffic ticket on the windshield. Gray flipped it free as he opened the car door for Adair, easing her in skillfully. She didn't think of protesting. She needed the support of a good solid seat beneath her knees, which were feeling oddly like custard. Gray's impetuosity dazed her. Once he had closed her in alone, she reminded herself with weak resolve that nothing must be allowed to happen. Nothing at all.

Gray threw her suitcase in the back. He opened his own door and folded his long legs into the seat beside her, unbuttoning his winter overcoat as he did so, for greater comfort and freedom in the car. With unerring aim, he jammed a key into the ignition, but he didn't start the engine at once. Instead he turned and reached for Adair with a low groan.

"Here's another of my priorities," he muttered as he folded her into his arms.

Adair's sanity remained intact for a fraction of time. She raised her hands to prevent the kiss, but instead felt a shock of pleasure as she placed her palms to his chest, between the parting of his coat, against the silky shirt he wore. Her fingertips thrilled to the unyielding wall of him, the feel of demanding maleness. As his mouth descended she forgot why her hands were there.

Her mouth melted helplessly beneath his subtle mastery, beneath the fingers that stroked her cheek and her hair and her ears, beneath the erotic persuasion of his kiss. His tongue dragged temptingly over the soft surface of her lips, parting them with no need of force. He explored the moist recess hungrily, his mouth wresting from her the responses he wanted, his own passionate need betrayed in the raggedness of his breathing, the heavy beat of his heart beneath Adair's palms. She was swirled into a world of eddying wonders, giving in to the sheer sensory pleasure of his closeness, his maleness, his ardor.

At length he moved his mouth to her temple, breaking the intimate contact. "Enough," he groaned thickly, pulling away. He had resisted with difficulty the desire to insinuate his hand beneath Adair's coat, to spread his fingers over the ripe, remembered sweetness of her breast. "Any more, and I'll be incompetent to handle a car," he breathed in a roughened voice. He clicked his seatbelt into place hastily, urgency returning to his movements. "Anyway, I'm too old to be carrying on in bucket seats in public places. The rest will have to wait until we're in my apartment."

As he flicked the ignition key Adair shrank into her seat, heart pounding. She was hardly aware of the several bystanders who were angling curious or angry glances at the Jaguar's interior. She was too alarmingly conscious of Gray's potent forcefulness, of the melting weakness that had overcome her in the moment of contact, of the dangers inherent in putting that explosive combination together in more secluded surroundings. Gray was making no secret of his intentions and it scared the hell out of her.

She knew the dinner was a promise she would have to fulfill at some time, but she made one last-ditch attempt to procrastinate.

"I'm supposed to meet my father and his new wife at their hotel," she said, some of her desperation creeping into her voice. "They're expecting me to eat with them tonight. I can't get out of it, and I wouldn't even want to try. I've never met my father's wife before."

Gray was adamant. His concentration now appeared to be fully devoted to putting the airport behind as swiftly as possible, but he spared time for a piercing glance at Adair. "They'll have to be told you have a prior date with me," he directed sternly. "I'll give you until seven o'clock to do your family visiting. What hotel, by the way? I assume that's where I'm taking you. When we get there, I'll have a quick man-to-man talk with your father and explain about your bet. He'll understand when he hears that the Clancy family honor is at stake."

Adair didn't want to tell him the name of the hotel. She felt as if she was damned if she did and damned if she didn't. Her hands were clammy with apprehension. There was an Alice in Wonderland surrealism to the whole situation, and she could think of no way out, especially as Gray's car would soon be exiting the airport complex, and she had to announce her destination at once. Damn Peggy for putting her in this position!

"No, I . . . on second thought, I'll get out of the dinner with my folks somehow. But I'd rather speak to them alone." With a sense of sinking unease because she was now certain that her hitherto successful deception could not possibly survive the weekend, she told him the name of the modest establishment where she would be staying. "If you'd just drop me off there, I'll take a taxi to your place."

To Adair's surprise, Gray agreed to part of her request with a brisk nod. He glanced determinedly at the digital clock on his car's dash. "Actually, I'm anxious to get back to that board meeting, which is still going on. However, you won't take a taxi. I'll pick you up on the dot of seven. And if you're not there when the desk calls up to your room," he threatened grimly, "I'll shout the lobby down. I can make a hell of a scene, I warn you, when I want."

So she would have to be in the lobby, Adair thought to herself, when he arrived. It wasn't a great solution but for the moment it seemed the only one.

"How was the raft trip?"

"Er . . . fine."

"Your enthusiasm is overwhelming," Gray said drily. "Dare I hope that you didn't have a good time?"

"Of course I had a good time! It was fantastic, wonderful, marvelous, but, but . . . if you don't mind, I'd rather not talk about it at all."

She thought she saw a faint grimace begin to form on Gray's face, but it was swiftly masked by an enigmatic expression. After that he kept his counsel and concentrated on the traffic. They passed Crystal City, a complex of high-rise apartment buildings on the Virginia side of the Potomac. Across the river, beyond its flat curving bridges, the gleaming white dome of the Jefferson Memorial could be seen, with the Washington Monument soaring toward the sky to dominate the view.

Gray negotiated Arlington Memorial Bridge and passed into the very heart of the capital. The greensward was sere and dry, the trees skeletal in the hitherto snowless winter; but otherwise the sights—the Mall, the Capitol, the White House—were by now familiar to Adair's eye. Perhaps the inspiring views had grown too familiar. Suffused with her consciousness of Gray and prickling apprehension about what lay ahead, Adair hardly saw them.

The hotel where Adair was staying was in the downtown area of the city. Gray didn't get out of the Jaguar when he dropped her off at the entrance. A doorman opened the passenger door of the car, ready to help her out. Gray restrained her briefly with one hand, his strong fingers closing over her arm.

"Wear something incredibly sexy," he murmured smokily, his dark blue eyes heating as they roved restlessly over Adair's face. "A tablecloth will do."

Adair might have been surprised at how swiftly Gray's expression changed when she vanished from view. A heavy scowl gathered over his brow as he sped off, tires complaining at the sudden spurt of speed. He had to get back to the vital board meeting he had walked out on in order to meet the plane. That dash to the airport, however, had indeed been a priority, for he'd had no idea of where Amelia Clancy would be staying, and no assurance that she would fulfill her obligation to call him.

It would have taken a thick-skinned man indeed not to be disheartened by the passage of time, the postcard that had come to Washington from the great distance of Baltimore, and the report from the Winterhazy steward, Anton, that Amelia had planned to meet someone for the flight to South America. For the past few weeks he had been trying to harden himself to accept the fact that Amelia was holding him at arm's length, possibly because of some other man.

Privately Gray felt that if his skin were as tough as he would like it to be, he wouldn't have responded to a last-minute phone call that gave no more than a flight number and a bare half hour to get to it. He would have left Amelia standing at the airport.

However, half to his own disgust, he had responded to the tardy encouragement—not only that, he had walked out on a boiling, seething hotbed of a boardroom meeting in order to make the rendezvous. The trouble he had gone to only firmed his determination to succeed with Amelia Clancy, come hell or high water. He intended to shoot the competition down, tonight if possible. And permanently if possible.

He should hate to have abandoned that board meeting for nothing.

Gray shut off thoughts of Amelia as his mind ricocheted back to the crisis he had left behind at the *Clarion*. He would not be able to exercise his stock options until the turn of the year, but things were reaching a showdown right now. In fact, when he had excused himself from the meeting, all hell had been breaking loose. Dolly Winterhazy had declared that she didn't like Gray's hand on the helm. And Bernard Winterhazy, good-natured but ineffectual in a fight, never dared to go openly against his powerful wife.

"Damn her all to hell!" Gray declared viciously, his knuckles turning white over the steering wheel.

Dolly was insisting on a new editorial policy: scandal and society pictures on the front page, supplanting the news of the day. It went against the grain of everything Gray believed in. If he had his way about the wretched society page—which for the moment he didn't—he'd cancel it altogether. It was an abomination of a page, a combination of manure and saccharin. Dolly had always controlled it, and now she was trying to spread her sickening mixture onto *his* front page.

He knew the reason for the sudden stand: she was trying to pressure him into offering himself as a sacrificial lamb. Dolly, who for all her faults had a devastating streak of honesty, had made no secret of her motives. Marina had deliberately neglected to take the Pill during a Caribbean cruise several weeks before and had gotten herself pregnant. She had expected that her partner, a vastly rich and equally spoiled young man, would propose when he found out about it. The man hadn't. Dolly wanted Gray to stand in at the altar to save the Winterhazy name, and she had confessed to him that her front-page ultimatum was blackmail. Blackmail, pure and simple.

Gray stamped on the accelerator, risking a traffic violation in hopes of getting back to the meeting while there was still time to alter its outcome. He did have his supporters on the board, others who, like him, believed in responsible journalism, but the large block of Winterhazy stock was outvoting him. It could outvote him even more emphatically at the annual shareholders' meeting next week. Another few days, and it was quite possible he would no longer be listed as publisher on the masthead of *The Washington Clarion*.

It was a dire three-way choice—give in to Dolly on the editorial policy; give in to Dolly on the marriage; or be fired. And if he was fired he would automatically lose his stock options, which had come with the job.

Marina Winterhazy was fully in favor of her mother's unpalatable ultimatum. The eight-week pregnancy had not interfered with her unflagging interest in men, with Gray himself highest on the list of prospects she was still anxious to ensnare. The months—no, years—of attempting to drag him into her bed had not discouraged Marina, partly because she was a hard female to discourage. Unlike Dolly, she didn't feel that motherhood should necessarily entail marriage, but she did want Gray; in fact, she wanted him very badly indeed. If marriage was the only way to get him, Marina was quite prepared to marry.

Gray's hackles rose at the prospect of giving in to either of the Winterhazy women. Surely there were openings for unemployed publishers! And yet that prospect was the worst of evils, partly because he had labored long and hard to bring the *Clarion* to its present position of preeminence. After devoting most of his adult life to changing it from an inconsequential rag to a respected oracle of journalism, he almost felt the paper belonged to him. He had assembled a fine staff and they counted on him.

Besides, he owed a great debt for the Winterhazy shares he had acquired over the years. His debt was one of gratitude as much as anything. At this point he couldn't possibly back out of his agreements.

No, he couldn't abandon the *Clarion*. He'd have control soon enough, in one more month. In one way or another, he could swallow his gorge for that long.

He hoped he might yet gain some points by returning to the meeting, where one or two board members, normally Winterhazy supporters, had been wavering in the balance. If he failed to convince them, he would be forced into a temporary retreat—until the turn of the year. But there would be no retreats on any front until he had put up one hell of a fight.

Adair checked into her room, unpacked, and tried to contact her father and her new stepmother to let them know she had arrived. She couldn't reach them in their room. Either they were out or they had requested that calls be held. Because of her evening's date, Adair decided not to leave a message with the switchboard. She would try again closer to the dinner hour.

With time on her hands, she spent some minutes thinking over the implications of her present perilous situation. Gray knew where she was staying; he knew her father was also there; he had actually met her father many years before. If he tried to phone at any point and couldn't locate an Amelia Clancy, he would most certainly ask for Lamont Clancy. It was improbable to think her secret could safely survive the weekend.

She remembered the *Clarion*'s society page with its gushing and its shabby innuendos, and shuddered.

If worst came to worst, what would the consequences be? A minor scandal probably wouldn't cost Doug his job; it took too much to train an astronaut. But it could very well mean another delay, putting him on the shelf until some future mission, in order to make sure his home situation hadn't caused instabilities in his character. She thrust aside reflections about how this would affect her and tried to consider how it would affect others. Doug would be deeply disappointed, and so would her father.

She considered her father's disappointment first. These past few months had torn some old blinkers from Adair's eyes. Since the return of that one hazy memory of conquered fear, she had done a good deal of thinking about her father. Still loving him, but no longer blinded by unquestioning devotion, as she had been in her teens, she recognized the unfairness of what he had asked her to do five years before. She had accepted the challenge to return to Doug, as she had accepted other challenges, simply because she couldn't bear to disappoint the father she worshiped. And yet hadn't she disappointed him anyway, simply by being female?

For some minutes she examined this unvarnished truth. Her father's attitude toward women had always been that of a dyed-in-the-wool chauvinist. He saw their weaknesses, not their strengths. He treated Adair's sisters as if they were china dolls, breakable and not quite bright in the head. As a youngster, Adair hadn't wanted to be treated like that, so she had battled to conquer fear, to accept challenges, to take life on the chin, to be a tomboy. She had won her father's respect—or so she had thought. But if she had really had it, wouldn't he have respected her need to break up a marriage that could bring her nothing but unhappiness? Was his view of women so condescending that he thought of them as no better than adjuncts to allow men to fulfill their greater destiny?

Ruefully, with thoughts of the five difficult years behind her, Adair realized it must be so. And perhaps her own actions only proved her father's thinking. She had indeed behaved like the weaker sex in allowing herself to be persuaded into a sham of a marriage, a course of action she had known in her heart to be wrong.

If worst came to worst, her father would simply have to live with his disappointments. She couldn't help him, and perhaps she should never have tried.

And Doug . . . what about *his* disappointment if there was another delay? Yes, he had behaved like a tomcat and hurt her badly, but that was five years in the past, and there were other things to consider. Over the years, tomcat inclinations excepted, she had grown into a comfortable relationship with him. It was impossible to share a roof with someone, to see him day after day, without developing strong ties. He was straight with her and she was fond of him. Besides, he had labored long and hard to earn his place in the sun—studied technology, toughened his body and his mind, submitted to needles and tubes and tests and indignities of every sort and size. There had been sensory deprivation chambers and air-pressure simulators and excruciating sound frequencies to suffer. There had been machines that made a milkshake out of the bones, heat chambers that parboiled the blood, and human centrifuges with incredible G-forces that flattened the face to a caricature and practically drove the stomach back through the spine. There had been constant attempts to unearth any small chinks in his courage, flaws in his judgment, lapses in his coolness, failings in his morale, faults in his physique. And even when he passed all tests with flying colors, as he had perforce to do, there had been new skills to acquire, vast amounts of complex scientific knowledge to accumulate, the inner politics of NASA to contend with; and all of these things put fiendish pressures on nerve and muscle and mind.

And there had been delays. So many delays, so many disappointments.

With a small sense of surprise, Adair realized how much her priorities had changed over the years. The prospect of her father's disappointment no longer troubled her unduly, but the prospect of Doug's disappointment did. He deserved his moment of glory, and he had already waited too long.

At last she ran a bath, hoping it would soak away some of her inner tumult. It didn't. The sight of her own nakedness was a disturbing reminder of how little she understood her own femininity, how incompletely she had explored the possibilities of her sexuality. One short hour in a Learjet had taught her all too dramatically how much she had underestimated her own potential for passion, how few defenses she had against a sexually attractive and sensually accomplished man like Gray.

She closed her eyes and melted at the very memory of the molten feelings she had experienced. She imagined that the bathwater moving over her skin was Gray's mouth. She wondered if the final release, which he had withheld from her, could be more beautiful than what she already knew. . . .

Angry at herself for allowing fantasies that caused

her flesh to grow weak even when she was wholly alone, Adair climbed from the bath and thrust the perturbing thoughts from her mind. Of course she had given in to Gray on the plane! He had virtually blackmailed her into his arms that day, hadn't he? This time he couldn't threaten to kidnap her to Washington, because she was already there. And she simply couldn't allow herself to do any more experimenting with sex until after the promise to present a solid married front had expired.

Wrapped in a thin robe, she once more placed a call to her father's room through the hotel switchboard. He answered the telephone at the first ring.

"Roberta's been lying down," he told Adair. "She's still tired from our flight yesterday. No, no, she's feeling all right, she says. And no, you didn't wake her, she was just getting dressed. So! You made it into town, and only one day after us. Well, well. Great you could get here, Sunny."

Adair's earlier claim had been pure fiction. No family dinner had been planned, so no family dinner had to be canceled. She could have gone directly to Gray's apartment, and no one would have been the wiser.

"We were planning an early meal," her father informed her. "I've made reservations in the hotel dining room for an hour from now. You'll join us, won't you?"

"I'm sorry, Poppy, I have other plans. Could we meet for a drink instead?"

"Sure, in . . . well, just a minute, I'll check if it's all right with Roberta. She may not feel up to it."

Adair could hear him consulting with another voice, muted by distance. It was a warm, quiet voice, its cadence slightly hesitant. Colonel Clancy came back on the line. "Give us twenty minutes," he said. "We'll meet you down in the bar."

Adair had minimal preparation to attend to, for she had already applied such little makeup as she wore, and laid out her dinner dress. It was the same soft crepe she had scorched on the night of the Winterhazy party, now dyed to a very dark mink brown. She had salvaged it because its uncluttered Grecian lines suited her; she hated fussy clothes. Besides, as she contributed no money to the household budget, she disliked overspending on her wardrobe.

She gave herself a critical inspection in the mirror. The dark mink brown was a little dull, she decided, but not totally unflattering with the warm gold of her year-round tan and the honeyed streakiness of her hair. In any case, she had no choice; it was the only dinner gown she had brought to Washington. But the dip of the halter front and the low cut of the back prevented the wearing of a brassiere, and that worried her.

But she had to stand up to Gray somehow! She straightened her shoulders to a square line and regarded her reflection sternly, but realized that the aggressive posture only drew attention to the deep cleft of her breasts and the exact delineation of her nipples. Her neckline wouldn't deter a mouse, let alone a mature man intent on seduction.

It was then, while envisioning how easy it would be for Gray to insinuate his long, deft fingers into the softly plunging front, that she decided on a drastic course of action. Her putative marital state would protect her more surely than any brassiere would do. She would simply have to tell Gray the truth of her identity, and trust to his discretion about her penchant for hazardous aerial stunts, for playing the imposter, and for romancing behind her supposed husband's back.

And perhaps if he accepted that news in a reassuring way, with a firm promise of confidentiality, she would also tell about being long divorced from Doug. There was a bigger risk in that disclosure. NASA might conceivably forgive *her* behavior, but never Doug's. They would surely be very, very angry if it came out that he had been underhanded about his marital state for five full years. They might start looking to see what other secret faults he had, and Adair thought they could probably uncover a few.

Perhaps she shouldn't be trusting Gray at all. For a man barely past his middle thirties, he had done very well for himself, and it took a hard-headed, hard-hitting man to achieve such early and astounding success in the competitive jungle of journalism. For all she knew, that wry, dry charm of his was only the stock-in-trade of a totally unprincipled man, both in business and in bed. A man who had coolly threatened kidnapping might be capable of anything.

She hardly knew Gray Bennett, she reminded herself. She had been with him only . . .

"Three times," she said out loud, with awe and wonder. No, four, counting the meeting at the airport today. How was it possible to be so preoccupied, both physically and mentally, with a man she hardly knew?

No, she shouldn't be trusting Gray. But she had to, because she had the gnawing feeling that he was going to discover the truth about her identity anyway, before the weekend was through. Perhaps he would not betray the trust; perhaps her fears on that score were simply because she had seen too many other people, including at times her own father, pilloried in the press. And perhaps the *Clarion*'s society page promoted sleazy notoriety simply because Gray didn't bother paying it much attention.

With a heavy sigh, Adair turned away from the mirror, saying farewell to the reflection of an exceedingly troubled woman. It was time to go downstairs.

She was waiting in the bar when her father walked in, beaming, with his new wife on his arm. Adair's first impression was of a walking tent topped by short hair of an indeterminate brown, and a nice, shy smile. Roberta was not a tall woman, and in her state of advanced pregnancy she gave the impression of being almost as wide as she was high.

Adair rose to her feet, smiling. "You're Roberta. Hi, and welcome to the Clancy clan." Her eyes flicked humorously to the maternity dress. "Both of you!"

Roberta laughed gently. "Hello, Adair. Or should I call you Sunny?"

"Good heavens, no. I've been trying to outgrow that nickname for years."

Colonel Clancy solicitously held a chair for his wife before sitting down himself. Drinks were ordered at once—plain milk for Roberta, a bourbon and branch water for Colonel Clancy, and ordinary soda water for Adair, who was determined to keep her head clear for the evening that lay ahead.

As soon as the waiter had departed, Lamont Clancy placed his hand over Roberta's, looked at her fondly, and imitated the proud ear-to-ear grin of a boy who has just won a blue ribbon on his first field day. "Well, what do you think, Sunny? Isn't she a peach?"

Roberta blushed like one too. Evidently she was not quite used to male admiration, or perhaps she was simply too shy to hear public praise.

Adair voiced her pleasure, and then her concern about Roberta's condition. "I gather you have to be extra careful for the last month. No complications, I hope?"

"None at all," Roberta said softly.

"Complications, hell—it was a matter of simple miscalculation," Colonel Clancy announced triumphantly. He patted Roberta's hand. "It was just a little fussing about nothing, wasn't it, honey?" He turned back to Adair. "It turns out she's expecting a month sooner than we thought. In other words, the little fellow should be getting himself born in another week or so. Roberta's known that for a while, but she wasn't telling because she thought she mightn't be allowed to fly so close to her time. Isn't that the limit? She finally told me the truth this morning."

Adair shot a glance at her father, amusement mingling with annoyance. How could he believe Roberta was fussing, when she had kept that news so quietly to herself? It was also typical of her father's chauvinistic thinking that the unborn baby, because it was now labeled firmly as a "he," was going to "get himself born." How about Roberta's part in the whole procedure?

"Oh, by the way, Sunny, Amelia and Arden are both turning up tomorrow. They told me they couldn't come at all because of exams, so I suggested they make it a one-day expedition. They'll fly in from New York in the morning, fly back in the afternoon. I said we'd hike across the river and have lunch with them in some restaurant closer to the airport, to give us more time together." He patted his wife's hand again. "That's if Roberta feels up to it, naturally. You free to join us tomorrow, Adair?"

"Of course," she promised.

In the visit that followed, Adair found herself liking her new stepmother enormously. Roberta was hesitant and self-effacing, and she was not particularly pretty, but there was about her a warm, quiet, appealing charm. Colonel Clancy appeared to be quite smitten. Whether he was in love with Roberta herself, or with her condition, Adair wasn't quite sure. As the latter had preceded the marriage, she feared that it might be the major factor in her father's gallant devotion. He treated his new wife as if she were breakable and had to be handled with extreme care. But after all, wasn't that how he treated all women, Adair herself excepted?

All too soon, Colonel Clancy glanced at his watch. "We have to be on our way, I'm afraid. Early bedtimes are a must for the little mother."

It was the china-doll treatment again. Roberta apologized with an embarrassed laugh. "He's much too protective! Really, I'm not made of glass. But Lamont thinks I've reached the age where it won't be as easy as it ought to be, especially as this is my first child."

And his last, thought Adair as she watched them leave, gladness for her father mixed with a rueful reflectiveness, because she wondered if his devotion would prove strong enough to survive the disappointment, should another daughter be produced.

She stayed in the cocktail lounge because there was no reason to return to her room. Her coat was folded over a spare chair at the table, and besides, Gray was not scheduled to arrive for another half hour or so. To prevent any tangles should he appear earlier than expected, she had left the name Amelia Clancy with the clerk at the main desk, and asked that Gray be directed to the bar.

She was surprised and somewhat shaken to see him in the entrance of the cocktail lounge no more than five minutes after her father's departure. And she was shocked by his appearance. She was sitting near the door but he didn't see her at once, for the interior was dim. The entrance area, however, was well lighted, and there was a bright spot falling over Gray's scowling face. No softness tempered the harsh angularity of his features. His mouth was thin and grim, his jaw dangerously tight, his midnight-blue eyes so hard they seemed to glitter with an unholy light. Even the carved facial grooves appeared strange and different, like knife scars cruelly etched into his lean cheeks. She had seen him firm before, she had seen him hard before, she had even seen him angry before—but she had never seen him like this. He looked older and colder, a stranger to her eyes.

The harshness eased when he sighted her and came over to where she sat. He saw the emptied glass in front of her and picked up her coat at once. "Let's go," he said.

"Wait, Gray, there's something I should tell you before we go to your place. Won't you sit down?" She intended to make all admissions at once, in case he wanted to retract the dinner invitation. In *hopes* that he would retract it, she reminded herself—although she felt oddly confused about that.

He sat down heavily and eyed her askance. "Am I going to like it?"

"No."

For a moment Gray's mouth turned forbidding again, revealing that facet of him that had shocked Adair only moments before. It unsettled her because it so closely approximated her musings about the toughness it must require to survive in the journalistic jungle he inhabited.

"Then I don't want to hear it right now," he said harshly. "I've just come from a very tough boardroom fight. You can tell me later, after I've had a drink."

The waiter came and he ordered a double scotch on the rocks. Adair ordered nothing. "What happened?"

His lean face was set into dauntingly enigmatic lines. "We were hammering out a new front-page policy."

"Please tell me about it."

"You'd be bored by the details."

"Try me. Or is it confidential?"

Gray's eyes turned to her. They were hard chips, their depths impenetrable. "Of course it's confidential. I wouldn't be where I am today if I were in the habit of hanging all the dirty boardroom linen on the line, for everyone to see."

"Please give me a hint. Or do I have to wait to see your next front page?"

The waiter brought Gray's drink and he looked broodingly into it for a moment. "Yes, I suppose you'll be able to see that much with your own eyes, soon enough. Watch Sunday's paper for the big news! We're bumping an in-depth report on the International Monetary Conference, in order to break a hot story about who's purportedly sleeping with whom behind what Pentagon filing cabinet. From now on, that's the drill. News hot from the bedrooms of the nation. Sex, sob stories, sin bins, society bashes, along with scandals and shockers of every sort and description. If controversy doesn't exist, we'll invent it."

"And this is *your* policy?"

His tone was clipped, discouraging her curiosity. "The *Clarion* is my baby. As long as I'm publisher, I'm personally responsible for the newspaper's policies—all of them."

"I can't believe you'd stoop so low!"

His eyes were vaguely hostile as he stared back at Adair. "Perhaps you would if you knew my reasons," he said at last, lifting his glass. His voice was so utterly cynical that Adair felt chilled.

Gray glanced back, saw the horror on her face, and realized he should not have allowed himself to sound so bitter. In truth, at the moment he was feeling more than a little resentful toward Amelia Clancy, because his unreturned feelings for her had had no small part in his eventual decision. He also felt frustrated that he couldn't tell her about the minefield of choices he was trying to pick his way through, with at least one of his options eliminated on her behalf.

He wiped the bitter expression from his face and spoke carefully. "I can see you're not in favor, and frankly it's not my favorite kind of journalism either. But it's only a one-month test. In January I may make a totally different decision."

"That's *sick!* I suppose you think putting all that slime on the front page will boost the *Clarion's* circulation!"

Gray tried to fight down the unreasonable surge of antagonism caused by her heated attack. He knew her reaction stemmed from not knowing the facts—but still, he wanted her to have faith; he desperately *needed* her to have faith.

And unless she did have faith, he would never be able to tell her anything at all.

His face became a granite mask, concealing the dilemma of his feelings. "I don't want to discuss it anymore. If you have objections, write a letter to my editor. He agrees with you, by the way."

Adair gazed at him and realized with horror that she could tell him nothing, nothing at all. How little she knew him, this hard stranger! Beneath the surface there was a core of steel, a cynicism and unscrupulousness that were deeply distressing. Thank God she hadn't told her story!

She couldn't deny that she had been toying with dreams of becoming romantically involved with Gray Bennett as soon as she was free to do so. But now, having seen a glimpse of his true nature, she decided she must have been suffering from moon madness.

She would have to brazen her way through the evening somehow, and during the course of it she would simply have to discourage him so thoroughly that he would stop paying attention to her altogether. She sat in complete silence while he finished his drink. She watched his thin face, still darkened by a difficult mood, and cursed herself for getting into such a compromising situation with a man so lacking in integrity.

Gray put down his emptied glass with finality, as if signaling an end to the brooding introspection that had possessed him. His hooded eyes darkened into a warm, intimate smile, as if he had moved into some different compartment of his mind. Once more, he had become deceptively relaxed, but Adair had been put on her guard. Warned by what she had seen, she knew she must not allow herself to be captivated by that easy surface charm.

Below the table, his hand closed gently over Adair's knee, his stroking thumb sending frissons of activity along her nerve channels. Wanting to resist the physical effect he had upon her, she moved her knee.

At her deliberate evasion, he didn't persist with the intimacy. His hand came above the table, its fingers lacing loosely with those of its mate, the posture of a patiently waiting man. "Well, Amelia? You wanted to tell me something I won't want to hear. What is it?"

Adair's voice was cold, chilled by knowledge of the things she had just discovered about his character. "Only that I'm not particularly hungry. Do you think Hoshu will be angry if I don't eat very much?"

Gray was astute enough to recognize the signals of rejection, but he ignored them. He didn't intend to remain rejected for very long. His lean face was bland, his normal suavity fully restored. "If he dares voice one word of complaint, I'll personally punish him tomorrow. He's not the only one with a mean karate chop!"

After what she had just witnessed, Adair could believe it was true.

Chapter Six

*G*ray's apartment was off Wisconsin Avenue, on a quiet side street overlooking a treed ravine. The advance of winter had long since stripped the bushes and branches of foliage, and in the dark their shapes were no more than graceful shadows, but the spare feathery outlines held the promise of a placid, almost countrified view. Adair marveled, not for the first time, that such enclaves of serenity and such vistas of open space could be found so close to the city's core. Elsewhere, Washington's pulse might beat with the frenetic pace of the nation's business, but in settings like this its great heart seemed fully at peace.

Gray let Adair into his apartment with a key, not troubling his manservant to come to the door. The balconied entranceway overlooked a sunken living room where soft lights glowed, and she looked it over with apprehension, hoping it was not about to become the scene of a seduction.

Central in the sunken area was an inviting conversation pit of deep, cushiony modern furniture, a dark warm mocha in color. Scattered on the fringes of the spacious room were a few well-worn antiques, the older pieces obviously not chosen by a decorator because they reflected not one period or one country, but several. An interior designer might have raised eyebrows at the melange—a wall of sliding Japanese partitions was not the perfect background for an old walnut sea chest and a pair of enormous branched candelabra, high as a man, that looked as though they might have been salvaged from an old church. However, in the spacious setting the end result was restful and uncluttered, a statement of personal taste and not merely the reflection of a decorator's dictates.

It was not so very seductive, she decided—except for those low lights.

"Do you approve?" Gray asked, noting her inspection.

Adair was maintaining the cool, distant manner she had adopted in the hotel cocktail lounge. "If you'd turn on a few more lights, I would. It's a little dim."

He reached for a dimmer switch near the door. "Better?"

"Much," Adair agreed coldly, with a short-lived sigh of relief. Before she had fully uttered it, Gray's fingers were at her shoulders to help remove her coat. He bent his head, and for some difficult moments his mouth hovered dangerously and suggestively close to her ear. She could feel his breath stirring each susceptible little tendril of hair, could feel her heart palpitating as his hands slowly slid the coat sleeves down the length of her arms. And then she felt the warmth of his long body closing against her spine, the lean hardness of him overpoweringly near.

"The trouble with bright lighting," he murmured huskily as his mouth dropped to her throat, "is that I can see you far too well now. From up here I have a tantalizing view of that well-lit neckline. I confess, it brings out the beast in me. Are you sure you wouldn't like me to adjust the dimmer switch again?"

She tensed, ready to rebuff the advance, but relief arrived when Hoshu emerged from the kitchen, putting an end to the intimacy.

Gray backed off and introduced her to his manservant, at the same time handing over Adair's coat. Hoshu was younger than Adair had expected, even younger than Gray, she guessed. He had a squat powerful torso, squat powerful legs, and long powerful arms. His hands looked lethal, but he had the smile of a saint.

"Miss Clancy is the lady I've been telling you about, Hoshu," Gray explained.

Hoshu expressed his approval with a big grin. "This one okay sure, boss," he declared before heading back to the kitchen. "Okay sure," Adair was to learn, was Hoshu's favorite expression. At the moment she hardly noticed it, because she was too busy dealing with the sensations evoked by the phrase "this one." It implied that this was not the first time Hoshu had passed judgment on a female guest—a reminder to Adair that she must not allow the evening to reach the conclusion Gray expected.

Impelled by his fingers at her elbow, she walked through to the conversation pit, nerves jumping at the light contact. There was no chair in the grouping, so when Gray freed her arm she circled a low, handsomely carved coffee table to put some distance between them. She sank into a deep sofa. For the moment, to her relief, Gray didn't make the obvious move of also circling the obstacle. He remained on his feet, looking down at her with a lazy, satisfied smile on his lips, as though he had at last gotten her exactly where he wanted her to be.

Adair hunted for an innocuous topic. "Hoshu doesn't look the type to be a gentleman's gentleman," she said.

"He's not. In Japan he worked as a karate instructor. I met him during a tour of the Orient a couple of years ago, and he asked for a job simply because he wanted to get to the States. His intention is to open a karate school one day, as soon as he learns enough of the language and gets his naturalization papers. Then, when he's a solid citizen, he'll arrange a mail-order marriage with some hometown girl and bring her over. Won't you, Hoshu?"

Hoshu had entered in time to hear the comment. He grinned as he approached with a tray of drinks—thimbles of warm Japanese rice wine, and an earthenware jug for refilling. "Yesss," he said. "I okay sure ask for good cooking wife, you see. She works for you, please?"

Gray laughed easily, as if he had heard the request before. "We'll see, Hoshu. By then I may have a wife of my own to make decisions of that sort."

Hoshu's eyes darted to Adair. "Okay sure, you bet," he said cheerfully. "Dinner in one hour, boss. When ready, I ring." His feet were soundless as he departed on the deep-pile carpeting. To Adair's dismay, he detoured to the dimmer switch on his return to the kitchen, and once more the lighting became alarmingly intimate.

"That's better." Gray heaved a fake sigh. "Now I can't see you half as well. I tell you, that low neckline of yours is maddening under bright lights."

Adair knew Gray was only playing skillful verbal games, but all the same the comment stopped any protests she might have made. Overly conscious of the delineation of her breasts, she felt she would be asking for his mocking inspection if she requested a return to brighter light.

Gray moved around the coffee table to where Hoshu had placed the tray. He handed a tiny glass of rice wine to Adair and kept one for himself. "Well, what shall we drink to?" he asked, his voice casual. "Now that the old dare is finally dealt with, we'll have to find a new one."

She slanted a cool glance up at him, conscious that his movement had brought those muscled legs within inches of her own. Her voice was frigid, her manner discouraging. "I can't think of a new one."

"There must be some challenge to throw out in this toast," he taunted. "I should hate to bore a woman who lives as dangerously as you do."

Her gaze dropped again, for she found his long legs in their impeccably tailored trousers less disturbing than the view of his mockingly sensual half-smile. "I've given up living dangerously. I've decided I like the quiet life."

"Thank God. I was hoping the weeks of running the Amazon rapids would cure you of thrill-seeking forever." His sardonic tone changed to a soft murmur as he added, "Correction. All but one type of thrill-seeking."

Adair tried to put conviction in her voice. "I don't want any thrills tonight, thank you," she said crisply. "I had quite enough in the Amazon. From now on, I prefer everything tame."

Gray laughed softly. "Everything? Including men?"

Adair forced herself to maintain a cool, distant expression. "Especially men," she said. She recognized a tendency for her eyes to drift toward his virile thighs, and fought it. She needed no reminders of his maleness.

"First bring out the beast in a man, and then tame him?" Gray's amused misconstruction was deliberate. "I warn you, with me you're going to have your work cut out for you—I'm feeling very untamed this evening. However, to please you, we'll drink to the toast you propose. Here's to the taming of me! Now drink up while your saki's warm."

Adair felt a strong need for something to quell the riot of inner butterflies. The ease with which Gray twisted her words unbalanced her. Would he confound all her defenses as easily?

All too aware of his ability to make her melt at a single touch, she decided it was best to confront the matter head on, before the first touch came. She looked up, challenging him with her eyes. "I'd like to rephrase that toast. Here's to you being totally tame," she said, lifting her rice wine, "starting right now."

He raised a dark sardonic brow and intentionally misinterpreted. "I hadn't actually thought of starting the taming process right now," he murmured, "although we can if you insist. Hoshu said we had an hour before dinner."

Adair felt her cheeks heating beneath his provocative suggestion. "No matter what you may think, Gray, that old dare of yours wasn't a package deal. It included dinner—not bed. If I had my choice, I wouldn't even be here." A little of her anger crept into her voice as she added, "Especially now that I know what an unprincipled businessman you are!"

His face became a mask, unreadable. "Perhaps

you'll change your mind before the evening's through."

"I'm never going to fall into your arms, Gray."

"It seems to me you already have, on a few occasions."

"Because you overpowered me . . . or surprised me . . . or took advantage of me in some moment of weakness. Why, on the trip to Dallas you even blackmailed me. Anyway, old responses have nothing to do with tonight. Don't you know enough to keep hands off when a woman isn't willing?"

"I can try," he said drily, "although it's going to be a great strain on the wild, savage, uncontrollable animal in me. Especially as I'm still suffering from the brutal frustration of fending off your unwillingness in the Learjet."

She flushed, knowing she deserved the sarcasm. "I'm not willing tonight," she said. "It's a woman's privilege to change her mind."

Gray's eyelids drooped as he measured her. "And a man's privilege to get her to change it back again," he muttered unsettlingly. "However, I promise not to attack you physically—at least, not unless you start sending out signs."

"I won't be doing that."

Gray laughed huskily. "Well then, shall I suggest a new dare? From now on, any part of your body that puts out a willingness signal is fair game. For instance, if you part your lips in a certain way, I can't be expected to restrain myself from using them. Agreed?"

She compressed her lips and glared at him.

"Are you so afraid you might issue invitations that you don't dare accept my challenge? Very well then, if we can't come to some agreement, don't expect me to behave in a civilized fashion. You'll have to take your chances on being overpowered, surprised, taken advantage of, and possibly blackmailed—or simply attacked with the savage, sensual lust that happens to accompany my present state of frustration. If you don't agree to the dare, I'll have to assume that's what you want."

"I'll agree," she said tightly. "But don't expect any of those willingness signals you talked about."

"And of course, if you fall into my arms again, all of you is fair game. Now, to go back to my undrunk toast." Gray lifted his tiny glass of rice wine. "Here's to the taming of . . . both of us."

At last, with his own thimbleful of rice wine downed, Gray dropped to a sitting position beside her, ostensibly to refill the glasses. Adair sipped at her heated wine, glad that no strong cocktails had been proffered. The saki was weak, but its warmth was soothing, a perfect balm for her painfully tangled emotions. At least she had extracted a promise of sorts, which ought to get her safely through the evening.

For half an hour or so Gray chatted easily and engagingly, putting disturbing conversation aside in favor of dry anecdotes about his early life. Although fascinated by parts of the story, Adair tried to pretend a cool disinterest. Gray was a self-made and self-educated man, she gathered, with a widowed mother and several sisters. At seventeen he had started as an office boy in a Winterhazy daily in Des Moines, and by the age of twenty-two he had become its acting editor-in-chief. "For two weeks," he added, "but for one reason or another the two weeks stretched into a year. Then Bernard Winterhazy brought me to Washington simply because the Des Moines circulation was rising, unlike everything else in the Winterhazy chain."

"And how did you boost the circulation there? The same way you're doing it at the *Clarion?*" There was a sting in Adair's voice.

He returned her gaze levelly. "By being damn good at my job," he said in a quiet voice, and turned the talk to their common interest in aviation. Commenting on her ability to recognize old planes, he drew from her an admission about her interest in collecting old photographs on the subject. Soon she was talking without constraint, her enthusiasm for the subject overcoming the cold antagonism she had been trying to cultivate.

"I even managed to dig up a photo of the Wright Brothers that's never been published. It's a little blurry, but not bad. And I have a grand World War One collection. Von Richthofen with his Fokker triplane, Eddie Rickenbacker with his Spad 13. And it all started with an old scrapbook my father owned."

"How on earth do you find time for all this collecting, with the busy life you lead?" he asked curiously.

Adair answered with an ineffectual shrug, unable to tell him that without the hobby her life would be very empty indeed. She fell silent, belatedly realizing how skillfully Gray had penetrated her barriers. He was far too good a listener, she reflected, deciding to leave the burden of conversation up to him.

For a time he spoke about his own hobby, collecting antiques. He had done a good deal of traveling, it turned out, and many of his finds had been discovered in faraway places, in disreputable condition. Adair's coil of tension began to unwind again, and after a time she even found herself forgetting her antagonism long enough to smile at his colorful and witty description of a flea market in Hong Kong.

The respite was not to last. Suddenly falling silent, Gray draped his right arm loosely along the back of the couch, his wrist connecting with Adair's hair, but so lightly that she could feel only the faintest of stirrings whenever either of them shifted in the slightest degree. She would have moved, but didn't want to admit that she even felt the almost imperceptible contact.

Gray had stopped talking altogether and Adair felt too unnerved to speak, for fear her voice would betray the breathless feeling that had suddenly assailed her lungs. She knew Gray was watching her with close and fascinated interest, using silence as a weapon. His lack of communication contributed to her building tension. She felt his eyes inspecting her, but didn't dare look at him in return in case he saw some sign of the willingness he was watching for. Every once in a while he moved his wrist fractionally, as if curious to see what response the movement might arouse.

"Odd," he observed at last, "you seem to be in a state of high tension. If I didn't know better, I could almost swear that something is exciting you unbearably right at this very moment. Surely not my simple description of a flea market? Your breathing is remarkably irregular and contradictory. Shallow one moment and deep the next—a fascinating pattern. I wonder if your pulse is as erratic?"

She darted an alarmed glance at him as his left hand moved, finding the little pulse-point beside her ear. The pressure of his fingers was gentle but definitive, unerring in locating the soft and vulnerable spot. "Mmm. Just as I thought. A willingness signal."

"No—"

"Don't move. Remember our bargain? Your ears are fair game now."

She clamped her mouth closed as his lean face started toward her, but a kiss was not his goal. His head bent to her ear and he whispered, "I've been wanting to do this properly for a very, very long time."

Behind her head, his right hand adventured closer to the nape, and his far-reaching fingers started a soft stroking at the earlobe unattended by his mouth.

She felt incapable of movement. She could feel his lips nibbling at the little tendrils of hair beside her ear, catching them on his tongue. The flickering movements grazed her cheek lightly, moistened the surrounding skin. The erotic teasing was only a foretaste, for soon he captured the entire lobe gently with his teeth. His tongue touched its tip, tantalizing the wildly sensitized pleasure site. The damp rubbing pressure increased slowly, until Adair closed her eyes. Although her lips remained firmly locked, still obeying some lingering reserve of willpower, she made a low moaning sound deep in her throat, in answer to the sheer shock of delicious sensation. While aware of the ear's possibilities, nothing in her past experience had prepared her for a stimulation as ardent and tender as this.

"And now your throat is mine," Gray breathed, his mouth dropping to claim the curve of flesh from which the sound had emitted.

His lips grazed the long golden curve of exposed skin, and his tongue delved into the delicate, vulnerable hollow formed by the collarbone. And she could not even deny that he had earned the privilege, for the little animal throbs of pleasure were still purring helplessly in the low reaches of her throat.

Adair's lids were closed, but Gray's were not. He saw when her body sent out its next visible message.

"Interesting," he murmured. "Another willingness signal. One I've been waiting for . . ."

Drugged but not yet wholly oblivious, Adair opened her eyes in time to see lean brown fingers sliding toward the parting of her halter neck. Through the clinging veil of crepe, there was no mistaking the exact delineation of her nipples, already stimulated to thrusting arousal although they had not even been touched. They were taut peaks, the telltale rigidity visible to the naked eye. She tried to twist away, but Gray murmured, "Fair game, remember? Now your breasts belong to me, whenever I choose to use them."

"Gray, no . . ."

"Don't squirm," he murmured, "or I might think those hands you just put on my chest are another invitation."

His lips returned to her earlobe while his feathering fingertips tantalized the flesh at the edge of her dress. Making no sudden assault upon her breast, his palm was toying with the curve of exposed cleavage. Her skin enjoyed a delirium of sensation beneath the slow, deft handling of the swelling softness. Desperately she reached for strength in the moment when she saw his fingers edging beneath the verges of fabric, for she wanted the caress to become no more intimate than it was.

"Stop, Gray. If Hoshu walks in . . ."

The torn words brought Gray's moving lips away from her ear, but it didn't change the dangerously suggestive insinuation of his hand. It advanced another inch, flirting at the edges of the nipple.

"Hoshu knows better than to interrupt," Gray

murmured, moving his mouth again. "Mmmm . . . you taste like lemon and honey. Here . . . and here . . . and here . . ."

His downward trail of soft little licks was taking him toward her breast, while his right hand had started to tug gently at her dress, first step to easing the halter front off one shoulder altogether. Adair found the will to stiffen into total resistance. If Hoshu knew better than to interrupt, it could only be because he was familiar with seduction scenes exactly like this. She pulled away. The sudden movement jerked her dress shoulder, still in Gray's hold, down over one arm. It fell, revealing the unsunned creaminess and the rose-ate peak.

Gray made no effort to prevent her retreat. Confidence unshattered, he merely leaned back on the sofa and took to open admiration of what his advances had uncovered. His eyes smoldered as they took in the ripe curve, lingering with unabashed interest on the tellingly firm nipple. "Breasts, throat, and ears," he taunted. "I wonder what part of you will be willing by the time dinner is over?"

Face hectic with the high flush of desire, Adair started to fumble herself back to decency. How *could* she have let him get so far, after all her lectures to herself?

Gray's long legs were indolently outstretched, ankles crossed in a posture of total relaxation. "No hurry," he drawled. "There's plenty of time for you to get changed."

Adair's eyes widened into a question.

He rose to his feet, unfolding to an imposing height. "Yes, changed. Hoshu will be offended if you don't put on traditional costume. There's a kimono waiting for you in my bedroom."

"I can't—"

"Of course you can," Gray contradicted, lifting her to her feet. His eyes were amused. "Believe me, it leaves a great deal more to the imagination than the suggestive necklines of North American fashion. Besides, how can you sit on the floor in that slender skirt of yours? In deference to Hoshu, I converted my dining room to Japanese seating style. That means mats instead of chairs."

Adair conjured up a mental image of a kimono, with its long sleeves, long skirt, heavy fabric, and possibly the tight girding of an *obi*. Maybe it wasn't such a bad idea at that. At least Gray wouldn't be able to see some signals of arousal.

She followed him along a hall to his bedroom, ready to bolt should he make a false move. In her mind was a guilty realization of exactly how deeply she had been affected by something as relatively simple as a kiss of the ear, the caress that had started the whole chain reaction. Couldn't she find one shred of real resistance in her entire misbehaving body? She had to!

He halted at an utterly masculine room, as simple as the rest of the apartment. Built-in shelves of books served as a headboard for the large double bed, the book jackets lending color to the otherwise subdued setting. Gray held the door open for Adair but didn't enter himself. "I'll give you five minutes," he said. "Call if you need help."

She was halfway into the woman's kimono, a heavy, supple apricot-colored silk woven with subtle peacock designs in golden thread, when it occurred to her to wonder how many other women had worn it. A bachelor wouldn't keep such an article of apparel in his apartment unless he made a habit of entertaining the opposite sex. Besides, expertise with female ears must take vast practice to achieve. How many times in the past had women come to change in Gray's bedroom? The thought put a sour taste in Adair's mouth, but it helped fix her resolve.

There was no traditional *obi,* only a light sash. Adair yanked it firmly closed before stepping out into the hall, feet silent in the flat little slippers that had also been provided.

Gray was leaning against the far wall, arms folded as he waited. To Adair's disturbance, he had changed too—his long kimono of dark brown cotton was far simpler than hers, but highly suggestive to her sensibilities. His feet were bare but for flat leather thongs, and that led her to believe there were no trousers beneath.

His eyes darkened when he saw her. "Extraordinary," he murmured. "I was right, that color is absolutely perfect for you. You glow in it."

Adair gave him a sharp look but didn't comment. Did he think she was naive enough to believe he had chosen the color especially for her? And if he had plans to slip the loose garment off her shoulders at some point in the evening, she had plans to confound him. She had left her own dress on, under the kimono.

With no more touching, Gray led her back to the living room, toward the wall of sliding Japanese screens. He slid back the partition to reveal the Japanese-style dining area he had promised—a low lacquered table, seating mats on the floor, a spare arrangement of pussy willows in a low bowl, all of these things conveying an utter simplicity that seemed to blend ease with formality. The area had a direct passage to the kitchen. Hoshu had entered via this route and was already waiting behind the low dining table, smiling. He was holding a small gong in one hand, about to sound it.

"Awready now. Okay sure good timing, boss!"

Adair saw that the seating mats were on one side of the table only, presumably so that Hoshu could present his masterpieces from the other. With little choice in the matter, she lowered herself to a mat. The narrow brown dress beneath the kimono caused a decided restriction of movement, but she managed to achieve a reasonably comfortable position, with both legs tucked to one side. With her feet angled toward where Gray would have to sit, the position would put a little distance and a minor barrier between them. He would have trouble, she hoped, reaching her ears.

Gray came down cross-legged, looking far more at ease than she. His voluminous robe covered everything, but Adair was utterly conscious that no sign of trouser cuffs could be seen at his naked ankles. A few inches of his lower leg were visible, and her skin prickled at the sight of the tiny dark hairs curling on firm flesh.

All the same, with Hoshu close at hand to prevent any untoward intimacies, she began to lower her mental barriers and contemplate some culinary adventures during the meal ahead. She had never tried Japanese cookery.

"All this is going to take a very long time," Gray advised her as Hoshu placed the first dish in front of them. "If Hoshu is up to his usual standards, there'll be about twenty-five courses, each more delicate than the last. This is a salmon appetizer, if I'm not mistaken."

After Hoshu had confirmed that it was, he retreated to the kitchen to put the finishing touches to his next dish. "It's raw," Gray warned. "The way the

Japanese prepare it, thinly shaved, it's very delicate and delicious and doesn't taste like fish at all. But if the thought alarms you, just say so."

"I'll try anything once," Adair declared rashly, her mind on the paper-thin slivers in front of her. They were beautifully presented, with delicate little vegetable flowers and curls adorning the plate.

"Just as I hoped," Gray murmured smokily, giving her words more meaning than she'd intended.

Beside Adair's plate, North American eating implements had been provided along with the customary chopsticks. Although unfamiliar with the latter, she chose to try them. However, the tiny shavings of fish eluded the ivory sticks. "I don't seem to have the proper control over these things," she sighed at last, in frustration.

After watching her awkward efforts for a few amused moments, Gray leaned closer and altered the placement of her fingers. His hand remained closed over hers longer than strictly necessary. "I hadn't planned to teach you control of any kind tonight," he said disturbingly. "I hope it's not catching."

Adair extricated her fingers and gave him the most discouraging look she could conjure up. "I think I can manage now, thank you." And with some increased degree of efficiency, she actually managed to scoop a delicately flavored morsel into her mouth. She smiled at Gray coldly. "It's all a question of practice, isn't it? I imagine by the time this meal is through, my control will be quite good."

Gray chuckled. "I wouldn't count on it," he said. "Ah, Hoshu, here you are again. What do you have for us this time? Sushi?"

The miniature morsels, mostly crab and tuna rolled around a delicate filling of rice, were served with a fantastic sauce of hot green mustard. Adair's mouth watered at the first taste. Tempura followed: crisp, lightly battered bits of quickly fried vegetables, each a tiny adventure in eating.

Adair found what safety she could in Hoshu's frequent presence, which prevented too much intimate talk. The quiet movements and occasional clatter of dishes in the nearby kitchen contributed as well to a temporary sense of security. Her concentration on the chopsticks also helped, eliminating the need for answers as she manipulated food to her mouth. Her skill improved as the meal progressed.

She found many of the tastes exquisite and the presentation, on eggshell-thin, translucent dishes, charming. In the subsequent offerings there were more varieties of fish and seafood and many delicately slivered vegetables, some raw, some marinated. There was seaweed, its iodine taste strange to the tongue but not wholly unpalatable. Only the octopus repelled her, and Gray ate that for her.

"I'm not too keen on it myself," he admitted with wry honesty after he had downed the contents of her plate. "However, anything to spare Hoshu's feelings."

Adair spoke rashly, with a sudden flare of anger. "You're not so careful of everyone's feelings! What about those people who'll be seeing their private lives laid out on your front page next week?"

Gray's face changed to a mask. "At the moment," he answered carefully, "I'm more concerned with my own private life. Now think of something important to talk about, like how long you're staying in Washington."

"I'm leaving tomorrow," she lied promptly.

"Again? I'll simply have to think of some way to make you change your mind, won't I?"

"You can't," Adair said flatly. The burst of annoyance had reminded her that she intended to squelch Gray's expectations forever, before the evening was through. It would be easy enough, and she wouldn't even have to lie. She turned and looked at him squarely. "There's something you should know, Gray. There's another man in my life."

Gray's fingers grew still on his chopsticks. "Serious?"

"Yes, serious." She challenged him with level amber eyes and a chin tilted at a defiant angle. "Very serious indeed."

Gray's mouth hardened, and something in the determined set of his jaw reminded her of the ruthless stranger he had been in the bar. "So am I," he muttered.

Adair's lips felt stiff. "Perhaps I should have told you about him before, Gray."

"Exactly why are you telling me now?"

It was a time for truth. "Because I have no intention of getting involved with you. After tonight I won't be seeing you again."

The clench of muscles around his mouth indicated obduracy. "I intend to change your mind about that."

"You may win your boardroom battles, but you won't win this one."

For the briefest of moments his eyes glittered, but the hard expression was swiftly hooded. His face relaxed. Once more he was the man of charm, affable and urbane, but Adair knew what deep and muddy currents lay beneath that easy manner.

"Another dare?" he asked with amused derision, the words soft and compelling. "Very well, then, I accept. I don't mind a challenge. In case you haven't guessed it by now, I never give up anything important without one hell of a battle. And I warn you, I intend to use every weapon at my disposal."

Involuntarily Adair shivered, sensing the steel beneath the softness. She had known from the start that Gray Bennett was a dangerous man. But this dangerous?

As the final course was brought, Gray made a sardonic observation particularly unsettling to Adair. "Amazing how you've managed to eat so well, considering your lack of hunger. I suspect it has something to do with the Oriental way of eating. In Japan they don't like to mingle their tastes—they savor each one separately. The meal is like a succession of appetizers, each of them leaving a person hungry for more. It's very much like the type of love you've been asking for this evening, don't you think? One course at a time, and each tiny experiment only whets the appetite for the next."

Hoshu arrived with tea, rescuing the moment. Adair escaped the necessity of answering Gray by delivering some effusive and well-deserved praise for the excellent dinner. Hoshu appeared to be delighted with the flattering comments, not the first he had heard during the course of the meal. He left the teapot in Gray's care. "Next time okay sure better, Miss Clancy," he said happily, vanishing back to the kitchen on velvet feet.

A silence fell over the table as the tea was sipped. A dish of small sweets had been placed on the table, but they didn't tempt Adair's appetite. Several minutes passed before she became aware that there were no more sounds from the kitchen, not even the muffled movements of slippered feet. Lifting her face from the tea cupped between her hands, she cocked her head, listening.

"Hoshu's very quiet," she remarked.

"And very efficient," Gray added drily. "He's finished now; he always cleans up as he goes along."

Apprehension trickled down Adair's spine. "Where is he?"

"He's gone out."

She tensed. She had not heard the click of the main apartment door, but she had no reason to doubt Gray's word. Hoshu's departure had probably been prearranged, in order to set the scene for romance. She glanced at her watch and saw that it was still early, only a little past ten. "In that case, I think you'd better drive me back to the hotel right now."

"Not yet," Gray said quietly, putting down his teacup and shifting to a half-reclining position. With his head propped on one arm, he took to studying Adair, whose ankles still extended defensively in his direction.

"You sent Hoshu out just to clear the decks for action!" she accused.

"Exactly," Gray agreed coolly. "I told him to go for a walk. Now calm down, for I refuse to drive you back to your hotel until we've had a chance to explore the latest willingness signal you just sent out. I see a decided curl to your toes."

"I'm calling a taxi."

Adair started to rise, but Gray's firm fingers closed over an ankle, preventing any withdrawal. "For the moment, fair lady, your feet belong to me. You can't leave until I've used them. And your ankle is trembling too—very erotic part of the body, the ankle . . ."

His eyes turned to smoldering coals, their heat felt in every inch of Adair's skin. He lifted her foot slowly and removed the small embroidered slipper, throwing it aside. "You made a terrible mistake leaving your own dress on underneath," he murmured with pretended direness when he saw the added obstacle. "And you should have removed the nylons too. Their taste is not to my liking."

"Gray!" But her anguished cry prevented nothing, for he bent his dark head to her ankle and seized it softly in his teeth. He growled low in his throat, and then his tongue assaulted the silken surface, dampening the flesh beneath. His fingers moved in a slow, sensuous circle over the sole of her foot, drawing an audible gasp from Adair.

"Odd," he muttered against her ankle. "I could swear that the trembling has traveled all the way up your leg . . . a very revealing signal indeed."

"No," she protested. "Don't . . ."

His hand slid upward on her calf, and his lips began to explore farther afield. Shock waves reverberated up her leg, and the slow progress of his hand did nothing to help. Insinuated intimately, it inched her layers of clothing upward, following the track of the quivering she could not conceal. The extra dress seemed small protection now. His stroking fingers had reached her knee and were still traveling. His mouth began to follow. . . .

"Very willing knees," he breathed huskily.

She could not have said how she came to be in a reclining position, with Gray prone beside her, exploring the willingness of her legs. She closed her eyes in an agony of indecision. She heard herself moaning, but it was the sound of passion, not of protest. Explosions of sensation invaded her skin beneath the damp trail of his conquest. His kisses were like small flames licking along the surface of her silky nylons, driving her mindless with their seductive tenderness.

And then his fingers began to tug gently at her

waist, pulling at the flimsy nylon casing that was the only thin barrier to his lips.

She overcame the sweet urge to surrender and began to fight in earnest, only to find herself freed as swiftly as she had been seized. Gray pulled away and watched her straighten her skirt with soft laughter in his eyes. "I don't think the competition can be half as rough as you've led me to believe," he murmured. "I have the strong impression that most of you is quivering to be properly kissed."

"You . . . you animal!" she declared, covering her flustered state with the worst accusation she could think of. Her color was high, her nerves as well as her clothes in total disarray.

"Is that a compliment?" he drawled.

His cool control, so in contrast to the tingle of heated blood his caresses had sent through her veins, enraged Adair. "No!"

"Do you know you're twice as lovely when you're angry? You look so beautifully aroused."

"I'm not aroused!" Trembling, she started to rise to her feet to race to the partition, hoping to put the dining room and Gray behind her. Uncoiling from his reclining position, he came to his haunches. In her haste to stand up, Adair caught her foot on a fold of the long kimono. With the narrow crepe dress confining freedom of movement, she spilled forward to find herself where she least ought to be.

Gray's arms had broken her fall, and they closed around her. Enfolded by his male strength, she lay there panting, shuddering into submission, all her desire revealed in the aching vulnerability of her eyes, the tremble of her parted lips. A tumultuous need swelled inside her, obliterating thought. Close against the lean hardness of him, held by his arms, with the sweet stimulation of his recent caresses still fluttering through her limbs, she could no longer deny the strong attraction his virility held for her. Nature and need were stronger than she, and defiance had changed to defeat.

As he reacted to her yielding softness, Gray's smile faded, and a dark tormented passion took possession of his eyes. "My God, Amelia," he groaned thickly, "how can you be so damn cruel?"

No longer able to sustain the pretense that he was not as aroused as she, he dropped his dark head to her throat, scorching her soft flesh with hot, hungry kisses that soon led a path toward her mouth. Their lips parted and met with a clinging, wildly passionate thirst, while their hands searched each other's shoulders with urgent abandon, both shamelessly seeking a deeper closeness that no kiss could truly achieve.

She felt Gray lifting her, sweeping her toward some inevitable destination. With her mouth still melded to his and her supple body supported by the strong surround of his arms, her exhilarated flesh was incapable of protest. She was in a world of pure sensation, a world where nothing mattered but the probing mastery of his mouth, the intoxicating scent and taste and texture of his maleness, the feel of his muscled shoulders beneath her clutching fingers.

The bed where he laid her was his own. He came down beside her at once, his mouth still ravenous on hers, leaving no moment of freedom that might restore her to her senses. Flooded with pure physical pleasure, Adair was beyond reason. Her passion-glazed eyes no longer saw Gray as predator, only as partner in a whirlpool of sensory experience that became more delirious with each passing moment. She was lost to herself and to him, and the compelling need that washed through her drove her mindlessly toward a passionate conclusion she had never properly achieved. No caution told her to stop, for her own awakened sexuality and Gray's powerful attraction had swamped her resistance.

She gasped with a startled shock of pleasure to feel his aroused maleness pressing hard against her, the potent contours palpable even through a barrier of cloth. Gray heard the gasp and the submissive moan that followed it. "It's you who turn me untamed," he muttered fiercely in her ear. "You, you, you . . ."

When he undressed her, lips roaming passionately over her ears and her throat, she made no protest but that of impatience, the low, sweet groaning of a woman longing for fulfillment. When he slid the confining nylons from her legs, her hips lifted to make the task easier for him. She hardly felt the air strike her naked breasts, for his mouth was there—his lips avid and restless, seeking the hardened tips of passion, his flickering tongue awakening wild and wondrous sensations as his hand adventured downward to stir an even deeper response.

He freed her in order to undress. Long past the point of no return, Adair was conscious only of intense excitement when he parted his own robe. He was unclothed beneath the kimono. He slid it swiftly from his shoulders, revealing the spare structure of flesh and muscle, the firmness of chest, the strong arousal that excited her so. A light dusting of dark body hair drifted downward toward his lean, sinewy stomach, and she dared to reach out and touch it, wanting to feel its texture on her fingertips.

Groaning, he pressed his naked length against her. "You little tease," he muttered thickly. "How do you expect me to be patient after that?"

She didn't want patience. She wound her arms

around his neck and clung, surrendering all the softness of herself to the ultimate deed she wanted. His hardened body pressed close against her, his bare chest prickling against breasts still stimulated by the dampness of his mouth. Readying her for the conquest, he smoothed her hips, his long, strong fingers hurried but gentle on the awakening flesh. In a prelude to the fuller possession his maleness demanded, he once more claimed her lips in a probing, masterful kiss.

Bzzzz. The sound was sudden and intrusive, a sharp reminder of the world that existed beyond the circle of Gray's arms. Adair stiffened as if dashed by icy water.

The sound came again. And again. The third time it went on, and on, and on. . . .

And so did Gray, whose lovemaking had not halted with the noise. She felt his shoulders tense beneath her fingers, but after a brief halt his mouth and his hands merely redoubled their efforts. His impatient fingers pushed her thighs apart, preparing her for the moment of possession.

But reality had intruded along with the harsh note of the buzzer, which sounded as though someone might be leaning on the doorbell. Adair was aghast. What was she doing? Why was she submitting to this possession by a man she didn't trust—a man she ought to fear? Had she gone utterly mad?

Gray had swiftly levered his body over hers, and although no union had yet been accomplished, his naked weight now pinned her to the bed. She felt him poising. Staggered by her easy submission to his seduction, Adair began to squirm beneath him, evading the finality of union.

Gray's powerful hips came to rest over hers. Unwilling or unable to continue without her compliance, he lifted his head. "Forget it," he muttered. His breathing was harsh and heavy, his voice clogged, his thin face seared by desire, his dark eyes heavy-lidded with unslaked passion. Driven by the immensity of his unsatisfied need, he pinned her hands to the pillow when she started to push him away.

"Oh God, don't do this to me," he rasped thickly. "Whoever it is, they'll give up. They'll go away. I can't stop now."

But Adair could stop now; her sanity had been restored. However, she knew she couldn't fight Gray's strength, should he choose not to release her manacled wrists. She could think of only one easy way to extricate herself from the wildly compromising position in which she found herself, like someone who wakes while sleepwalking to find the body teetering on a precipice.

"I'll answer, Gray. It must be Hoshu. Perhaps he's forgotten his key."

The person at the door was not going to give up. With a deep groan, Gray at last rolled away. "If it's anyone else, tell 'em to go to hell!"

Adair snatched the embroidered kimono and wrapped herself with shaking fingers as she hurried to the door. She didn't care whether it was Hoshu or not. Whoever was down there in the lobby, male or female, Japanese or Siamese, tinker, tailor, soldier, or sailor—whoever was there was going to gain instant and unquestioning admission.

She flicked the intercom and heard a female voice. "Gray?"

Adair didn't hesitate. "Come on up," she answered, and leaned on the button that would soon bring salvation right to the front door. She supposed it must be some woman friend of Gray's, and that made

her doubly thankful for the interruption. Oh, God.
How *could* she have so forgotten herself?

She waited by the entrance, shivering with nervous-
ness and a sudden chill after her narrow escape from
the bedroom, clutching the kimono to herself without
realizing that its sash was unfastened. Although she
was decent, it could be seen that the robe had been
hastily donned. At the moment Adair didn't consider
the other woman's reaction; she thought only about
her own urgent need for an escape route.

A minute or so later the door knocker sounded.
Adair flung the door open and froze with recognition
and surprise. In the same instant Gray emerged from
the bedroom, still struggling his arms into his kimono.
He completed the task and looked up in time to see
the entry of his female visitor.

"What the devil!" he exploded, striding furiously
forward. He took the steps to the entrance in a single
angry leap.

But it was already too late. Marina Winterhazy was
well through the door, her slanted green eyes widen-
ing and then narrowing, catlike, as she took in the
revealing scene. "Well, well," she purred. "I seem to
have interrupted something. Could it be that sex has
been rearing its ugly head?"

Adair was in too much shock to think of all the
implications the other woman's arrival held for herself. Only one conclusion had reached her benumbed
brain: Gray must be having an affair with Marina
Winterhazy, whose platinum hair, pointed face, and
sharp almond eyes she had recognized in the first
instant.

"Get out, Marina," Gray said tightly, yanking the
door wide again.

Marina was in no hurry. Her eyes roved thoughtfully from Gray's bare feet to Adair's. Then they lifted to take in Adair's dishabille and continued onward and upward to examine her kiss-swollen lips and disordered hair. "So my good saint Gray is a secret sinner," she observed sweetly.

"Get out," Gray rasped, shaking with rage.

Marina smiled lazily. "I will—in a moment. I came because Daddy told me about the board meeting, Gray. I saw your car below so I knew you were home. I thought you might be ready to . . . talk."

Gray bit out his words through clenched teeth. "You have a hell of a nerve, Marina. Isn't it obvious I'm in the midst of entertaining another woman?"

"Oh, yes, it's obvious. Very obvious! And the method of entertainment looks . . . very interesting too. But don't worry, Gray darling, despite my prior interest in you, I'm not the jealous type. In fact, I'm fascinated to know there's another woman in your life"—her lips curved into a small, wicked smile— "besides me."

She was watching Adair with narrowed feline eyes. Her voice was arch, sophisticated. "I'm amused to discover your weakness for blondes with interesting backgrounds, and Mama will be too. But maybe I won't tell Mama, Gray darling—if you ask me very nicely. You know what a terrible gossip she can be when she has something scandalous to talk about."

Marina paused, her eyes sliding meaningfully to Gray, while she let the inference sink in. "When you think it over, Gray," she finished sweetly, "you know where to reach me. I'll be waiting for your call."

Sauntering to the door, she turned to Adair with a saccharine smile. "Nice to see you again, Mrs. Anderson. Do say hello to Digger for me. I hope you recovered from the spilled drink?"

Adair was still not thinking straight, but she had her pride. "Yes," she said coldly, and the door had closed behind Marina before she realized just how much she had admitted.

Now there would be no more fooling Gray.

Chapter Seven

G ray's face had turned to chalk beneath his tan. He was staring at her with a thunderstruck expression, every muscle in his lean body rigid with disbelief. His knuckles had whitened with the tightness of his fists. "You can't be," he said in a hoarse voice.

Adair's embattled heart felt as if it could bear no more. Although alarmed for herself and the jeopardy in which she had placed Doug's career, she was wrenched by an even deeper feeling—a reaction to something she saw in Gray's expression. Fearful at the sudden strength and depth of this feeling that pierced her, she thrust it aside, unwilling to analyze it for the moment. This was not the time to experience strong feelings of attachment to a man who now had the knowledge to create havoc in her life.

She had to brazen it out, because there was no other way. "But I am," she said levelly, closing her kimono more firmly, this time with the sash.

"You can't be!" The hollowness in Gray's face had changed to ferocity. His fingers closed over her upper arms, digging hurtfully through the heavy silken sleeves. He shook her shoulders, his fiercely clenched teeth bared like an animal's. This time he bellowed the words. *"You can't be!"*

Under his hands, she felt like a rag doll about to lose its stuffing. "You're hurting me!" she cried.

The shaking ceased, but Gray kept hold of her arms, his glittering eyes hard as gemstones. He remembered the Winterhazy party now with nightmare clarity—Marina angling for the astronaut; the deliberately spilled drink, which could have been intended to put a wife out of commission; the slight evasiveness about names during the encounter in the laundry room. And then the elusiveness since. But she couldn't be!

"Are you married to Digger Anderson?" he demanded angrily, but the volcanic fury of his voice could release only a small portion of the lava-like frustration that was seething inside him.

Under attack, Adair opted for defiance, a trait she had inherited from her father. Her eyes flashed and her chin rose to the challenge. "I told you there was another man in my life, and now you know who! And you know why I didn't want to sleep with you! And why I let that . . . that woman interrupt what was going on tonight! I'm not Amelia, I'm Adair. *Mrs.* Adair Anderson. Now please let me go!"

"But you can't be Adair! She phoned! I know her voice! She—"

"That was my friend Peggy! Both times!"

"Oh, God!" Rage and pain battled in Gray's voice, and rage won. He released her, but smashed the flat edge of his palm with furious karate force on the heavy cast-iron balustrade surrounding the elevated foyer. Under the onslaught it buckled by a fraction but didn't break. The passionate eruption gave some small relief for his feelings, but it offered none for his hand. How could he have been so damn stupid? And why had she been so damn sly?

"Why the hell didn't you *tell* me?"

Emotion caused her words to stumble. "Because I . . . I didn't want my flying antics put out in the p-purple press! And if you do it now, I'll never forgive you!"

"*Flying* antics!" With a laugh so bitter it might have been a curseword, he ran a hand around his neck and cast tortured eyes to the ceiling. "Doesn't it occur to you there are far more damning things than *flying* antics?"

"That's damning enough! Doug might be pulled off the space shuttle if you were to print the whole—"

He blazed through her sentence, his eyes returning to impale her like blue lasers. "I do have some scruples! Don't you trust me at all?"

"I can't—" she cried. And then, stopping herself short, she realized what Gray had said. Scruples? He laid claim to scruples? Had she been wrong in thinking him bereft of principles? Perhaps his newsman's ruthlessness didn't include the betrayal of personal friends.

She spoke more calmly. "I was afraid you might print something about me practically committing aerial hara-kiri. If NASA knew, they might consider grounding Doug, because an astronaut's wife isn't supposed to run around causing him concern of that kind, especially just before an important mission. He's been training for this space shuttle for nearly five years, waiting his turn. I couldn't forgive myself if he lost out now."

Gray's caustic response lashed back at her. "Don't

you think NASA might be equally upset if they heard about what happened tonight? That kind of scandal would hardly put a husband into a fit frame of mind for a space mission!"

Adair's eyes dropped with shame. "Yes," she admitted as strong remorse overcame other emotions. A part of her ached to tell Gray about the long-time divorce, and yet she couldn't. At this point, she didn't dare trust Gray any more than she had to. He knew too much already, and she was feeling sick that her impulsive behavior had put so much of Doug's future into his hands. Gray was explosively angry with her, and in his anger, those scruples he claimed might give way to a stronger motive, the desire to punish her for her deception. It would be all too easy for him to use the weapon of his knowledge.

"All I can do is beg you not to use what you know," she requested in a muffled tone.

For a moment Gray stared at her in mute disbelief as he swallowed the unpalatable extent of Amelia's— no, Adair's—mistrust in him. She had deceived him from the first, so she must have doubted his ethics from the first.

She was asking for a promise of confidentiality. Even had he wanted, he could not have given it now. "Marina knows about tonight," he reminded her harshly.

Adair wet her lips, head still penitently bent. "Perhaps, for you, she'll keep quiet. I got the impression that she . . . that you . . ." She couldn't bring herself to finish the implication, but it didn't have to be voiced. The word "affair" hung between them.

Too angry with Adair to correct the impression, Gray contradicted nothing. His mouth turned to a bitter slash as he pressed back the hurtful, hateful things he wanted to say. He was damned if he was going to deny a liaison with Marina. He wasn't lily-white; he'd had other affairs. Besides, mistrust was a two-edged dagger. Adair had kept her personal life to herself, and so would he.

Adair stumbled on, feeling sickened by Gray's failure to deny involvement with the other woman. "Marina did say she wouldn't tell her mother, if you asked. That didn't sound as though she intends to blurt everything out."

That hardly helped Gray's frame of mind, for it evoked all the bitterness of his recent dealings with the Winterhazy women. His blood curdled as he realized that his distasteful concession of this afternoon had not removed all threats after all. It would be a whole month before he could wrest back control of editorial policies, and a month was more than ample time for Marina to use the new weapon in her possession. A Damoclean sword hung shivering over his head, and Adair's actions had brought it slicing down to within narrow inches of his scalp. The scalp Marina wanted.

Gray was silent for so long that Adair finally glanced up again. He was looking at her strangely, his lips compressed and the muscles of his face still struggling for control. At last he said curtly, "Go and get dressed. I'll call a taxi for you."

"Gray . . ." She stretched out an imploring hand, eyes huge with pleading. She was asking for his simple assurance, because in response to her request he had given no promise to protect her privacy. And yet she also needed something more from him . . . or perhaps needed to give him something . . . exactly what, she wasn't sure.

He wrenched away, turning his back. His shoulders

hunched as if to close her out. "Go and get dressed!" he grated savagely. "Can't you see I need you out of here? I have some heavy thinking to do."

Adair opened her mouth to say more, but no words emerged. Faced with the dangerously suppressed emotion conveyed by Gray's tense spine, the word "sorry" moved unspoken into her mind. But she didn't say it, because it sounded far too lame.

That night sleep did not come easily to Adair. She tossed and turned, fighting battles with her hotel pillow, living a thousand tortures in her mind. There were so many unknowns, so many "ifs" the future might bring. If Gray decided to use his knowledge . . . if Marina Winterhazy talked . . . if Doug was scrubbed from the upcoming mission because of her foolish, free-wheeling behavior.

So much depended on Gray! And that was the biggest "if" of all, for as far as Adair could discern, he was in a position not only to publish discrediting stories if he chose, but also to extract a promise of confidentiality from Marina Winterhazy. It nauseated her to know the two of them were entangled romantically, but that was another matter, an unruly feeling that resulted from her basic emotional responses to Gray, and not from her rational mind.

Her rational mind told her that Gray had the power to hurt her; it also told her that after what had happened, he might want to. While shepherding her down to the waiting taxi, his face had been a stony enigma. Adair had admitted that she would be in Washington for the rest of the weekend and had given him her room number at the hotel. "I'd appreciate some warning if you're going to put any of my crazy behavior into your newspaper," she had said when they reached the sidewalk.

For a moment, in the uncertain shadows of the street, she had thought his eyes looked bleak. But perhaps it had been her imagination, for his voice had been so acid that it was almost painful to hear. "Maybe. Don't count on it," he had said. He had returned to grim silence as he handed her through the open door of the taxi.

That piece of parting cruelty could only have been a deliberate decision to keep her in suspense. At least, that was what her rational mind told her. And yet her emotions told her something else.

But that was crazy; Gray might be angry but he couldn't possibly be as upset about this as she was.

Oh, why did her emotions have to be so hopelessly tangled where Gray was concerned? She didn't understand them at all. Restless in her bed as the long night wore on, she trooped the feelings out one by one, trying to put them into perspective.

There must have been some modicum of trust at first, she realized. If instinct had warned her strongly against Gray, she would not have given way to a reckless impulse and agreed to the afternoon of flying. Or would she? She had never been one to back away from risks.

Her real mistrust had started, she decided, on the afternoon of stunt flying. It had been a day for the discovery of fear: the near-brush with death had awakened all sorts of cautionary instincts she hadn't known she possessed. The old half-remembered fears had been only a part of it, for there had been new fears too—fear of Gray's physical hold over her senses, fear of the extraordinary sensations he was awakening in her, fear of an involvement she wasn't ready for, fear that she might have been subconsciously trying to attract Gray with her daredevil stunts.

Had the fear become mistrust because she hadn't

wanted to admit to fear? Not admitting to fear was ingrained in her by her upbringing. To her rumpled pillow she admitted it now: "I've been afraid . . . afraid . . . afraid . . ."

Afraid of what? His background of journalism was the obvious, and she avoided thinking about that, because she had the feeling her fears went far deeper than Gray's power to hurt her through the printed word.

What else was she afraid of? His physical attraction, of course. He affected her so strongly that she could never think straight when he was around; in fact, she usually stopped thinking altogether. The fear was well-founded, as tonight had proved. One touch from him and her backbone evaporated, all the hard-earned spunk of her youth dispersing like an insubstantial mist. "The weaker sex," she told her pillow bitterly.

But there was something else, something deeper and stronger, some truth she had been avoiding, a fear so deep-seated it hardly bore thinking about. Why didn't she have the courage to think about it?

She forced her mind to return to that moment in Gray's apartment when she had felt herself attached to him as if by an unseen force. The power of that feeling had frightened her. It was as if there had been a series of links extending in an invisible, unbreakable chain, with one end of the chain forged right into her heart.

Adair sat bolt upright in bed, shivering even though she wore pajamas and the hotel room was not cool. Was she in love with him? Was that what she was afraid of?

"Oh, damn," she groaned, now in true anguish. Of course! And no wonder she had been afraid to examine her feelings! There was an immense contradiction in them. Being in love, she had wanted to be a woman in the fullest sense, to be desired and admired and respected for her femininity. And yet, somewhere deep down, there had been the fear that being a woman would earn her no respect. Her father's long-time chauvinism had left its scars.

"Oh, God," she said in agony, turning back to bury her head in her pillow. She was in love, wildly in love, desperately in love, and the whole thing was hopeless. She was in love and she hadn't wanted to admit it, because she had been sure that a woman could not earn a man's love and his respect at one and the same time.

And even recognizing all that, rationally knowing that love and admiration could go hand in hand, it was still hopeless. She didn't want to be in love with Gray. It didn't much matter if he admired her, because she couldn't admire *him*. Besides, the complications of the situation were immense. SNAFU, as pilots sometimes said.

"Situation Normal, All Fouled Up!" she declared, fisting her rumpled sheets.

Her pillow answered with what comfort it could, silently absorbing the hot tears she had been carrying inside since the moment of leaving Gray.

Exhaustion could not be allowed to interfere with the promise she had made for the following day. Adair hadn't seen her sisters for many months, and lunch at a restaurant near the airport shouldn't be overly taxing.

Adair met her father and Roberta in the hotel lobby, as agreed. A limousine had been arranged. Snow had begun to fall, and as they all climbed into the car Colonel Clancy did some gallant worrying about Roberta's lack of snow boots. Adair noted with half-hearted amusement that he was wearing none himself.

Lunch was an effervescent occasion, and Adair managed to join in all the family laughter, although for her the enthusiasm was difficult to maintain. Her heart felt like a stone. At least the dark smudges under her eyes weren't too obvious. She had applied makeup with far more care than usual to camouflage the previous night's ravages, for she didn't want to ruin the occasion for everyone else. She felt emotionally drained, but no one commented on her appearance, not even her sisters, who were usually very perceptive. And they could be quite outspoken when they wished, using—or abusing—their sibling privileges to pry. Her father looked at her once or twice with a mildly puzzled expression but asked no questions.

As the lunch drew to an end Adair felt that her pretense of normality had been successful. Her father's close looks, she decided, must have been because he wasn't used to seeing her wearing so much makeup.

Dessert had just arrived when Roberta said quietly, "Lamont, it's time to go."

"Go? Why, Amelia and Arden don't have to catch their plane for another hour at least. There's no need to worry your pretty little head, Roberta." He chuckled expansively. "Leave the worrying to me! Isn't that what men are for? I'll get them there on time." He turned to one of his daughters. "Arden, I'm sorry you're finding college so hard, but remember it doesn't much matter if you get through. No reason you need a degree! Now, if you were a man . . . well, there's a helluva difference when your whole future's at stake. Why, I remember one time when I damn near got booted out of advanced flight training at

Corpus Christi. A bunch of us guys got into some silly escapade that—"

Roberta glanced at her watch. "Really, Lamont—"

"Hush, Roberta. Stop all this female fussing. Now you gals will be shocked to hear this, but . . ."

Adair looked at her father and stepmother curiously. Roberta hadn't fussed since the meal began. In fact, she had been remarkably quiet, leaving most of the chatter to the talkative Clancys. Adair, with her new perception of her father, could see that he was being chauvinistic again.

". . . and when they found out I'd gone winging off with four broken ribs, a black eye, and a broken wrist, there was a helluva storm. A few million bucks' worth of airplane up there, and—"

"Perhaps you'd better listen to Roberta, Poppy. She has something really important to say."

Adair's firm interruption stopped Colonel Clancy in the middle of a sentence. He turned to Roberta with a gently indulgent smile. "I'm sorry, my dear. Have I been neglecting you today? It's only that I haven't seen Arden and Amelia for so—"

"It's time to go. To the *hospital*, Lamont, not to the airport."

Adair had to give her father credit. When action was called for, he sprang into action. It seemed only seconds until the bill was paid and the whole party was out on the sidewalk, now covered with a two-inch layer of white. It was still snowing, a slick wet snow that felt slippery underfoot.

Hasty good-byes were said, and in no time at all Amelia and Arden were tucked into a cab to return to the airport. The remaining three settled into the back of a larger limousine-size taxi for transport back to the city core. Adair pulled down the small jump stool,

leaving all the space on the large back seat for the two
main actors in the small drama that was unfolding.

The taxi driver eyed Roberta's voluminous shape
askance. "You in a hurry?" he asked nervously when
he heard his goal was a hospital, any hospital. "Streets
are a hell of a mess today."

Colonel Clancy was crisp and in full command of
the situation. "Fast as you can, but don't overdo it.
The lady's in no condition for a sudden jolt." He
patted his wife's hand. "Now don't fret, Roberta," he
said soothingly as the driver took off, expertly avoiding a skid.

Roberta was not fretting. She was sitting in total
quiet, ostensibly concentrating on the passing scene,
but Adair noted that her stepmother's eyes occasion-
ally flickered toward her wristwatch. Adair didn't like
the regularity of those glances. They seemed to be
timed a little too frequently, each of them accompa-
nied by a tiny compression of Roberta's lips.

"Are the pains too close?" Adair asked, drawing
her father's concerned attention too.

"No," Roberta said quietly and stopped checking
her watch.

The two inches of snow had caused Washington
traffic to grind to a slow crawl. The taxi driver was
doing his best, threading around halted cars when
possible, but short of sprouting wings on his vehicle
he could not travel faster.

Colonel Clancy was still patting hands and being
overly reassuring. "No need to panic, Roberta.
There's lots of time, even with this damn snow.
Remember, I've been through this before. There's
usually plenty of time after the first pain. Why, Adair
took ten full hours to be born."

Roberta was not panicking. She was simply sitting

there, staring out the window. Since Adair's question, she wasn't doing any overt timing, but all too frequently her eyes glazed and a dew of moisture broke out on her brow. Adair's admiration grew, for she realized her stepmother was doing a fine job of keeping her complaints and her worries to herself.

Colonel Clancy was droning on. Talking arrant male nonsense, Adair thought with a flash of annoyance—as if he had been through it all personally. She had the feeling her father believed, underneath all that soothing talk of his, that there wasn't so very much to this female business of childbirth. Adair could imagine his thinking: A man (being a man) could suffer pangs far worse than labor without turning a hair, whereas women (being china dolls) needed sympathy and lots of tender loving care, even when the situation wasn't critical.

They were passing parkland when the taxi skidded to a sudden halt, swerving to avoid a collision. Ahead, within the range of visibility, cars had stopped at strange angles. Nothing was moving. Horns started honking. Cursing, the taxi driver let himself out his door and stood on the running board, craning his head to peer at the situation.

"That is some pile-up," he reported gloomily as he climbed back in. "Must be a dozen rear-end collisions up ahead."

From her jump seat, Adair twisted to look at him anxiously. "You can't get through?"

"Not a hope. Cops'll have to sort this one out. Don't worry though, they're on the scene already. It shouldn't take long."

"Pull off the road," came a quiet command. The voice was Roberta's, the first words she had spoken for some time, and everyone turned and stared.

"Lady, there's no street to pull off on! This is a park, and there's cops ahead. I can't just drive over the curb and—"

"Now look, Roberta," Colonel Clancy said crisply. "You'll simply have to hang on. This is no time to lose your head. And this is no place to—"

"Now," she said firmly.

"Oh, my God," muttered the taxi driver, shaken. He started his ignition again. "Nothing like this ever happened to me before. *Ever.*"

As the car pulled out of the line of traffic and bumped over a curb onto parkland, Colonel Clancy was still fancying himself in control of the situation. "Hold on, Roberta, I know you're in pain but there's no need to lose your head. Just stay in the car and I'll fetch a doctor. There's got to be one around."

"Where?" Roberta asked mildly. "In any case, there isn't time." She bit her lip as a new film of moisture appeared on her brow. "Instead of running off on a wild goose chase, Lamont, you can start by taking off your coat."

She leaned forward to the taxi driver, who had braked to a halt under a feathery snow-clad tree, in a highly illegal place. A policeman was already trudging toward the taxi, looking weary and thoroughly exasperated. "Leave the car running, please," she requested. "I want the heater on. And would you mind hanging my husband's coat over the window? Stay out there to keep everyone away. Perhaps the policeman will be good enough to help you."

"Sure thing, lady," agreed the badly rattled driver, grabbing the greatcoat and leaping out of the car as if only too grateful to escape.

"But I don't have a clue what to do," Lamont Clancy complained, sounding helpless for the very first time in Adair's memory.

Adair felt exactly the same way. "Neither do I," she echoed.

"Well, I do," Roberta said calmly. "I haven't worked for the Red Cross all these years without learning a thing or two." Her brow creased until a new pang passed. It looked like a bad one, for when it was through her forehead was bathed in moisture.

"Good God, Roberta, there's no way I can—"

"Hush, Lamont! I know you can't." Then Roberta announced to her two helpless helpers, "Adair is going to deliver the baby for me. Don't worry, Adair, I'll tell you exactly what to do. And as for you, Lamont, either make yourself useful by holding my hand—hard as you can—or get out there in the snow. And stop looking at me as if you're dazed out of your wits!"

Chapter Eight

The hospital maternity ward was finally reached, after the fact, with the help of traffic police, an ambulance, and several sirens. For Adair and her father, there were two anxious hours in the waiting room. At last they received a full medical report.

"I believe it's safe to say your wife's no longer in critical condition, Colonel Clancy," the doctor reported gravely. "At this point, I doubt she'll need another transfusion. But she's very weak, still suffering from trauma, and there are a few medical procedures still to attend to. You can see her in half an hour or so—but only for a few minutes. She's been through a great deal. Take it from me, Colonel Clancy, your wife is a most remarkable woman."

After the doctor had left, Adair had the feeling her father had hardly heard. He was still looking stunned by the quick onward march of events over which he had no control. Adair had the notion he was half in shock; that he had not really taken in much of what had happened, since witnessing the difficult and near-fatal birth.

She wondered whether, in all the terrible worry about Roberta, he had actually assimilated the other fact that must have been a terrible disappointment to him.

"She's a beautiful baby, Poppy."

"I . . . oh, yes," he said absently. But he appeared drained, and his mind was elsewhere—with his wife. "Yes, it was a girl, wasn't it, too bad . . ."

After serving as midwife, Adair wasn't about to commiserate with her father about the baby's sex. She was too proud of her handiwork to apologize for it. "The doctor said it hasn't hurt the baby a bit to be born in a taxi. She's hale and hearty, all eight pounds of her. And Roberta's going to be all right too. You must have heard the doctor say that."

Lamont Clancy's head dropped into his hands. "I didn't know," he whispered, his voice hoarse and upset. "Oh God, I didn't know it would be so hard for her . . . so damn hard . . ."

"Poppy, you mustn't worry. The hemorrhaging has stopped and Roberta's been given a transfusion. She's going to be *fine*. The doctor said so."

". . . and she just kept telling you what to do, as if everything was all right . . ."

"It *is* all right, Poppy, thanks to Roberta. The doctors said all her instructions were letter-perfect."

". . . and she could have died just like that . . ."

"But she didn't! Don't you understand, Poppy? It wasn't easy for her, but it's over now. She's in good hands."

". . . and not a whimper out of her, not even

when . . . oh God, worrying about the *baby* and not about herself . . . and it was so damn difficult for her . . . my God, if anything happens to her . . ."

Adair took her father's hands in her own. She looked at him earnestly, waiting until he lifted his head. His eyes were haunted and old. "You're married to a very remarkable woman, Poppy. If she wasn't, she wouldn't be alive right now. Roberta is quiet, calm, and courageous. And she's not a quitter. After what she went through, do you think she's going to give up *now?*"

Colonel Clancy blinked and seemed to come out of his worried fog. He shook his head, sounding more positive. "No. No, you're right. She won't give up. She can't give up!"

"The doctor says she's a fighter, she's going to pull through," Adair repeated, in case he was still in doubt. "And she's so very happy about the baby—you must remember that."

"She was so weak, so weak . . ."

"Roberta was happy to have a lovely, healthy little girl. Don't you think she'd want you to be happy too?"

Adair's father was still too concerned about his wife to think about his new child. After a choked moment he said, "I love her, Sunny."

"I know you do." Moved by the simple statement, Adair felt moisture gathering behind her eyes. But then, surprising herself, she burst out, "But damn you, Poppy, you should also be busting your buttons with pride that she's the mother of your daughter!"

Adair's father stared at her as if he had only half heard.

That evening Adair placed a call to Poughkeepsie to advise her sisters of developments; she also phoned

Houston to inform Doug of the eventful birth. "I've decided to stay on in Washington for a couple of extra days. Just until Roberta is one hundred percent."

"Roger," Doug said, but he sounded utterly gloomy.

"Is something the matter?"

"Hey, what the hell is this, an inquisition?"

Adair was startled by the sudden vicious attack, so unlike Doug. "Just asking," she said stiffly.

After a second of silence he apologized gruffly. "Sorry, kid. Grumpy from missing my breakfast bacon and eggs, I guess. Or maybe I'm just hung over. Listen, don't worry about a thing. I'm managing just great on my own."

Adair had considered making minor confessions on the telephone, just so Doug would have some advance warning if all hell broke loose in the Sunday *Clarion*. But he sounded so unaccountably depressed, so upset, so different.

"I'll be back as soon as possible," she promised, adding a new worry to her load. Again that night, despite severe exhaustion after the tense and trying day, she had little peace.

By the following day Roberta was well out of danger. Adair and her father shared a taxi to the hospital at the start of Sunday visiting hours. Lamont Clancy planned to spend the rest of the day at the hospital, but Adair remained in Roberta's room for a few minutes only. An overload of visitors was no help to a patient recuperating from a severe shock to the system, as the difficult and dangerous delivery had been. However, Adair spent the better part of half an hour peering through the glass of the nursery, feeling a proprietary pride in the baby she had helped to deliver. She thought her new half-sister was lovely, despite a wrinkled red face, scrunched-up eyes, a healthy howl, and a totally bald head.

That enjoyable half hour was a diversion from thoughts that remained difficult in almost every other regard. Tiredness didn't help, and Adair's head was throbbing by the time she left the hospital, the headache perhaps induced by the caterwauling of new arrivals in the maternity ward.

On returning to the hotel, she bought a copy of the Sunday *Clarion*, something she had guiltily avoided doing while in her father's company. No headline leaped out at her. She stopped at the hotel desk long enough to instruct that all calls be held, unless they came from the hospital. In the elevator, which she shared with several other passengers, she put off closer inspection of the front page. But as soon as she reached her room she scanned it with anxious eyes, to find . . .

Relief. The only scandal in sight was something to do with a major tax scam, but that was big news of the day and had been making headlines everywhere. The front page looked much as it had always looked— there were stories about Congressional committees, upcoming conventions, employment statistics, Arab influence, Russian intervention. The report on the International Monetary Conference had survived. If there was a single word about Adair Anderson, she couldn't find it.

With trembling fingers, she turned until she found the society and gossip section.

And there, staring back at her, was a picture of Gray. And beside it, a portrait of Marina.

WINTERHAZY HEIRESS TO WED, proclaimed a bold headline. A story followed, but Adair couldn't read it. Her head started to swim dizzily and nausea hit her in the stomach with the impact of a kicking mule. She put the paper down and ran to the bathroom, but only a dry retching resulted. As she had eaten nothing since the previous noon, it was not so surprising.

At last, unrelieved and finding that there was no relief to be had, she bathed her face in cold water to shock herself back to control. In her mirror she saw the dark marks, almost like bruises, that appeared beneath her eyes when the concealing makeup was removed. Then she staggered back and lay down on the bed. Her distress was emotional, not physical, she realized, although the exhaustion of two near-sleepless nights and the strain of worrying about Roberta were undoubtedly also contributing to her state.

Gray and Marina, Gray and Marina, Gray and Marina. The ghoulish refrain kept hammering through her brain, like the pounding of nails in a coffin. All other anguish paled in comparison. Gray and Marina . . .

Adair woke with a start, feeling as if she had been tumbling at ever-increasing speed through a black and endless emptiness, a hole with no bottom, a nightmare with no end. She was in a time warp, free-falling toward some ultimate nameless terror. The room was dark, so the sensation was not at once dispelled. She was disoriented and couldn't remember falling asleep.

A sharp rapping noise intruded on the dark silence, causing a confused realization that this was the second time she had heard the sound. In her dream it had seemed like the close report of a sonic boom, contributing to the sensation that she had fallen through the speed of sound. And then she remembered where she was. Was Poppy back from the hospital with more news of Roberta? Still heavy with sleep, she fumbled for a bedside lamp. "Coming!" she called.

A glance at her wristwatch told her it was only six o'clock. Darkness must have fallen not long before. Her father probably had dinner on his mind, and Adair realized it would do her good to eat something herself. She was not hungry, but her stomach was concave with emptiness. "Coming!" she repeated, moving more swiftly.

The softly gathered wool skirt she had worn to the hospital was badly rumpled, her fawn sweater twisted on her body. She straightened them while she stumbled to the door, her unbrushed hair spilling about her shoulders. In the moment before opening the door, she composed her face as best she could. She hoped sleep had wiped the black smudges from beneath her eyes.

"I'm sorry, Poppy, I was . . ." The unfinished words trailed off as her sleep-drugged mind took in the fact that it wasn't her father at all.

Gray's eyes were cold. "I've been trying to get you on the phone all day to set this up. However, I won't apologize for the sudden appearance. If you're shocked to see me, remember you have no corner on unpleasant surprises."

He walked in without invitation, passing Adair to gain the main part of the room. He remained on his feet and stood surveying the room with its plain blonde oak furniture, its one dim light, its disordered bedspread. Finally his eyes dropped to the copy of his own newspaper lying askew on the floor, still opened to the society page. And then he turned to Adair, who had remained standing by the door, marshaling her wits. "I see you've already read about it," he said, his tone serving notice to Adair that the encounter was not to be an easy one. "Well, shall we talk?"

She closed the door quietly and moved to within safe distance of Gray, all systems now on full alert. "I don't think there's anything to talk about," she said, her voice cold in response to his chilly manner.

His eyes raked her with something akin to contempt. He sounded utterly cynical as he bit out, "You might start by thanking me for keeping your name off the front page—and every other page too."

Adair was momentarily jolted, realizing how much her preoccupations had changed after reading the news of Gray's engagement. She steadied herself by sitting down on the room's lone chair, using its armrests as if they could help her hold on to herself.

"Thank you for keeping my name off the front page," she said. But pride had prevented any warmth from creeping into her voice, and she knew the stiff thank-you was not enough. She looked up at Gray and said quietly, with more gratitude, "I really mean that. I should have told you at once, but I've had a lot of other things on my mind."

Gray bent to lift the fallen newspaper. "This story, for instance?" he asked with intense bitterness. He quoted from the column which Adair had not read. "'An antique gown, worn by three generations of Winterhazy brides, will be the cynosure of all eyes at a January wedding certain to be the social event of the winter season . . .' Surely that society claptrap can't be of any concern to you."

Adair swayed at the discovery of the wedding's imminence. She had the feeling her face was very pale, and with the opened newspaper as evidence of her interest, there was no point pretending to Gray. She bent her head, evading his eyes, remembering her debt to him, trying to keep her voice level. "Yes, I confess I was perturbed, especially considering the way you tried so hard to have an affair with me. How long have you been engaged to Marina?"

Gray's voice was caustic, acid with the need to

inflict a part of the hurt he himself had suffered. "If you'd read the story, you'd have some idea. Fourteen bridesmaids have been chosen, and Dolly Winterhazy's guest list is already six hundred names long."

"You should have told me you were getting married next month."

He flung the newspaper on the bed with a gesture of angry disgust, and his blazing eyes came back to her. "And you should have told me you'd been married for years! Don't fling accusations of infidelity in my face without looking into your own sins!"

Conscious of how much she owed Gray for not using hurtful information in his possession, she tried to keep her words reasonable. "But I wasn't looking for an affair, and you were."

Her unemotional response only enraged him further. "Don't pretend innocence! You were damn ready for me every stage of the way! Oh, a little artful pulling back now and then, but isn't that all part of the big come-on?"

Adair looked up, stung by his opinion of her. "No! Sleeping with you—or anyone!—was the last thing on my mind."

Once, Gray might have believed her, but the cruel revelation of the other night had ripped the veils from his eyes. He had had a couple of restless nights himself, thinking over each small detail of their acquaintance, starting with the encounter in the laundry room. Knowing her identity now, he had been able to make a number of educated guesses, and none of them were flattering to Adair.

His lips twisted with scorn. "Oh? Why else would a married woman go around without a wedding ring? That's the biggest dare of all—a challenge for every interested man you meet to do his damnedest to get

you into bed. A dare from Adair . . . ironic, isn't it?
You're well named for the risky life you lead! I should
laugh but I'm too damn sickened to do anything of the
sort. It must be hellishly dangerous for you, having
such a high-profile husband. No wonder you wanted
to protect your precious identity! Keep the liaison
short, sweet, and anonymous. No wonder you were so
badly thrown when I figured out who your father was!
You were ready to back out then, weren't you? But
instead you pretended to be your own sister, and put
me on hold. Did it amuse you to find yourself getting
away with it? And why did you decide to carry
through? Was Houston growing too tame?" He
paused and drove his next words into her as if they
had been a dagger. *"Or were you settling some score
with your husband?* To put it more plainly, was it
boredom or just plain bitchery?"

"Neither! I—"

But Gray was not finished with his scorching con-
demnation. Interrupting, he flung more words at her,
each as forceful and hurtful as a slap in the face.
"Don't bother inventing motives for yourself, for I
have them well figured out now! I know your husband
plays around. But in my book, getting even for a
partner's infidelities doesn't excuse a thing. And don't
tell me you didn't have an affair in mind, or you
wouldn't have sent word that you were coming to
Washington! Only a first-class bitch would pull that
kind of stunt just before her man heads for outer
space!"

Adair sat in shocked silence. How could she defend
herself? Much as she might want to, she could not
now tell Gray the truth of her relationship with Doug.
And to explain to him that Peggy had phoned on her
own initiative seemed a pale excuse. Besides, Adair

didn't yet comprehend why Peggy had done that, breaking all promises. How could she explain to Gray something that she didn't understand herself?

He glared at her, the jaw muscles of his lean face working murderously. "It all fits together, doesn't it—a cheating husband and a wife who wants revenge, but has to get it on the sly. My God, I was stupid not to see it from the start! I suppose you were being a little coy at the Winterhazy party, in case I happened to stumble onto your true identity before the evening was through? Then giving me the address in Houston . . . it must have been very amusing, for a female who flirts with danger!"

"It wasn't like that," Adair said, but the protest was shaky, carrying no conviction.

"And the trip to Dallas! If you were so anxious *not* to have an affair, why were you begging me to make love to you that day? Then your reaction to the new newspaper policy. No wonder you were upset! But you weren't quite ready to cancel the scene in my apartment, were you? Oh, it was all very well done. Pretending to hold me off. The warning that you wouldn't be seeing me again, so I wouldn't expect a continuing entanglement. Then tripping into my arms, so you could later claim you had simply lost your head . . . as far as I can see, the only thing not in character is your letting Marina through the door." His dark eyes slithered over her contemptuously. "But then," he sneered, "you thought it was Hoshu, didn't you?"

Adair was bristling under his accusations, but still trying to maintain control. Her voice was tight. "I've told you, I wanted an interruption. And I didn't want an affair."

His eyes glinted with disbelief. "And exactly how

long have you been walking around with a bare ring finger?"

She took a tighter grip on the arms of her chair. "Five years and a few months," she said, forcing her voice to remain level. "I took my wedding ring off the day I learned that our marriage vows meant nothing to Doug."

"My God, five years." Gray sucked in his breath, casting anguished eyes heavenward as he fought to contain his explosive emotions. And this was the woman he was trying to protect? The woman whose actions had driven his back to the wall? He thought about Marina and Dolly Winterhazy and all his bizarre maneuverings of the previous day, and his temper exploded, no longer a volcanic eruption but an entire mountain of rage blasting apart under the stress.

"In five years exactly how many sleazy affairs have you had, trying to get back at that womanizing husband of yours?"

Adair's temper was reaching flashpoint too. She leaned forward tensely, her flushed face raised to Gray, countering his blistering attack. "You know nothing about my marriage! I haven't had any affairs! I'm not a slut, and if you knew the whole story you'd—"

But Gray was beyond listening or caring. "I don't want to hear it," he lashed back. "With your need to avoid publicity, would you admit the truth anyway? In any case, I haven't come to listen to more lies. You owe me something for the hell you've been putting me through, and I've come to collect."

He reached down and seized Adair by the arms, yanking her to her feet and jerking her against his body in one swift movement. In the same fluid motion, he wound a hank of her hair around his hand, tightening it painfully to hold her face still.

Adair gasped once to recover her lost breath and clamped her lips closed in the moment before his mouth impacted with smothering force against hers. She fought the embrace as best she could, but one arm was locked against her body, and her knees were still weak from hunger and stressful days. With her free hand, she tore at his hair, using fingernails in an attempt to wrench his face away from hers.

Slowly, inexorably, his lips pried hers apart, and his invasive tongue began to wreak havoc with her inner mouth. His kiss started in rage and pain and bitterness, a probe to punish her, to hurt her as deeply as she had hurt him. But Gray had not expected such resistance. As her ineffectual struggles continued he found no satisfaction in the conquest of a struggling woman. And so his kiss changed, became the deeply arousing act of a lover who seeks his promised due. He wanted her response. He demanded her response!

And because she could not help herself, she gave it. Slowly, inexorably, her fingers lost their ferocity, until they were twisted in his hair not to withhold, but to hold. Slowly her softening mouth yielded and molded to his demanding passion, until her kiss was as ardent as his. And slowly, inexorably, the weakness in her knees trembled upward to find its center elsewhere.

Even before he laid her on the bed and stripped her of her clothes, her resistance had slipped away like a palmful of water escaping through opened fingers, leaving behind only tiny beads of knowledge that she should not submit so easily to a man who held her in open contempt.

But it was not contempt she saw in the lean face hovering over her unclothed body, only a dark, embittered desire. She felt shackled by her own terrible weakness, but she made one last attempt to forestall his loveless possession. Eyes pleading, she asked, "How can you do this, Gray? You're engaged to another woman."

Gray paused on the verge of leaving the bed to remove his clothes. "Am I?" he mocked. "Then that makes us almost equal. A fiancée for me to fool, and a husband for you. I wonder which of us is cheating more?"

Anguished, Adair tried again. "I don't want this, Gray."

As he loosened his tie, his contemptuous gaze raked her limp, quivering nakedness. His eyes were bitterly cynical. "You're not fighting it very hard."

"It's no more than surrender. Is that all you want from me? Don't you care about my feelings at all?"

Above the shirt buttons he had started to undo, his jaw tightened momentarily. "What makes you think surrender is enough? I want a great deal more than that from you."

Thinking he meant revenge of some other kind, Adair felt her mouth go dry. "What else can you possibly want?"

He looked at her for a long moment and then said in a strangely hoarse voice, "Everything. I want everything. You're a passionate woman, Adair. I want all the fire, all the fury . . . everything."

He rose and turned his back while he undressed, swiftly divesting himself of jacket, shirt, shoes. Adair watched, pain tugging at the invisible chain lodged immutably beneath her breastbone, while desire washed through her in great waves too powerful to be resisted by her embattled body.

She heard the sound of his descending zipper, saw

his trousers fall and his lean, hard hips emerge. The sinewy flanks, virile as his shoulders, still concealed the power of his aroused strength. She swore to herself that if she could not find the will to fight, she would at least deny him the openly passionate response he wanted.

He turned and came crushing onto the bed beside her. "This time, if there are any interruptions," he warned, "you're not answering the door. I'll kiss you into silence if I must!"

When his strong arms tightened around her, Adair tried not to respond. She locked her hands at her sides in order to keep them from wandering. Even if she was carried away by passion, she mustn't allow him the triumph of knowing.

"Don't fight it," Gray ordered hoarsely, feeling her stiffness. "You're only fighting nature. Give in to yourself . . . give in to me . . ."

She closed her eyes to deprive herself of one sensory stimulant. Her lashes and her lips trembled. "I'll give you nothing except what you take," she whispered.

His laugh was soft and cynical, erotically uttered against the ear his lips had started to tease. "I wonder how much you'll be able to withhold."

His next long, searing kiss caused her senses to spin crazily. Overcome by the hot passion of his mouth and by the feel of the muscled nakedness stretching alongside her on the bed, it was not long before her disobedient hands crept around his shoulders. She denied him nothing when his fingers coursed over her body masterfully, wresting from her responses she didn't want to give. She groaned and sobbed out her need when he fondled her breasts as if he owned them, manipulating the taut crests with the familiarity of a man who can see and feel visible proof of his power. She arched and moaned when he stroked a slow downward path past the hollow concavity of her waist, branding each inch of her as his. She writhed beneath the hand that explored the contours of her hips, and her eyes flew open when his fingers at last claimed authority over a goal that was helpless to resist him.

She whimpered with desire and clenched at Gray's hair, seeking to bring his hovering face down to her own. His mouth moved into passionate union, anger and anguish forgotten in the searching, scorching penetration of his kiss. He pushed her legs apart and raised his lean, sinewy body over hers.

With a swift thrust, he made her his. His male body was driven into impatience by the deep frustrations of these past months, but the release he so desperately needed was less important to him than the admission he wanted from Adair. And so he grew still, kissing her hungrily but forcing himself to wait for the satisfaction he craved. It was not submission he wanted, not even passion, but total surrender.

At last she could bear it no longer. She twisted her head to free her mouth. "Make love to me," she begged, gasping with urgency. "Please, Gray, please . . ."

"Tell me more," he grated thickly. "Little words, lover's words. What would you say to a man you cared about? If you want me to continue, tell me how you feel about me. Pretend if you must!"

"I love you," she whispered, trembling at the power she was putting in his hands.

"Tell me again, again, again . . ."

He stroked her hips and her breasts, feeling the fire leap and burn in her flesh, listening to her speak the

false words, until the roaring of his own body's needs
overcame the deep and desperate needs of his mind.
He started to move rhythmically, and soon they were
both fused in a furnace of hot, impassioned kisses and
twining, tangling limbs.

Perhaps Adair had escaped the full knowledge of
her womanhood for too long. The explosion of pure
sensation was a wild metamorphosis, lifting her to
peaks of ecstasy, sending her hips straining higher for
a continuation of the long, shuddering delight, bringing cries of wanton pleasure to her lips. But she did
not tell Gray she loved him again, for she had
confessed it too often already.

He rolled away from her as soon as it was done. He
lay with his back turned for a time, muscles taut as he
tried to fight his difficult feelings under control. When
able, he rose and pulled on his clothes. Adair watched
him with anguished eyes. She pulled a sheet over her
breasts, suddenly ashamed of a nakedness that had
seemed so right only a few short minutes before.

It seemed a humiliation that he had not spoken of
love as he had forced her to do, that he had taken
everything from her. All the passion, all the fire, all
the fury . . .

"Why did you want me to say that?" she asked, her
throat hurting.

He was standing by the bedside, now fully dressed.
He turned and looked down at Adair, his face hard
and proud. "Anger, cheated desire, outrage at being
duped . . . can't you imagine my motives?"

"Oh . . ." The choked word could not express the
awful pain of her feelings. It was as though he had
deliberately yanked at the invisible chain within her,
dislodging a vital part of her heart. She wanted to
weep, but pride was the only thing she had left, and
she gathered it around her like a cloak. "I can't

imagine what satisfaction you'd get out of hearing cheap lies," she said.

Gray had started to walk toward the door. He halted before he reached it, and turned back. For one fleeting moment something bleak and terrible entered his voice. "Very little," he said. "I got very little satisfaction at all."

Chapter Nine

*A*dair remained in Washington for two more days. She reminded herself that life must go on as usual, but only during visits to the hospital's maternity ward did she manage to convince herself that it would. There, faced with the renewing surge and cycle of humanity, entranced by a newfound fascination with beginning life, and sustained by the proud memory of her own vital part in one of the births, she could find some relief from the despair engendered by Gray's callous treatment of her.

The baby was still unnamed, but otherwise doing very well. Adair was not allowed to hold her half-sister, who remained in the nursery area during visiting hours; but even through a wall of glass the tiny, aimlessly clutching fingers reached out to capture her heartstrings.

During visits to Roberta's room Adair was less distracted, although she managed to maintain a facade. Roberta continued to improve rapidly. Her face was no longer bleached by severe anemia. She was sitting up, even walking a little, and the doctors were allowing her to nurse her baby. When Roberta reported that particular piece of news, eyes shining with pride, Adair found herself fighting a surge of despair and envy. Did her own life hold only emptiness from now on?

She ate most meals with her father, usually in the hospital cafeteria or in some nearby restaurant. He seemed unusually subdued. As he was no longer worried about Roberta, Adair could only surmise that he was making efforts to deal with his feelings about producing another daughter. As her sympathy on that score was by this time nonexistent, in his company she often slumped into silence.

She couldn't impose on Roberta with visits as lengthy as her father's. And so there were hours when Adair was alone, with little to do, and no heart for shopping or sightseeing. In those solitary times, scuffing aimlessly along streets where snow had swiftly melted, she drifted into deep depression. She thought sometimes about Gray's engagement to Marina Winterhazy and decided it must be simply a politic arrangement—a marriage of convenience to consolidate the Winterhazy empire, with no particular love on either side. Otherwise, both of them would have reacted quite differently during the confrontation of the other night. Gray's upset had revolved around Adair's deception, not around being found by his fiancée *in flagrante delicto*. And Marina had seemed oddly triumphant, not distressed at all. Perhaps Adair should have been comforted to realize that Gray's feelings were not involved with Marina, but somehow, the thought brought her no peace of mind.

Her final dinner with her father, in the back booth

of an indifferent restaurant near the hospital, soon descended into its usual gloom. There was some desultory talk about plans: Adair was to return to Houston the following morning, while her father and Roberta would be departing for Canada as soon as mother and child were able to travel. It would be some time before Adair saw her father again, but she couldn't rouse herself to try for a restoration of their once-warm relationship.

Therefore she was startled when her father unexpectedly said to her, toward the end of the meal, "What's troubling you, Sunny?"

"Nothing, Poppy." But she couldn't fool him completely; he knew her too well. "Actually, I guess it's been a bit of a strain these past few days. The birth, the worry, and then . . . I've been feeling I should get home to Doug. He's been sounding a little low on the phone, ever since I told him I'd be staying on for a bit. Not that he really minded, considering Roberta's condition, but—"

"It's more than that," her father said, his eyes suddenly sharp. "You weren't yourself during that lunch with Arden and Amelia, and that was before the birth. I was very concerned about you, Sunny. I've never seen you look so damn . . . defeated. I would have asked you about it before, but I've had a lot on my mind."

Suddenly, against all pride and habit, tears started to form in Adair's eyes. Not since babyhood had she cried in front of her father, and she didn't want to start now. Tears were feminine, tears were weak, tears were something her father would scorn. She rose to her feet and mumbled excuses, intending to dash to the washroom.

His fist closed over her wrist. "Sit down," he

ordered in his best military voice. "You had a trip to the ladies' when we first came in, and I'm not letting you get away from me so easily. What's troubling you?"

Adair sat back heavily because she had no choice. Her wrist was too well shackled, and she didn't want to make a scene. In the back booth, hidden by a high partition, there was no one to see the tears fall but her father—but he was the one person who mustn't be allowed to see. She shaded her eyes with her free hand, a feeble attempt at concealment, for the tears, once started, wouldn't stop. They oozed down past her fingers, sliding into visibility on her cheeks.

He said with unnatural gentleness, "Are you afraid to let me see, Sunny?"

"Yes."

He released her wrist, leaving Adair free to fumble in her purse for a tissue. Her father sat in silence, putting no pressure on her to talk for the moment. At last Adair managed to stem the flow, but even after the tears had stopped she avoided looking at her father.

"What's upsetting you?" he asked after a time.

"I'm not going to tell you."

"Something is," he pressed.

"At the moment . . . oh . . ." She glanced up, some of her old spunk returning. Her chin jutted in tomboy defiance. "At the moment I'm just damn upset at having you watch me! I refuse to be considered a member of the weaker sex!"

He answered slowly. "And that's why you won't unload your troubles?"

"That's why."

Lamont Clancy heaved a deep sigh. "Then perhaps I'd better tell you what's been on my mind for the past few days. It's a little hard for me to discuss, but turn about is fair play, and I want to hear what's bothering you."

Adair compressed her lips. "Whatever you say, I'm not telling, Poppy."

He looked at her for a moment, his expression sad and speculative. "I'll take the chance," he said finally.

He signaled for two cups of coffee and fell briefly silent until the waitress had brought them. "Well, to start off, I don't mind admitting that this whole thing, the taxi crisis I mean, has hit me pretty hard. Of course, I've been mulling it over a lot, but I've also been thinking about something you said soon after the kid was born—after we got Roberta to the hospital. At the time it didn't seem like much, but when I got to thinking about it, it hit me like a ton of bricks."

"I can't remember saying anything in particular."

"About being proud of Roberta. How I ought to be busting my buttons . . . well, frankly, I have been. I am so damn proud of her it hurts. But what hit me, what really *hit* me, was that I can't remember ever having that kind of respect for any other female in my life." He paused, then added in a hoarse and humble voice, "It's hard as hell to admit this to you, Sunny, but that includes your mother, much as I loved her. And in some ways it includes you. Oh, I was proud of you, all right. You were a pretty spunky kid, but I used to sometimes think that if you were a *boy* . . ."

Adair winced, not wanting to hear this part. "I know all that, Poppy. I've always known it."

He looked into his coffee cup for a moment, then lifted his eyes again. They looked pained. "It was a helluva way for me to feel," he admitted. "A helluva way. And now, when you refuse to tell me your problems, it sort of . . . brings it all home. You never did whine about your troubles, did you? Any more than Roberta did the other day. And you had enough guts for a dozen boys. I remember your first parachute jump. You fell against the hatch, broke your wrist just before you went out—and it was the hand you had to use to pull the D-ring. But you didn't say a word. The instructor saw what happened and shouted out to stop you, but it was too late . . . out you went. I was down on the ground, watching and waiting. When I got to you, you had passed out."

Adair's attention had been riveted by the things her father was saying, but she sat with a carefully neutral expression, unwilling to betray the fact that he was touching her deep emotions in any way. So that was the memory . . . pain and terror . . .

She had been a teenager at the time, not so very young, but she must have blocked out the incident because she didn't want to relive the fear. She remembered the broken wrist well enough, but she'd had the confused notion that it must have been sustained during the landing. She and her father had never discussed the details.

"I feel sick with myself for spending all those years wishing you were a boy. I should have been busting my buttons just because you were you! But dammit, I didn't *know* that women had it so tough. Weaker sex, hell. What I'm saying is that Roberta opened my eyes. Taking all that like a man—" He stopped himself short and laughed self-consciously, embarrassed by his lapse into chauvinism. "Anyway, you know what I mean. A woman shouldn't have to be brave in a man's ways, when she has to be brave in her own. I'm saying I should have accepted you for yourself. I understand that now, and seeing you with a few tears in your eyes isn't going to change the way I feel about you. Which is, by the way, damn proud. Is any of this making sense, Sunny?"

Adair nodded. "Yes, it makes sense." She added in a burst, "But if you really mean all that, you might try calling me by my proper name. I'm a woman, Poppy. A *woman*. And proud of it! I have nothing against nicknames, but I'd prefer not to have a boyish one."

Her father had the grace to flush. He bent his head, looking penitent. "What I'm trying to do, Adair, is admit to a lifetime of error. That's damn hard for a man like me. But I think I've got the idea now. It's the person a man should take pride in, not the gender."

Adair was touched. She knew it was difficult for her father to apologize at any time, but it must have been doubly hard when he had to admit to a lifetime of wrong thinking. Again, he started to question her about her problems. Encouraged by his new sensitivity, she soon admitted that she was unhappily in love, giving him the sketchiest of details and no names. "It will never work out, Poppy. At the start I didn't tell him about Doug, you see. And when he found out I was a married woman, he . . . well, he has a terribly low opinion of me now."

"But you're not a married woman."

Adair's little laugh was despairing. "Yes, but he can't know that, can he?"

Her father's answer was slow and heavy. "Perhaps you should have told him."

"And what if *that* came out? Doug would be on the carpet for sure. NASA would hardly thank him for lying all these years. Anyway, I made a promise to you, and I'm sticking with it."

"Then I release you." He added with some humility, "I realize I should never have asked."

"Thanks, Poppy, but it makes no difference now. I wouldn't let Doug down under any circumstances. Besides, this . . . man . . . is engaged to someone else. By the time the space shuttle mission is over, he'll be married." The wedding date, Adair had seen on a closer reading of the story, was shortly before the start of the mission. "The whole thing doesn't have a hope."

Her father regarded her sadly. "I really have done you in, haven't I? I have to make another admission, Sunny . . . sorry, I mean Adair. If I'd had a son whose new wife was sleeping around, I'd have told him to get out, and pronto. I'd never have asked for the kind of sacrifice I asked of you. And I don't think a son would have made it." He gave his head a small shake, as if clearing it of old notions, and added in a hoarse, disturbed voice, "These past five years with Doug must have taken a hell of a lot of strength."

Adair grinned to lighten the mood. "Only when Doug started getting frisky," she said. "And thanks to you, I knew exactly how to deal with that. Remember those lessons in self-defense?"

Her father managed a smile, too, somewhat more uncertain than hers. "You females are really amazing creatures, you know that?"

Adair was pleased to hear him say it, but she wasn't convinced of her father's total conversion. She said softly, "I hope that means you're not too disappointed about having another daughter."

"Disappointed . . ." Suddenly Lamont Clancy's eyes were suspiciously watery. He straightened his shoulders and slapped the table to draw attention away from them. "Hell, I'm busting my buttons with pride!"

Weekday working hours were in force when Adair returned to Houston, so the ranch house was empty. Not wanting idleness, which only aggravated her deep depression, she changed into jeans and an old shirt and dove into activity—unpacking, cleaning up the considerable mess Doug had left in the kitchen, making his unmade bed, throwing a load into the washer, starting some dinner preparations.

The phone rang when she had been home for little more than an hour. "Hi, Adair?" It was Peggy, with sounds of small children in the background. "Listen, honey, I can't wait to hear about Washington. I've been dying for the phone to ring. Why didn't you call?"

Normally Adair might have phoned Peggy soon after her return, simply to unwind and find out what had been happening in her absence. But at this point her feelings for her friend were not particularly kind. She could not forget the broken promise and all the heartache it had caused. "I've been busy," she said.

"If my work can keep, so can yours. Why don't you drop everything and come over for coffee?"

"Sorry, Peggy, I can't. I've just finished putting an apple pie in the oven."

Peggy squawked. "Hardly in the front door, and already an apple pie in the oven? I don't believe it."

"Freezer variety," Adair said. "I didn't make it myself, but now that it's cooking I do have to watch the timer. Look, can we talk another time? I have a lot of things to do. Besides, I'm not much in the mood for gossiping."

"Just one quick question, then, before I expire from a terminal case of curiosity." Peggy's voice became artfully casual. "Anyone meet you at the airport?"

Adair stiffened. It was the very question she had hoped to avoid. "Sorry, Peggy, I've got to go. My pie's burning."

She hung up, not particularly caring that the excuse wouldn't wash, especially since the pie had been frozen. As far as she was concerned, Peggy could crawl walls with her curiosity. And if she sensed Adair's displeasure—well, it would do her good to ponder about that. Perhaps she wouldn't be so quick to meddle another time.

Doug appeared at the usual hour, the bang of the front door advertising his arrival. Adair went into the hall to greet him. He was already removing his jacket, first stage to making himself at home. "Hi," she said easily, digging her fingers into the hip pockets of her jeans.

"Hi." He smiled at her warmly. As he loosened his tie he added gruffly, "Sure is good to see you, kid. This house feels empty when you're not around."

"I heard the car and I fixed you a drink."

"That's a pal. I could use one."

They moved toward the living room, decorated to Adair's taste in unpretentious, restful earth colors. "Dinner's ready, too, any time you want it. I didn't know if you were going out tonight."

"Hell, no. Your first evening back?" Doug sank into his usual armchair. "I'm going to make like a homebody."

These were the small amenities that made the pretended marriage work—the friendly welcome, the easy smiles, the camaraderie, even the choosing of Doug's favorite pie as a fitting gesture upon her return. After the anguish of the past few days Adair found the rituals oddly comforting. With Doug, she didn't have to do much pretending. Except on those odd occasions when she had to fend him off, he put few emotional burdens on her.

But he was not quite himself today. He asked the polite questions about Roberta and Adair's father, but seemed abstracted when Adair gave the answers. His few smiles, when she spoke about the new baby, were forced.

Adair was watching him closely. "Something's bothering you, Doug. Anything I can help you with?"

Silent at first, he leaned forward to rest his elbows on spread knees. His head was lowered, his drink cradled between both hands. He spent a moody moment swirling it. "Yeah," he said at last. "You can give me a pretty big piece of help, but I'll get to that later. I want to deal with the bad news first. I've been scrubbed, Adair. I'm through, done, finished. Booted out!" He laughed bitterly. "Abort one astronaut! And five years of my life down the damn drain!"

"Oh, no," she whispered, shocked. "Why?"

"Because I'm rapidly developing tunnel vision! I thought I could fool them, but they did another medical last week, and . . . my God, can you feature it? They told me on Friday. After all that work, all that trying . . . and then to lose out because I can't see out of the corners of my eyes! My God, I don't even need *glasses!*"

Her heart went out to him, because she understood what a truly great blow this was. For the moment she wasn't thinking about her own wasted years; she had already spent too many hours contemplating the futility of her past and her future. She listened with deep sympathy as Doug talked on, relieving some of his bitterest feelings.

He admitted that he had suspected his growing deficiency. "It started creeping up on me just after we were in Washington. My God! If only they'd sent me up two years ago . . . if only there hadn't been so many delays, so many technical problems, so many budget cuts . . ."

Adair felt for him, and yet she understood NASA's reasons for disqualifying Doug. A man with tunnel vision, a condition affecting peripheral sight, might miss some vital signal on the outer edges of the highly

complex instrument panel. Doug was not only finished as an astronaut, he was finished as a pilot.
"Oh, God," he groaned, "it's like being told that
you've . . . been emasculated. Lost your manhood. I
couldn't say that to anyone but you."

Dinner came and went, apple pie came and went,
five hours of talk came and went. Near midnight
Adair was still listening, and Doug was still dealing
with his deep despair, although he was somewhat
calmer.

"Sorry to talk your head off," he apologized, "but
I've been needing a listener. The others . . . well,
they were sympathetic, sure, especially Guy Wishard.
But I could feel them all saying to themselves *'I'm
glad I'm not him.'* And I was angry because I wasn't
them. So I couldn't get into a lot of the stuff I've been
telling you."

"I wish I hadn't been in Washington." And for
more reasons than one, Adair thought. And then she
remembered Roberta and the baby and the panic in
the taxicab, and took back the wish. There was at
least one reason—one new, bald, red-faced bundle of
a reason—that made the trip worthwhile. Adair didn't
think her father, who had been so upset about
Roberta, could have handled the grave situation
alone.

"Not that I could have really helped you, Doug,"
she added with a sigh.

"You might be surprised how much you do," he
told her in a low voice. Then he looked up, his eyes
troubled. "Kinda makes me understand what wives
are for. And I haven't even dealt with that part of my
feelings yet. Can you listen a little longer?"

"Sure," Adair agreed, tucking her feet back into
the chair.

Doug took a deep breath. "I know all this puts an

end to our arrangement along with everything else, and frankly, right now that's just about the last straw. I'm going to ask a favor, kid. Will you stick with me for just a little longer? Another month or so? Until I get over the worst, decide what I'm going to do."

It wasn't hard for Adair to say yes. "Of course. If you hadn't asked, I'd have offered."

Doug nodded acknowledgment but was silent for some time. Finally he said, "God, Adair, if you knew how I've been needing you. I never thought about it much before, but you know—I sure as hell made a good choice when I picked you. Wrong reasons, right girl. I loused it up, and now I wish I hadn't. All those other females, they . . . well, they sure didn't seem like much help these past few days."

Adair could understand that. There would be little joy in minor conquests while dealing with a major defeat. But she also imagined that Doug would be back to casual liaisons as soon as the worst of the disappointment was over. She didn't bother pointing it out, because at this moment he probably felt as if he would never know joy again in his life.

Doug leaned forward tensely, his expression earnest. "I said earlier I was going to ask you something big, and here it comes. Don't interrupt because I want to get it all out before you dive in with an answer. Would you consider trying again? I mean, really trying? Ring and everything? I know I haven't given you much reason to think it would work, but . . . well, a man's got to settle down sometime. Have kids. Raise a family. Put down roots. I couldn't promise to be perfectly perfect—I won't lie about that, and you wouldn't believe me anyway—but I'd sure try a hell of a lot harder than I did five years ago. What else can I say? Dammit, Adair, you know all my faults too well. I may not be a great husband, but I think I'd be a helluva good father. I like kids, and they like me." He laughed ruefully. "Crazy, isn't it? Now that I don't need a wife for official reasons, I find myself needing one anyway. Just *needing* one. Needing you. Don't give me your answer now, because I don't want it to be no. But think about it seriously, huh?"

Adair dismissed the notion out of hand, although she wouldn't have told that to Doug. He had quite enough on his plate for the moment, and she thought it best not to add to his big helping of disappointment. There would be time enough to turn down his suggestion when she saw that his eye, while following some other female, had recovered its customary gleam. And that would happen soon enough, once he got over the severe blow to his ego.

She phoned Peggy the next day, having concluded for herself that she had been a little hasty in her estimation of her friend. "Do I owe you an apology?" she asked.

"You sure do," Peggy said in heartfelt fashion, "and I'm coming over to get it right now. So put it on the hob, please, a nice big pot of it. Extra strong."

Adair laughed. "What, the apology or the coffee?"

"Both," said Peggy. "And pop a little humble pie in the oven while you're at it, hmmm? If you've cleaned out the cinders of the frozen apple, that is."

"That excuse was a bit much, wasn't it?"

"A bit much! I could smell your slow burn from ten blocks away! But at least you satisfied my curiosity. You wouldn't have been so damn mad at me if no one had been waiting at the airport!"

Ten minutes later Peggy was at the door, with little Tommy in tow. His weight was now such that Peggy had not brought a playpen, so Adair laid a collection of pots, pans, and wooden spoons in the center of the living room floor. She and Peggy were accustomed to talking over the din.

When they had settled, Peggy got to the heart of the matter at once. "I guess by now you know Doug's news, or you wouldn't have phoned to apologize." She made a wry face. "Ghastly, isn't it? For Doug, I mean."

"Yes," Adair acknowledged. "I'm sorry, Peggy. I should have known you wouldn't break your promise."

"Actually, I was in a terrible bind. Guy told me last Friday, not long after your flight took off. It wasn't up to me to phone long-distance and let you know about Doug, so I didn't dare phone you at all. On the other hand, I didn't want you to waste those days in Washington. So I just . . . took the bull by the horns. I thought you might be able to figure out for yourself that there had been some change on the home front. God, I feel bad about Doug. And Guy does too. What's he going to do?"

"I don't know."

"He should be able to stay on with NASA as . . . no, Tommy, no! *No!* Take that out of your mouth at once!" Peggy lunged forward to rescue a book that had been on a coffee table, its handsome leather binding now bearing the imprint of several small toothmarks. "No, no, no," she warned sternly, putting the book back on the table. Hanging on to the edge of the coffee table, Tommy stood on unsteady legs and looked at his lost prize longingly, his pudgy fingers wavering toward it.

"Put it out of reach," Adair suggested.

"Good heavens, no. Well, that is, if you don't mind the risk. He has to learn not to touch. I'll watch. He won't get away with it again."

Moments later, feeling the weight of his mother's

disapproval, Tommy collapsed back onto the floor and crawled back to his pots and pans. A happy uproar soon filled the room.

"It's when you *can't* hear them that you have to start worrying," sighed Peggy. "Well, where were we? Look, let's not talk about Doug. It's too depressing. I know exactly how Guy would feel if the same thing happened to him. And I don't want to hear about babies and taxicabs, either—Doug gave us a report about that." She leaned forward expectantly, her eyes sparkling with curiosity. "So tell me about being met at the airport. I figured if that hunk of man wasn't still interested, he wouldn't meet your plane. And he did meet it, so . . . well, start talking. Tell me everything, everything, everything. Within the bounds of decency, of course."

Adair was ready to field the question, which she had expected. "Decency is practically all there was to it," she lied. "Yes, he came to the airport, and yes, we had dinner. His main purpose in seeing me was to let me know that he's engaged to another woman. He's getting married next month. The formal announcement hit the paper while I was in Washington."

Peggy struck her forehead and cast her eyes at the ceiling. "Wouldn't you know! Too late! And don't say I didn't tell you so!"

"I would have let him slip through my fingers anyway, Peggy. I decided he wasn't—"

Tommy had made good use of the one instant of upward-cast eyes. "No, no, no!" Peggy raced across the carpet in time to avert catastrophe. Expertly catching a vase of dried flowers on the fly, she also whipped a handful of its contents away from Tommy. "He's teething," she explained. "Everything goes in the mouth."

"Don't worry about the flowers."

"I'm not! I'm worried about *him*. What if some of these berries were poisonous?" She turned from restoring the floral arrangement in time to see her son's pudgy little body scrambling across the room, his new goal a sharp letterknife that had fallen unnoticed to the floor. "No, Tommy, don't touch!" she shrieked. "No, no, no! You'll put out your eye and *Mummy says no!*"

Needless to say, Adair didn't have much trouble evading Peggy's questions.

A week later NASA held a press conference to announce the change of plans. Naturally the major part of the attention was focused on the astronaut who would be taking Doug's place, but there were also a lot of probing questions for Doug himself. Adair, watching the whole thing on TV, had to admire his cool. One or two members of the media behaved like hyenas tearing at a carcass to find the last shreds of flesh. With their questions, they tried again and again to goad Doug into betraying the full depth of his disappointment. They were looking for weaknesses, not strengths. Doug survived the grueling conference with flying colors, betraying nothing except his ability to take disappointment in his stride.

"I was so proud of you," Adair said afterward. "Some of them were awful, weren't they! I guess you're glad it's over."

"It is over, isn't it? All over." Doug's public performance had given way to private depression. "From now on, I'm yesterday's news."

It was cold comfort to Adair to realize that in the future neither Doug's doings nor her own would be of any interest whatsoever to the press. The time for that worry had passed, along with the need for it. "You mentioned on TV that you might resign your commission and move into private industry. Is it true?"

"What else is there for a failed astronaut? It's a fact that I want to move away from Houston. Sure, they'd give me some safe cushy job at the Space Center, but it would be like living hell to stay. Perhaps now that the news is public, I'll get an offer or two."

For Adair the morning with Peggy, near catastrophes and all, was producing an unexpected result. Or perhaps it would be more exact to say that several things, taken together, were producing a result. Peggy's preoccupation in dealing with Tommy's boundless energy; Adair's new half-sister; her twinge of envy for Roberta; the emptiness of her own future. And Doug's straightforward suggestion.

It could not be said that Adair thought about these things consciously, but as the days passed with no ease for her heartache, she found herself desperate for something to fill the great void in her life. Old photographs of Morane monoplanes and Gloucester Gamecocks no longer seemed enough. Her far-flung correspondence had become a burden, for she found her attention wandering too easily and too often. The occupation was far too solitary and quiet to distract her, and she badly needed distraction from her personal problems. She photostated some of the material, sent it off to a publisher who had expressed interest some years before, and thrust the project from her mind.

It was not an occupation that Adair needed, but a preoccupation.

It was over the holiday season, while decorating the tree with Doug's help, and burdened with thoughts of how lonely the following Christmas was going to be, that she realized, with a sharp sense of surprise, that she was actually considering Doug's suggestion seriously.

Sinking back to the floor in a welter of ornaments, she watched him climb a stool to affix the traditional star to the top branch. Could she really be thinking what she was thinking?

Yes, it was all there in her head. Going round and round and round almost unnoticed, like a moving barber's pole on a busy street. Occupied with her heart, she had not understood what was going on in her head. She realized she had been wondering whether comradeship would be enough. Whether Doug might actually, miraculously, settle down to some extent. Whether he would make a good father.

He *was* good with children, she knew. And he was a pleasant companion. And he didn't lie to her. And he really had a lot to recommend him, all those good qualities of courage and stamina and intelligence that had gotten him into astronaut training in the first place, over hundreds of other candidates. And she believed he would try far harder the second time around.

Gray was the great passion of her life. In her relationships with people, Adair was not a changeable person, and she knew she would not fall so deeply in love again. And yet she needed warmth and meaning in her life, something to fill the bleakness of a future that stretched ahead like a desert landscape, drought-stricken and unendingly empty. Her feelings for Doug couldn't equate with her feelings for Gray, but at least there was real caring in the friendship they had developed over the years. A small oasis in the desert.

She thought of Roberta's baby and of pudgy little Tommy and of Peggy's other children, and knew she didn't want to forgo the experience of motherhood.

She couldn't give Doug an answer yet—that needed
a great deal more thinking about, for the possibility had only now risen to the forefront of her
consciousness—but she did want to prepare the
ground. He had been honest with her, and perhaps it
was time to accord some honesty to him. If she should
decide to accept his offer, she wanted him to be fully
aware that she was in love with another man.

That night, after the tree was decorated, she told
him of her deep feelings for Gray. She told him that
those feelings had culminated in an affair. As to the
reasons for the relationship's failure, she was far more
honest than she had been with her father. It was quite
easy to tell Doug the plain truth, edited but essentially
unchanged. And she was grateful to him afterward.
Even knowing of her lapse from grace, he didn't
attempt to follow her to bed.

Yes, Adair decided; he was trying.

In early January, Doug was offered a job that
caused the first burst of enthusiasm Adair had seen in
a month.

"Technical consultant for a movie," he announced
triumphantly. "It's being touted as the greatest thing
since *Star Wars*. And look at the *salary!* My God, it
makes an astronaut's pay look like a pittance! They
want me to start right away, soon as I can unattach
myself here. Oh, the work may be a little dull after
flying, but . . . hell, you know it might be just the
thing?"

Hollywood hype aside, Adair thought Doug would
find the complete change stimulating. He must have
felt that the prospect was exciting, too, because he
accepted the offer almost overnight, conditional on
his prompt release from the service. For him, if all
went well, it would mean hurtling headlong into a

move; for Adair, it would mean an almost instant decision about her future. Doug started to press for her answer, and she promised she would give it as soon as possible. "Within days," she said, but the days began to stretch.

Doug's quick release was easily arranged. NASA, having failed to tempt him into staying on in a senior but sedentary capacity, was smoothing his way into civilian life. For a pilot, the problem with peripheral vision was reason enough for a medical discharge. The Houston house was put on the market, and the need for Adair's decision became urgent. "Soon," she told Doug.

"What are you going to do?" Peggy asked Adair when she heard of the impending move.

"Maybe go with Doug," Adair said, not meeting her friend's eye. "We might actually remarry."

Peggy looked skeptical. "And what about all those Hollywood cuties that are going to catch his eye?"

"What about them," Adair returned indifferently.

Just before the launch of the space shuttle, Adair accepted an invitation from the Wives. It was to be in the nature of a farewell luncheon. Peggy, who wanted to give the lunch in her own home, had pressed to have it at once, in case Adair had to move from Houston while her husband, Guy, was in space.

After five years of friendship, it was for Adair a poignant occasion. "I'm going to miss that bunch, Doug," she sighed later in the day, during the ritual pre-dinner cocktail. "You know something? In their own way, all those women are absolutely remarkable. Peggy especially. It's the first time I've ever seen her in a panic."

"A panic? Good God. It won't help Guy to—"

"If she's worrying about Guy, she's keeping it to herself. Husband heading off for outer space, and what's she in a total terror about? The TV crews that are starting to camp at her door!"

Doug laughed, and Adair was pleased to hear him sound so much like his old self. Moments later he reported to her that on leaving the service, he would be receiving a signal honor. The following week a citation and medal were to be presented at the White House. The private presentation had been intentionally planned to coincide with the space shuttle mission. Doug had been advised that it was intended not only as a consolation for lost opportunities, but as an occasion to mark his excellent service record, in particular the many times he had risked life and limb for his country during his years as a test pilot for highly hazardous experimental planes.

"You're invited to the White House too," he told Adair.

"But I won't go." She rose and walked to the window. She stood there, looking out at the suburban street disconsolately, wondering whether it was fair to ask Doug a favor.

"What is it, kid?" he asked kindly. "Are you hankering to see that man in Washington?"

"No, I'm not hankering. And I don't intend to hanker in the future—his opinion of me is too low. But I'm wondering if you would do me a favor while you're in Washington. Could you contact the *Clarion* and find out if he's married yet? Or you could phone the Winterhazy house and ask."

"The people who gave that dizzy party? What would they know about it?"

"Didn't I tell you? Marina Winterhazy is the blushing bride. You must remember her."

"Remember . . . ! My God, and this guy has a low opinion of *your* morals? I can't—"

"Look, Doug," she said wearily, "just do me a favor and find out if the big event has actually transpired. It should have, by the time you go to Washington."

He agreed, and added after a moment's thought, "Is that all that's keeping you from reaching a decision about me?"

"Yes," she admitted. "It's the only thing. Not that it really matters, but it's a mental roadblock I'd like to get out of the way. I'll give you a positive answer as soon as you get back." She turned back to Doug, dredging up a light smile. "And if he's married, Doug, then my answer to you is . . . yes."

"And if he's not?"

Adair's smile evaporated. "I imagine it will still be yes," she said. But her voice choked a little, and again she turned unseeingly to the view. It wasn't fair to let Doug see how terrible she felt.

Chapter Ten

$\mathcal{W}$ith Doug in Washington and no reason to immerse herself in photos of antique planes, Adair spent a good deal of her time watching the TV coverage of the space shuttle mission. The launch had gone perfectly, the astronauts were performing splendidly, and there had been no failures of the sophisticated equipment. Moreover, according to Peggy, the hardest test of all had been passed. "I didn't totally freeze up on TV," she said with awe, on the phone to Adair immediately after her first interview.

"How could you, with all the no-no-nos you were handing out to Tommy, and the hugs for Tilda's hurt knee? The kids were wonderful! Peggy, you're so . . ."

But how could she say "lucky" to a woman whose husband was out there in space? "You're so natural on TV I don't know why you ever worried."

For a moment there was relative silence on the

other end, although Tommy's bangs and gurgles of delight could be heard as he played around Peggy's feet. How Peggy could be pensive in the midst of all that, Adair did not know.

"You know, Adair, in a way, that worrying about TV is the best thing in the world. It stops me from dwelling on other things. Frankly, I used to get in a cold sweat when Guy was flying for the navy. I wouldn't dare say that to the Wives, because they're so damn *cool* about it. I wouldn't want to get them all worked up."

"Did it ever occur to you they might feel exactly the same way? And that *you*, Peggy Wishard, look as if you're the coolest of them all? A stranger would swear you didn't have a worry in the world—well, except for Tommy, Tilda, and Susan."

"Me? But—" Peggy's small astonishment ended in a laugh. "You're right, I don't really have a worry, or I shouldn't, because there's no point in . . . Susan, honey, will you please move the cord of the electric kettle out of Tommy's reach? . . . No point in . . . *no, Tommy, no!* Hot, hot, hot!"

As the phone clattered down at the other end, Adair could not help a wry smile. She mused that Peggy's little worries very effectively took her mind off the big one. Would the solution work in her own case? Would she learn to live with Doug's foibles? She thought she could, if she married not with hope and shiny-eyed optimism, as she had done at nineteen, but with realistic expectations and a far, far better understanding of the man to whom she was committing herself. In part because of the recent dreadful dashing of hopes, Doug had matured too. Adair knew he liked her and admired her, as Gray would never do. To her, that was of vital importance. It might be cynical to plan a life without love, but it seemed she had no choice. Love had planned a life without *her*.

"Half a life is better than none," she said out loud, with a feeble attempt at finding humor in a situation where no humor existed. Doug would be home from Washington in a couple of days, and her final answer to him was due.

He phoned first thing the following morning to advise her that he would be returning that same evening, a day sooner than expected. After hearing a short report on what had happened at the White House, Adair asked about his arrival time. "Around suppertime, I guess. But make some kind of dinner that will keep, in case I'm a little late. How about that great *boeuf bourguignon* of yours? And break out a bottle of wine."

"That sounds like a celebration."

"It is. You practically promised a yes."

There was a question she didn't want to ask, but knew she must, before Doug's return. "Did you . . . find out . . . what I asked you to find out?"

"Oh yeah, I nearly forgot to tell you. I phoned the Winterhazy house yesterday." He paused and added softly, "It's all over and done."

It was the news Adair had expected, but even expecting it didn't prevent the awful yanking of that invisible chain attached to her heart. But at least she now had some advance warning, and that gave her the rest of the day to prepare herself emotionally. If she was going to accept Doug's proposal, she simply couldn't be gloomy about it.

Doug's voice, careful a moment before, became cheerful again. "Look, kid, stow the blue jeans for tonight, huh? Do something extra nice for the scenery. Remember that big new salary of mine, and buy something if necessary. To put it to you straight, honey, if you're going to accept a proposal, the least you can do is set the scene for romance."

Adair tried, although her heart was not in it. After a flying trip to the supermarket, she spent the rest of the morning in the kitchen. Another apple pie—this time made from scratch—went in the oven. With vegetables cleaned and beef simmering, she arranged the flowers she had bought, great sprays of carnations in the living room, a low bowl of roses against the white tablecloth in the dining room. Dark red roses for love and romance.

Oh, God, could she really bear to go through with it? And yet she knew she would. And she would make it a good marriage too. Going in with her eyes open, she had no right to withhold anything from Doug.

She had saved the afternoon for her personal preparations. After driving to the neighborhood shopping center, she determinedly walked into the most expensive fashion store in the place. Doug had said to do something nice for the scenery, and she intended to. After trying on practically everything in the store, she achieved her purpose in the beaded, flowing silk of a wickedly extravagant caftan—half hostess gown and half negligee, for its publicly respectable exterior concealed a privately daring chiffon nightgown that was soft, seductive, diaphanous as gossamer, and by far the sexiest thing Adair had ever owned. The color of the two-piece outfit, a glowing warm bronze, did marvels for her complexion and her hair.

More time was spent mulling over a cosmetics counter, trying to choose makeup to enhance the new outfit she had bought. Urged by a persuasive and helpful saleswoman, she also indulged in an expensive perfume.

In another store she purchased some frothy under-garments, more feminine and frivolous than anything she had bought since shopping for her bridal trous-seau at the age of nineteen. She refused to let herself contemplate the fact that she would prefer to be buying such things for another man's eyes. Or she tried, but it was hard not to think of Gray.

Next came the beauty salon, where she had made an appointment to have a new cut and professional blow-dry to the simple, flattering style she preferred. As she had been fitted in at the last minute, her appointment squeezed between others of longer standing, the treatment took longer than she had expected. A manicure, the first in her life, also caused some delay.

It was growing late and she was in a hurry when she let herself in the front door of her home. Still clad in jeans and a checked shirt, she raced down the hall to her bedroom, dumped the parcels, and hurried to the bathroom to run a scented bath. She had just turned on the taps when she heard a man's voice behind her.

"Mind if I watch?" asked a low, vibrant voice.

She straightened to attention as if burned, and wheeled around. Gray was leaning against the door, his thin face wearing a warm, amused smile that was not echoed by his eyes. The eyes were dark blue pools of desire, deepening as they roved over her face. Gradually the smile faded from his lips. He reached for her, breathing hard, but already Adair had snapped away, out of his reach, acting out of reflex despite her state of deep shock.

"Don't touch me!" she cried, feelings of hysteria rising in her throat. She remembered only too well how Gray's touch always affected her.

His hands dropped. He flexed the fingers for a moment, then pushed them into his trouser pockets as if to keep them out of mischief. "You're right," he said. "We should talk first. May I start with an apology for my behavior last time we met? I can only plead temporary insanity."

Adair was still benumbed, staring at him with sick disbelief. Why had he come, and today of all days? She tried to steady her voice. "What are you doing here?"

"I came to see you."

"I d-don't want to see you." She recovered enough to bend and turn off the taps, a mechanical movement that allowed her a moment's thinking time. When she rose, she was no calmer, but her wits were no longer in total flight. "You'll have to go. My husband could be home at any minute. I can't . . ." Anguish began to rise, causing pain to appear in her amber eyes. "Oh, God, Gray, why did you come? *Why?* Whatever's happened between us, it's in the past. I don't want to see you, touch you, think about you . . . I can't *bear* you walking into my life, just when I'm trying to put it together again."

"I thought I might be able to help with that."

"You can't—except by staying away from me." She licked her lips and added, "I . . . I love my husband."

Gray's thin face had become skeptical. "I didn't fly all the way from Washington to listen to crazy nonsense. I've had enough pretense from you to last me a lifetime, and now I want to hear a little truth."

Struggling to cover her feelings, Adair tossed back the streaky mane of her hair and resorted to angry defiance. "The truth is I want nothing more to do with you, ever! Now get out! I don't want you here when Doug gets home. What would he think?"

An ironic twist lifted Gray's lips. "The worst, probably," he suggested sardonically. "Entertaining another man, and in the bathroom too . . . shall we go into the more neutral territory of the living room? It seems a more sensible place to talk."

"I don't want to talk! And what's more—" she started furiously, and then paused as a new question occurred to her. Her eyes flashed and narrowed. "How did you break into my house, anyway?"

"I'll answer that question when you come and sit down. I'd like to start exchanging a few facts, instead of all this fiction." His eyes flicked over the bathroom. "I have an aversion to major scenes in minor rooms, laundry rooms excepted. I'm aiming for a comfortable chair, and I refuse to move out of it until we've had a good long talk."

"If my husband walks in—"

But Gray had already walked out, leaving Adair alone with her heated words. In a few moments she followed because she had to. Every nerve was vibrating wildly, and she began to wish that Doug *would* walk in. He already knew about Gray anyway, and his presence would offer moral support.

Gray had draped his rangy frame into Doug's favorite chair, a positioning that helped put a cold steel into Adair's resolve. She came to a halt in the entrance to the living room. "How did you get here?" she asked coldly.

"By Winterhazy jet."

"And from the airport?"

"By taxi."

Without a word, Adair walked to the kitchen and placed a quiet phone call to the local taxicab company. "Ten minutes," promised the voice on the other end of the line. She went back to the living room, unhurriedly switched on a few lights, and then drew the curtains against the fast-gathering January dusk. She took her time with all the small rituals, each of which cut into the number of minutes she would have to spend in conversation. At last she sat down as far as possible from Gray, her distance causing a raised eyebrow.

"I could use a cup of coffee," he noted, "or even a drink, if you're offering."

"You won't have time for one," she said icily. "Your taxi's going to be here in about eight minutes. If you don't go when it arrives, I intend to ask the police to show you out. Preferably all the way to the airport."

"That doesn't leave much time to deal with the complications of our relationship, does it? Besides, although I did fly the jet down myself, I doubt if I can locate my co-pilot—he took off for a hot night on the town. I can't possibly return to Washington tonight."

"That's your problem. You're not staying here."

Gray leaned farther into his chair. "Eight minutes, you say? Well, I'll try to cut it short and get right to the heart of the truth. First, about you and your husband—"

"Leave my husband out of it. Instead, think about you and your wife! Marina may have been amused by your carrying on when you were still a bachelor, but I don't imagine she'd be quite so amused by this."

"Ah, so you want to start with the truth about me? That's not hard. I don't believe I've ever told you a lie."

"Don't you understand, Gray? When it comes to you, I am simply . . . not . . . interested."

He sighed deeply. "Changeable woman. Well, then, as you're not interested in me, I'm forced to go back to the subject of you and your husband. Not such a bad fellow, Digger Anderson. We had a nice visit this morning."

A new shock touched Adair's eyes. "You . . . were speaking to . . . Doug?"

Gray nodded, confirming it. His dark eyes shone with amusement. "He came to see me at the *Clarion* this morning. Is there some reason you wouldn't want the two of us to connect? Frankly, he said some very flattering things about you. What a good wife you'd been, how you'd stood by him all these years, how I was wrong to think you'd been playing around. I admitted to him that I had made a lot of nasty accusations during our last scene. It was anger talking, and frustration, and despair. For a time I admit I wanted to hurt you, simply because I . . . but let's go back to the subject of your husband. It was he who told me the spare key to your front door was outside, under a flowerpot. That was right after he hung up from phoning you this morning—from my office."

Adair was faint with incredulity. "From . . . your office?"

"Nice of him to set the whole thing up for me, wasn't it? Oh, by the way, he won't be back in Houston until tomorrow evening."

"Then . . . but I don't understand . . ."

Gray's small smile mocked her gently. "I admit, it's not every woman's husband who would play Cupid for her, especially when it puts an end to the hopes for his own proposal." Gray paused, letting that statement sink in. "But then," he added softly, "he seems to feel he owes you an enormous debt. Five years of loyalty is a lot for a woman to give, especially when she's not a wife."

"You know," whispered Adair.

Gray's voice was quiet. "Yes, *Miss* Clancy, I know."

They sat and looked at each other as the precious seconds ticked by. At last Gray remembered the coming taxicab and Adair's ultimatum. He had no assurance that she would not throw him out; he had as yet made no revelations about himself. He glanced at his watch, frowned at the passage of time, and said, "Aren't you going to ask why Doug came to see me?"

Adair was struggling with her confused feelings. "I . . . I asked him to find something out. He . . ."

"He didn't have to see me to find that out. He already knew the answer to your question, because he had phoned the Winterhazy house. When he heard Marina and I weren't married, he decided it was worthwhile trying to patch things up between you and me. And that's why he came to see me."

"Not married?" Adair choked out. "But Doug said . . ."

"He said it was over and done. He meant the engagement." Gray spoke swiftly now. "I was black-mailed into the arrangement with Marina, and also into the newspaper policy you didn't like. I want you to know that before I propose. I should hate you to turn me down because of your opinion of my scru-ples."

A soaring happiness was beginning to take wing inside Adair, but the swift progress of Gray's disclo-sures left her head spinning. Gray was not married; he knew now that she was not married; he intended to propose . . . but she simply sat and stared at him, stunned.

Gray's eyes darkened. He rose and moved slowly closer to Adair, speaking as he prowled across the room. "I realize you couldn't possibly guess that I had a proposal in mind. But frankly, that's why your . . . your ex-husband set the scene for an evening of romance. He has your interests at heart, and he knows my intentions are incredibly honorable. They've always been incredibly honorable," he added in a husky, deeply emotional voice, coming to a standstill beside her chair.

Outside, a car honked. Adair rose and slipped past Gray, who made no move to stop her. She pulled a curtain aside to peer through the picture window. It was the taxi, and the driver blinked his lights to show that he had seen her.

Gray frowned at the interruption, which had come just at a vital juncture, when he had been planning to take Adair into his arms. "I'll pay him off," he said brusquely. He strode toward the door.

Adair's reaction was instinctive. "Gray, no! Tell him to wait. Tell him to put his meter on. He won't mind, if he knows it's a trip to the airport."

Gray's head jerked back to her, his thin face harsh with incredulity. He stared at her, thunderstruck. "You can't send me away now," he rasped.

She went across the room to reassure him. When she put her hands on his shoulders, she could feel him grow rigid with pain. When she laid her cheek against his suit jacket, she could see the agonized flexing of his fingers at his sides. His voice became deathly quiet, deeply pained. "Oh, God, Adair. If you intend to turn me down, don't touch me. It's only torture."

She lifted her face, mouth tremulous and happiness spilling luminously from her eyes. "Oh, Gray. Don't you see? This house is another life—my life with Doug. I wouldn't feel right to let you into this life, when it's not the life I intend to share with you. Yes, I'm sending you away—but only because I'm going with you. Tonight. To Washington. And I'll be your co-pilot on the flight. Can you tell the taxi driver I'll be about ten minutes?"

During the flight, with instruments and night flying conditions to occupy their attention, the time was not ripe for romance. Adair was still dressed in jeans and cotton shirt. She was breathless from quick packing, from putting the dinner away in the fridge, from leaving a hasty note for Doug. She had written that she would be back to pack up and clean out as soon as the house was sold. "The apple pie is all yours," she had added. "I owe you about a million of them. Do you know something, you big lug? I love you for what you've done!"

Once they were clear of the control tower and on the prescribed flight path to Washington, there was opportunity for Gray to tell Adair his own side of the story. Concisely and with clarity, he told her about the choices he had been faced with on the day of the board meeting. "I couldn't admit to any of this at the time, because I didn't have control of the chain. I do now."

Wonderingly, Adair considered what he had told her about Dolly Winterhazy's pernicious influence. No wonder the society page had been so wretched! "Then the newspaper policy was never your idea," she concluded.

Gray nodded briskly. "I had three options, none of them acceptable. I certainly didn't want to change the editorial policy, but I wanted even less to marry Marina. Perhaps you'll think I should have taken the third option and resigned, but I couldn't do that either—I'll explain why in a minute. At first I decided I had to give in on newspaper policy, temporarily at least. How could I have become engaged to Marina, when I was intending to propose to you? And yes, I was intending to do that—in fact, I started thinking about it as far back as last September. When you made yourself so elusive, I was damn frustrated. How can a man make an offer of marriage when he can't even get a proper date with a woman?"

Adair struggled to believe him. "But . . . the last

time I saw you, you said you'd been engaged to Marina for some time."

"I didn't say that, I simply misled you. It was true enough that Dolly had been making plans. But *I* hadn't. The engagement didn't come about until *after* Marina found you in my apartment. I don't deny that she'd been trying to get her hooks in, but how could we have been engaged? I was intending to propose to you that night."

"Oh, Gray," she breathed, darting a sideways glance at him. Her insides melted to think he had loved her even then. "Were you, really?"

"I certainly was. Why do you think I went to so much trouble to get you to my apartment, and to get everything right? If you doubt I'm telling the truth, ask Hoshu! He helped me choose the kimono, install the dimmer switch . . . good God, he knew I was obsessed with you. He couldn't believe it when I ended up engaged to Marina instead."

Adair was still not quite sure how that had come about. "And why did you?"

"Because she and Dolly threatened to put you into the news, as nastily as possible. At that point the Winterhazys still wielded the power of major shareholders. Actually the *Clarion* and the other Winterhazy newspapers weren't the only threat. Dolly has a lot of influence with every gossip columnist in Washington. She intended to spread the muck."

With the plane on automatic controls and on an even course, neither pilot nor co-pilot needed to be overly preoccupied, although there were always things to be checked. Adair glanced at the console before turning to stare at Gray. "You got engaged to Marina . . . for *me?*"

"Only as a stalling device. Actually, if it hadn't

been for my intention of proposing to you, that's the option I would have chosen in the first place. I knew Dolly Winterhazy wouldn't consider anything less than the biggest Washington wedding on record, and that meant it couldn't possibly be engineered in less than a month. A month gave me all the time I needed to get control of the *Clarion*. And once I had control, I knew I could dump Marina easily enough. That may sound heartless of me, but frankly Dolly and Marina deserve some heartless treatment."

"But . . . how did you get out of it so easily?"

Gray's eyes gleamed as he remembered. It hadn't been hard to get rid of Marina. Once in control of the *Clarion*, he had simply told her that he didn't intend to sleep with her—ever. He had added a long list of unflattering epithets about her sexual attractions. As Marina's reasons for marrying weren't quite the same as her mother's, she had had a small temper tantrum and thrown her ring at him.

Gray would never tell Adair, but according to Doug Anderson, who had been remarkably frank about his recent sexual exploits, Marina was up to her old tricks. For the past few days Digger had been having a high old time, and all of it in the Winterhazy coach house. "Marina had an abortion," Doug had reported to Gray. "Her third, she says. Wow! I wouldn't want to get hitched to a dame like that, but let me tell you, she is something else in bed. A real nympho."

Gray kept his explanations to Adair simple. "I told Marina I didn't want her, to put it mildly." A tiny quirk of amusement softened the edges of Gray's firm mouth. "And as for Dolly's threat of blackmail . . . well, there was still some risk that she would try to harm you, out of pure spite if nothing else. With engraved invitations mailed out and wedding gifts pouring in, she was apoplectic when the engagement broke up. However, she wasn't too hard to deal with. As I was by then in control of the Winterhazy chain, *I* was in command of what went into the gossip column. I simply turned the tables. It's amazing how many juicy little items of news Dolly Winterhazy didn't want printed—most of them to do with Marina. Once she saw the light, Dolly was quite happy to shut her mouth about you."

Adair laughed. "By then, I don't suppose she'd have been able to work up much interest in gossip about me, anyway. As soon as Doug became an ordinary citizen, he lost all his news value. And so did I."

"Dolly could work up a hot scandal about anyone, newsworthy or not. Several gossip columnists slaver over her, and they'll print practically anything she wants. She's destroyed quite a few reputable people in her time, simply by using arch innuendo. She even threatened to wield that weapon against her own husband years ago, when he tried to walk out on her. She invented some dirt about another member of his family—his sister, who happens to be a quiet and perfectly respectable nun—and she would have used it too. By the time she was through with you, the public would have been sure you were sleeping with everyone in NASA, right up to the top command."

"She sounds like a . . . a bitch!"

Gray laughed sardonically. "You have an incredible gift for understatement." His face sobered. "The only person I was sorry to disappoint was Bernard Winterhazy. He would have liked to see me marry Marina, although he understands why I wouldn't want to. Poor Hazy. He's a bitterly disillusioned man. The women in his life have made things hell for him."

Adair shot him a curious glance. "It sounds as though you like at least one member of the family."

"I do. And I owe Bernard Winterhazy a great deal—everything, in fact."

"I remember you told me he'd brought you to Washington."

"He did a hell of a lot more than that. Brought me up through the ranks, had faith in me, made me editor, made me publisher. It was he who wrote my job contract so that I'd someday gain control, not of all the Winterhazy assets but at least of the newspaper chain. Oh, he may pretend to his wife that it was a bumbling mistake, but actually he did it deliberately —and not just because he wanted the *Clarion* to become a good paper. He's a weak man, too weak to fight his wife in the open . . . but he could fight her by putting control into someone else's hands."

This was a trust that Gray would have betrayed to no one but the woman who was going to be his wife. If Dolly ever found out the truth of what had been going on, Bernard Winterhazy's life would hardly be worth living.

He went on, telling Adair the rest. "He not only wrote the stock options into my contract; he also loaned me the money to buy the shares when the options came due. Dolly doesn't know. With all the wealth they've inherited—the newspaper chain is just one small part—the Winterhazys are swimming in so much lucre she couldn't possibly keep track of it all. Over the years Bernard has loaned me millions of dollars, and all of it interest free. I don't even have to struggle to repay it. The dividends I've been receiving have covered my schedule of payments exactly. Now do you understand why I felt I couldn't quit? It wasn't the money, it wasn't the stock—I could have walked out a wealthy man in December. And it wasn't even the *Clarion* itself, although I have a very proprietary interest in that. My reason for staying on was much simpler, and it had to do with the trust Bernard Winterhazy placed in me. How could I let him down, when he was finally about to even the score with his wife?"

It was well past midnight, Washington time, when they reached Gray's apartment. Adair stepped inside the door and looked over the remembered scene: the sunken, tasteful living room, the ambience of serenity, the sense of age and agelessness achieved by the carefully collected antiques and the wall of Japanese screens.

Gray was close behind her, and he folded Adair into his arms without even taking time to remove her coat. "I've been waiting for a lot of hours to do this," he breathed as his mouth descended, to be met with an eagerness equal to his own. The fires between them flared, but only briefly. Hoshu arrived in the hall, clad in pajamas and yawning.

"Back awready, boss? So sorry, must be bad news—" But then he saw Adair, who had been half-hidden by Gray's long frame, and gulped back the rest of his words. He rubbed some sleep from his eyes, and his round melon of a face broke into a slow grin. "Miss Clancy says yes?"

Gray's arm tightened around Adair. "Miss Clancy says yes," he agreed, slanting a possessive smile down at his prize.

Hoshu burst into effusive congratulations. He offered to bring tea, drinks, or food to welcome the travelers after their long flight, but Gray refused. "I think we'd rather be alone, Hoshu."

The manservant took the hint. He left, with a few last words. "I okay sure bring breakfast in bed," he said fervently.

After the brief interruption Gray didn't try for a

renewal of intimate embraces. He led Adair along the hall to his bedroom and placed her suitcase on the bed. "If I'm not mistaken," he said drily, "Hoshu's already cleaned out half a cupboard and one chest of drawers for your use. He knew I had gone to fetch you."

Adair gave him an oblique, teasing glance. "You were so sure I was going to say yes?"

Gray's eyes turned briefly pained. "I've never been less sure of anything in my life." He stood and looked at Adair with a dark, aching question in his eyes. "This morning, when I heard that you were still . . . thinking of me, I couldn't believe it. I knew you'd been physically attracted to me—but how could any woman love a man who behaved as I behaved the last time we met? A man who forced her to say words of love he was sure she didn't mean? That night I felt as Samson must have felt, pulling down the pillars to bring about his own self-destruction. I still can't quite believe my good luck."

A strong man's vulnerability was a touching sight, and Adair had never seen Gray look vulnerable before. She wanted to express her deep feelings, to repeat the words of love and tell him that they had been spoken from the heart. But she also wanted this night to be perfect, and she wanted to save the words until Gray said them to her. "Can you leave me now, Gray?" she asked quietly. "I'll be ready very soon."

"Shall I pour you a drink? Fix you a sandwich?"

"No, thanks." They had shared a thermos of coffee on the plane and a takeout pizza bought before leaving Houston.

Gray left the room swiftly. Adair's preparations were simple but sensuous: the interrupted bath, the perfume, the floating negligee, the silken caftan. There were rueful thoughts about how she had chosen these things with plans for a different evening; and yet, while shopping, it had been with poignant thoughts of Gray on her mind.

She emerged from the bedroom before he returned, to find him in the living room nursing a balloon of brandy. He too had changed, and was now clad in the dark brown kimono he had worn during their previous interlude in his apartment. He rose to his feet when she entered, and his eyes smoked darkly as they raked her.

"You're so beautiful," he said in a low, disturbing voice.

Adair went to him slowly and reached up to stroke the long groove that sliced down one thin cheek. She wondered why she had ever thought him anything but handsome. "Not half as beautiful as you are," she whispered proudly, letting love shine from her eyes.

Gray emitted a short laugh, half astonishment, half disbelief. "I warned you, no more lies," he murmured, closing her into the circle of his arms. "I have a lot of sins, but handsomeness isn't one of them." His fingers threaded into her hair and he bent his mouth to find hers. "Accuse me of a host of other sins, if you wish," he muttered against her lips. "They're all there in my head. Lust, wantonness, covetousness, selfishness, carnal desire . . . and most of all, love . . ."

"Then none of the others are sins," Adair murmured in return.

And all at once their mouths were clinging, the hunger of the months unleashed by the urgent passage of their hands over each other's bodies. The kiss broke only to allow the whispering of urgent love words, all of them too long unsaid. And soon they led each other to the bedroom, equal partners in passion, both impatient to seal a union that would be for all time.

They sank to the bed, mouths still welded. Soon a
kiss was not enough, and little by little they began to
undress each other. The caftan went first, and Gray
sucked in an unsteady breath when he saw Adair in
the gossamer nightgown beneath. "Too bad it has to
come off," he said thickly, moving his parted mouth
against the sheer fabric at her breast while his finger
reached downward toward the hemline.

"No, Gray," she begged. "Let me undress you first.
Don't move a muscle."

He forced himself to remain almost as still as she
had requested. She accomplished the task as slowly as
possible, bathing his lean body with ardent kisses,
nibbling the crisp texture of his muscled chest, tasting
the salty tang of his skin, touching, stroking, holding,
using techniques of arousal taught to her by Gray
himself. Finally, driven to a frenzy of impatience, he
reached for her nightgown.

They made love with passionate abandon, both
whispering words of endearment into each other's
ears. They reached for the stars, and found the
heavens and the universe too . . .

"I love you, darling," Gray murmured for the
thousandth time as they lay spent but still united. He
started to shift, intending to relieve Adair of his
weight.

Her arms tightened to hold him exactly where he
was. She was reveling in the feel of his spare, sinewy
body draped over hers, in the intimate connection
they still shared. Gray was a part of her now, and she
was a part of him, and even though passion had
passed, the time for closeness had not.

"Tell me again," she said, her voice a low, contented purr. "Again, again, again . . ."

It didn't occur to her that the request echoed one

that Gray himself had made, not so very many weeks before. He lifted his head and touched her mouth with gentle fingers, only too pleased to fulfill her wish.

"I think I loved you from the very start," he muttered. His words came slowly, broken by the little line of kisses he was laying along her jaw. "I could have sworn it wasn't possible for a sane man to fall in love with a perfect stranger, even one with a beautiful chin like this. But then, I have to confess I've been half insane for months. I think the tablecloth did it." His mouth moved to a new part of her anatomy, the proud, soft curve of her neck. "Or perhaps it was the sound that comes out of this throat when you laugh, like water music . . ." His kisses kept traveling. "Or perhaps it was these freckles that made me fall in love at first sight . . . or this lovely tip-tilted nose . . . or the lemony taste of your hair . . . or this marvelous, impudent, sexy lower lip . . ."

"Gray! Now who's lying? You didn't taste my hair the first time we met! Besides, nobody falls in love at first sight!"

He bit her lower lip with mock ferocity, catching it softly between his teeth. "I did," he growled, nipping her until she pretended to cry out for mercy, as part of the sensual and thoroughly enjoyable little game.

He lifted his head again. "Coward," he said with a laugh.

With a chin that was still quivering from his ardent lovemaking, Adair managed to achieve the facsimile of a defiant jut. "I am not," she said, daring him to prove otherwise.

Gray looked down at her affectionately, his eyes warm. "I wonder if it's safe to confess to you now?"

"Confess what?"

"My most terrible sin. The real coward is me."

"What on earth are you talking about?"

"That day in the AT-6. You told me I mustn't touch the controls, and . . ."

"You bastard! You mean you *did?*"

"I guess you were a little too frozen up to feel me pulling on the stick."

"Cheat! Then I never did owe you a dinner date!"

"When a man's wildly in love and wants to live long enough to enjoy it, he does what he must," Gray sighed, his amused midnight-blue eyes mocking her tenderly. "Besides, I didn't cheat. You didn't ask whether I'd touched the controls. You simply conceded."

Adair glowered at him, hiding her relief and also her secret thrill of delight. It was wonderful to know that he had been wildly in love, even then.

"I'll make you pay for that for the rest of your life," she warned. She pulled his head down to hers and fastened her teeth firmly over his lower lip, digging in softly, rubbing her tongue against him, drawing out the exquisite torture until he groaned with pleasure. Soon she felt his body beginning to stir with renewed desire, just as she wanted it to stir.

"Coward," she murmured through her tight little teeth, daring him to do his damnedest.

MORE ROMANCE FOR
A SPECIAL WAY TO RELAX
$1.95 each

2 ☐ Hastings	23 ☐ Charles	45 ☐ Charles	66 ☐ Mikels
3 ☐ Dixon	24 ☐ Dixon	46 ☐ Howard	67 ☐ Shaw
4 ☐ Vitek	25 ☐ Hardy	47 ☐ Stephens	68 ☐ Sinclair
5 ☐ Converse	26 ☐ Scott	48 ☐ Ferrell	69 ☐ Dalton
6 ☐ Douglass	27 ☐ Wisdom	49 ☐ Hastings	70 ☐ Clare
7 ☐ Stanford	28 ☐ Ripy	50 ☐ Browning	71 ☐ Skillern
8 ☐ Halston	29 ☐ Bergen	51 ☐ Trent	72 ☐ Belmont
9 ☐ Baxter	30 ☐ Stephens	52 ☐ Sinclair	73 ☐ Taylor
10 ☐ Thiels	31 ☐ Baxter	53 ☐ Thomas	74 ☐ Wisdom
11 ☐ Thornton	32 ☐ Douglass	54 ☐ Hohl	75 ☐ John
12 ☐ Sinclair	33 ☐ Palmer	55 ☐ Stanford	76 ☐ Ripy
13 ☐ Beckman	35 ☐ James	56 ☐ Wallace	77 ☐ Bergen
14 ☐ Keene	36 ☐ Dailey	57 ☐ Thornton	78 ☐ Gladstone
+5 ☐ James	37 ☐ Stanford	58 ☐ Douglass	79 ☐ Hastings
16 ☐ Carr	38 ☐ John	59 ☐ Roberts	80 ☐ Douglass
17 ☐ John	39 ☐ Milan	60 ☐ Thorne	81 ☐ Thornton
18 ☐ Hamilton	40 ☐ Converse	61 ☐ Beckman	82 ☐ McKenna
19 ☐ Shaw	41 ☐ Halston	62 ☐ Bright	83 ☐ Major
20 ☐ Musgrave	42 ☐ Drummond	63 ☐ Wallace	84 ☐ Stephens
21 ☐ Hastings	43 ☐ Shaw	64 ☐ Converse	85 ☐ Beckman
22 ☐ Howard	44 ☐ Eden	65 ☐ Cates	86 ☐ Halston

Silhouette Special Edition

$2.25 each

87 ☐ Dixon	99 ☐ Dixon	111 ☐ Thorne	123 ☐ Douglass
88 ☐ Saxon	100 ☐ Roberts	112 ☐ Belmont	124 ☐ Mikels
89 ☐ Meriwether	101 ☐ Bergen	113 ☐ Camp	125 ☐ Cates
90 ☐ Justin	102 ☐ Wallace	114 ☐ Ripy	126 ☐ Wildman
91 ☐ Stanford	103 ☐ Taylor	115 ☐ Halston	127 ☐ Taylor
92 ☐ Hamilton	104 ☐ Wallace	116 ☐ Roberts	128 ☐ Macomber
93 ☐ Lacey	105 ☐ Sinclair	117 ☐ Converse	129 ☐ Rowe
94 ☐ Barrie	106 ☐ John	118 ☐ Jackson	130 ☐ Carr
95 ☐ Doyle	107 ☐ Ross	119 ☐ Langan	131 ☐ Lee
96 ☐ Baxter	108 ☐ Stephens	120 ☐ Dixon	132 ☐ Dailey
97 ☐ Shaw	109 ☐ Beckman	121 ☐ Shaw	
98 ☐ Hurley	110 ☐ Browning	122 ☐ Walker	

LOOK FOR A HARD BARGAIN BY CAROLE HALSTON AVAILABLE IN JANUARY AND SHINING HOUR BY PAT WALLACE IN FEBRUARY.

SILHOUETTE SPECIAL EDITION, Department SE/2
1230 Avenue of the Americas
New York, NY 10020

Please send me the books I have checked above. I am enclosing $_____
(please add 75¢ to cover postage and handling. NYS and NYC residents please
add appropriate sales tax). Send check or money order—no cash or C.O.D.'s
please. Allow six weeks for delivery.

NAME _____

ADDRESS _____

CITY _____ STATE/ZIP _____

Silhouette Desire
15-Day Trial Offer
A new romance series that explores contemporary relationships in exciting detail

Six Silhouette Desire romances, free for 15 days!
We'll send you six new Silhouette Desire romances
to look over for 15 days, absolutely free! If you decide
not to keep the books, return them and owe nothing.

Six books a month, free home delivery. If you like
Silhouette Desire romances as much as we think you
will, keep them and return your payment with the
invoice. Then we will send you six new books every
month to preview, just as soon as they are published.
You pay only for the books you decide to keep, and
you never pay postage and handling.